I0554042

She'd just told him the most amazing tale, and now she wanted him to leave her to face danger alone…

A shadowy figure sat on the table. A small flame appeared in the darkness as the silhouetted intruder lit a cigarette.

"That's it. I'm getting you out of here," Marie said. She grabbed Parker by the arm and led him away from the picnic table. Marie blasted another jolt of blue light into the woman, who collapsed to the ground, jets of white smoke swirling across her limp body.

A voice called out from behind them. "You have nowhere to run, *outsider*." Its tone was cold and mocking.

Parker turned to look, but Marie nudged him forward.

"Get in the car," she barked. This was not a request.

"But what about you?" he asked when he reached the car door and opened it.

"I'll be fine, just go."

"Who is that?"

"That's Seth. I'll explain later. Just go."

Why couldn't she just come with him? She didn't have to stay and fight. They could make their escape together. He was about to ask her to get into the car when Seth loomed behind her.

"He's behind you!"

Marie whirled around.

Seth took a long drag on his cigarette, the orange ember intensifying in the darkness. The small fire pulled away from his pale face, and he exhaled.

"Stop this foolishness, Marie. You can take your charge and run to the four corners of the earth, and I'll still be there, waiting."

Eighteen-year old Parker Austin, big brother and high school quarterback, dreams of glory on the football field. But a tragic shooting shatters Parker world. In a chilling span of sixty seconds, a mass tragedy wreaks havoc upon his life, family, and community. Although hailed a hero, Parker is horror-struck to discover that an incident from his past was the motive for the killings and he was the intended target. When someone threatens to get the one that got away, Parker finds himself hunted.

Help comes from an unexpected source—an angel named Marie. A spunky, impulsive guardian, Marie is dedicated to saving Parker at all costs, but will her love be enough to save him when the darkness comes for him? When Marie is confronted by a sinister nemesis who covets Parker's soul, a desperate struggle is waged over Parker's fate. With time running out, she must face her growing, but secret, affections for Parker that she can no longer ignore, affections that will force her to make the ultimate decision—sacrifice herself and all that she believes, or lose him to the darkness forever.

KUDOS for *Sunrise*

This is a wonderful story about a boy who has had to face very hard obstacles and who feels running away is the answer. Parker is a wonderful character, and the author does an amazing job of making you feel his pain. This is definitely not a book that makes you smile. It is a book of courage and finding faith. Marie is willing to give up everything to save her charge, Parker, but can she? The ending leaves you knowing there is more to come and I look forward to it. Although this is rated YA it is a book for any age. ~ *Linda Tonis, Paranormal Romance Guild*

This is a marvelous coming-of-age story about a young man who thinks running away will solve all his problems. The characters are realistic and charming. You can't help but feel Parker's pain as he struggles to deal with events beyond his control. A wonderful read that will appeal to people of all ages. ~ *Taylor Jones, Reviewer*

Sunrise is the story of love, courage, and tragic loss. It echoes the cry of innocent victims everywhere: "Why does God let such bad things happen to good people?" Filled with endearing characters, vivid descriptions, and tense fast-paced action, *Sunrise* is a chilling and exciting read for YA and adults alike. ~ *Regan Murphy, Reviewer*

SUNRISE

Scott J. Abel

A Black Opal Books Publication

GENRE: YOUNG ADULT/NEW ADULT/PARANORMAL THRILLER/ PARANORMAL ROMANCE

SUNRISE
Copyright © 2015 by Scott J. Abel
Cover Design by Taria Reed
All cover art copyright © 2016
All Rights Reserved
Print ISBN: 978-1-626944-95-4

Publication Date: JULY 2016

Published by Black Opal Books **http://www.blackopalbooks.com**

DEDICATION

To Jena, Ainsley, and Allie, who give me reasons each day to smile more and laugh often. May you never stop.

We can only appreciate the miracle of a sunrise
if we have waited in the darkness.

"They found him in town," Trajan said with a trace of nervousness not usually present in his voice. "Maybe there are others. Maybe they know?"

Curious, Seth squatted next to the man, though careful not to let his jacket touch the ground, and helped him sit up against a marble grave. He slid his fingers under the captive's chin and gently raised his head so they were face to face. "Hello, Yaris."

Yaris's eyes widened in recognition and his shoulders sagged as though his body deflated from a sudden loss of air.

A smile was hard to resist, and Seth fought it only for a moment. Grinning, he said, "It's been a long time. Let's see…when did Constantinople fall?"

Yaris looked away. Though the duct tape prevented him from speaking, he really didn't have to—the look in his eyes and his slack face said it all. Defeat.

Struggling to break free made no difference. Seth studied the gold halo firmly fixed to the top of Yaris's head and relished the irony. A device once used to capture and expel Seth and the others from paradise could also be used on its own kind. The beauty of the halo was that it also worked when they were in human form, confining the captive to the primitive, earthly body and depriving the celestial being of the ability to return home.

"That's okay, Yaris. I know you don't feel like reminiscing. Even when you pretended to be my friend, we never did see eye-to-eye on much, did we?" The rhetorical question stirred up the past and sent a clear message that nothing had been forgotten no matter how many millennia had elapsed.

"They found this on him," Trajan blurted out, clearly alarmed.

Seth twisted in his direction, slightly curious but more annoyed at the interruption.

Trajan withdrew an object from the zipper pocket in his vest and handed it to him.

Six inches in length and pointed on one end, to any human the gold device appeared like a shiny letter opener. But to an angelic being, it was a weapon.

Seth stood and squeezed the handle in the palm of his hand. The pointed end shot forward several feet, covered in a luminous fire that dripped from its blade.

"An angel sword, huh? Expecting close combat, are we?" He brought the blade forward until it hung in front of Yaris, the small flames illuminating his face. A drop of fire fell from the blade and landed on the captive's leg.

Yaris twitched and jerked from the burn and screamed through the duct tape as a small trail of smoke drifted upward from the wound.

"Oops," Seth offered. "How clumsy of me." A few snickers slid out of some of the nearby onlookers.

"Reductum," he said, and the fire-laden blade withdrew, the object resuming its original benign appearance. "I won't rub your capture in your face and make fun of your hopeless situation. All I ask is that you answer me honestly. Do that and I'll let you go. Understand?"

Yaris turned and cast a leery expression, dripping with doubt and defiance.

Seth leaned forward and slowly caressed Yaris's cheek with his index finger. "Make no mistake. You will leave scarred." A soft red glow emanated from Seth's finger, scorching Yaris's flesh with intense heat.

The prisoner threw his head back against the tombstone amidst a muffled scream. The odor of burning skin wafted between them. Tears of pain dripped from Yaris's eyes.

"I don't like hurting you. But I promise, you will live and still get to roam Creation if you cooperate and tell me the truth. Otherwise, I may have to turn you over to some of my more aggressive colleagues who are not as considerate and delicate as I am. Deal?"

Yaris's chest heaved in search of breath, and Seth waited for him to collect himself. After a moment, a pair of sad, forlorn eyes closed as Yaris nodded in agreement.

Seth ripped off the duct tape with a quick tug, causing the prisoner to shut his eyes and recoil. "Now, do any guardians know I'm here?"

Yaris lifted his bound hands and massaged the skin around his mouth. "No."

"Are any guardians alerted to our presence?"

"No."

"So, if I send my colleagues into town, they won't run into any surprises. Will they?"

Yaris shook his head.

"Say it."

"No, all right? No other guardians are out. Why would they be? I mean, what are you thugs doing here anyway?" Yaris cast a nervous look at the large group forming around Seth.

"You'll see soon enough." Seth slid a hand under Yaris's arm and helped him to his feet. He guided him to a seat on the tombstone behind him. "Trajan, Zyro. Sweep the town. See if there are any guardians waiting for us or anything at all that looks like we're heading into a trap. I've spent the past three years working for this, and I'm not about to have it spoiled at the last second."

The two lieutenants nodded and disappeared into the darkness.

A cold gust of wind swept through the cemetery, stirring up the few autumn leaves that littered the dry ground. Seth put on his leather jacket and lit a cigarette. Though bitter cold was a permanent condition, inhaling the warm, toxic fumes provided a feeble but temporary respite.

"You never asked me what I was doing here," Yaris muttered, his head bowed. "You're getting rusty in your old age." His tone carried a slight edge, like I-know-something-you-don't-know.

Seth flicked ash from the butt of his cigarette. "What else is there to ask? You're a guardian. You're in this backwater town to protect your charge."

Yaris slowly raised his head and his lips twisted into a slight grin. "Wrong."

Seth inhaled deeply from his cigarette, the tiny ember glowing just inches from his fingers. He pondered the possibility that Yaris had been up to something, but soon dismissed it. "Stop trying to be deceptive," he said, smoke billowing out with his breath. "We both know you haven't got it in you."

He nodded to a colleague who replaced the duct tape over Yaris's mouth.

After an hour had passed and Seth had smoked nearly half a pack of cigarettes, the two scouts returned.

"We've walked the streets of Briar Ridge, Seth. No guardians are out. None."

"Have our two heroes made it into town?"

"Yes."

"And they're with the pill popper?"

"As we speak."

So Yaris had told the truth, as expected. Seth couldn't suppress his grin. Three years of work was about to pay off. And even though that small amount of time hardly qualified as a blink of an eye, it still took great effort to manipulate lives and get all the pieces into place, especially while under constant scrutiny from the guardians. But if they hadn't caught on to what was happening yet, there was no way they could stop what was coming.

There was only one thing left to do. He stood in front of Yaris, still perched on the edge of the marbled tombstone. "Thank you for telling me the truth. Like I said, if you were honest with me, I'll let you go." He moved closer to Yaris until no more than a foot separated them. "The only problem is—I lied." With a sudden thrust of both hands, he struck Yaris with jets of red light in the chest. He tumbled backward off the grave and fell to the ground, muffled screams emanating through the duct tape.

Seth walked around the marble slab and threw bolt after bolt of hot light into Yaris until the writhing, screaming guardian caught fire from head to toe. The flames cast an ominous flicker of light around the crowd that closed in to watch. Smoke danced upward into the cold night air, carrying with it the stench of burning flesh.

Seth's henchmen watched the burning of Yaris's corpse in silent enjoyment until Trajan finally stepped forward. "What are your orders?"

It was time. Seth stepped away from the small fire and observed, with quiet satisfaction, the unsuspecting town one last time. Its last night of ignorance, its last night of living and believing in the illusion.

"Let it begin."

CHAPTER 2

Marie knew she shouldn't appear, and she'd probably get in trouble for it—she'd been warned more times than she could count But the thrill and intimacy of seeing Parker proved far too strong. Besides, if she really was on thin ice with Markus, there was only one way to find out.

Really, what was the harm in appearing in the dead of night with everyone asleep? In an unexceptional small town, where nothing exceptional ever happened or was expected. That was the beauty of remote communities like Briar Ridge—isolation relegated them to the world's margins, where they were hardly noticed.

With a shrug of indifference, she appeared in the front yard of the red brick house next to Parker's. Heavy mist matted her clothes against her like a wet paper towel. She took a slow, deep breath of the sweet, crisp smell of approaching rain. Her eyelids half closed from the relaxation-inducing scent.

Cloaked in darkness, she moved in silence, her steps timed with each gust of wind and rustle of leaves. Nothing—no sound, no shifting of shadows—hinted at her approach despite her physical presence.

Marie continued her stealthy advance toward Parker's house. Her pulse quickened when it came into view.

Three large oak trees shaded the front yard, obscuring

part of the house, but as she walked closer, she could see more. Except for the white brick, it was a carbon copy of the other ranch-style houses in the neighborhood—long, with a low roof and attached two-car garage on the side. Flowerbeds flanked the front door and overflowed with holly bushes and shrubs. Small lights illuminated a wooden sign carved in the shape of a football with number "12" and "Parker" painted on it. A basketball hoop stood to the side of the driveway, the telltale sign of young people inhabiting the home. A thick row of trees bordered the driveway as an informal property divider.

She snuck across the front of the house, and the corners of her mouth turned up in a grin. Although she knew Parker was sound asleep in his room, she couldn't help but glance at the windows in the hope of seeing him. Who knew? Maybe he'd wake up and shuffle to the kitchen for a late night snack. Dark brown hair tousled from the pillows, deep ocean-blue eyes glassy with sleep, bare feet dragging him across the cold linoleum floor in his boxers…

Her chest heaved, and a dreamy sigh escaped past her lips. It was so easy to get lost with him, unlike any of her previous charges.

Marie shook her head. *C'mon. Snap out of it. Concentrate.* There would be time enough for dreaming.

Maneuvering into the thick row of oaks and pecans, she crept underneath their low, heavy branches to get out of the mist, sweeping long strands of wet hair from her eyes. The space under the trees wasn't as wet, but that would change soon with the increasing pit-pat of raindrops falling through the leaves above.

She stood parallel to the house and took up her post for her routine vigil. The thought of sneaking into the backyard and watching Parker through his bedroom window while he slept proved tempting. The nights were long and tedious, and she had to pass the time somehow, but she soon dismissed the idea. There was, after all, a point at which thin ice gives way for sure.

The rules were archaic, but simple: don't harm your charge and stay in the background. Direct involvement complicated matters. The preferred method was to work behind the scenes, unobserved. Subtlety was key, though with Parker the urge for direct contact was strong—too strong, perhaps. Although the rebuke had been heavy afterward, she'd gotten away with it once, years ago, with much success. But Parker probably didn't remember. He was very young then, while contact with him now could be problematic. Still…

Her ears tingled as her inner radar picked up a familiar presence from behind, among the trees' dark shadows. *Hello, Jacob.*

He didn't make a sound, but she sensed him. A glance over her shoulder revealed nothing but tree trunks and darkness. Jacob wouldn't show himself unless he wanted to be seen. She turned around and continued gazing at the house.

Jacob watched the home, too, but she felt him glancing at her as well. She felt the staring, the annoying sense of disagreement emanating from him, but that's how he operated. That's how all the guardians operated, really. Being an exception could be fun, but sometimes it left her with a sense of isolation, even inadequacy especially in their company.

Undeterred, she continued her observation of the house against the backdrop of gentle rain.

Her eyes drifted to the black Pontiac Firebird in the driveway. She remembered the day Parker got the used car for his sixteenth birthday and how the first ride he gave went not to his girlfriend or to any of his other friends, but to his eight-year-old sister. She smiled at the memory.

"Why have you appeared, Marie?" Jacob's voice was soft, almost a whisper, yet it carried a distinct trace of irritation.

Marie sighed. "I've appeared because I like it. It helps me relate to my charge." She'd known Jacob for ten years, ever since he'd been assigned to guard Parker's sister, and she sensed him shaking his head. Better to get the disagreement over with—otherwise, it would make an already very long night insufferable.

"So spit it out already."

"I'm not looking for an argument. I'm curious why you've appeared just to watch your charge." Curiosity wasn't in his tone—more like snobbish disapproval. Another hint that her presence in the guardian ranks wasn't embraced, merely tolerated.

A small huff escaped from her. Resignation weighed down her shoulders. *Not this conversation again.*

"Just because my approach differs from yours and everyone else's doesn't mean I'm wrong." The constant defense of her actions was getting tiring.

"How long have you appeared?" Jacob asked.

"Not long." Obviously he'd been watching for some time, looking around, observing for potential dangers. If caution could be measured, Jacob would score off the charts. *You're so uptight and by-the-book. No wonder we don't get along.*

He finally emerged from the darkness and stood next to her. "A storm is coming."

She turned and studied her colleague for a moment. The glasses he chose to wear made him look young and a little mousy. "There, that wasn't so hard, now was it? See, a little rebellion now and then can be a good thing."

Jacob's eyes narrowed. "I'd be careful with that line of thinking." He turned back to the house and shook his head. "*Extrarium*," he muttered under his breath, though louder than he probably intended.

There it was—*outsider.* As many times as her colleagues had thrown that word at her, she would've thought she'd be used to the insult by now, but the reproach still stung. She twisted the toe of her boot into the damp ground, felt the sod give way. All she ever wanted was to be accepted. After all these years, was that so much to ask?

She looked at the branches overhead and squinted as a

silver raindrop fell into her eye. She wiped it away with the back of her hand as the precipitation intensified. The ground under her feet grew wetter, the wind more menacing as it whipped through the treetops. Bluish-white streaks of lightning shot across the dark sky like sinewy fingers, followed by a distant rumble of thunder.

"You really shouldn't appear so much. It's not safe. Uriel and Markus wouldn't approve."

"Uriel and Markus? You mean you and everyone else. Contrary to rumors, I don't appear human as often as you think," she shot back. "Besides, I can handle Markus."

"Oh, that's right. I keep forgetting you're his favorite."

She cast him a sideways glance, lips slanting into a smirk. "Really, Jacob?"

He shrugged his shoulders. "Hey, I'm just stating what everybody knows."

"Well, he only favors the best, I guess."

He removed his spectacles, took out a handkerchief, and wiped the lenses. "Very funny."

She grinned. "You're the one who started it. If you can't—"

The hair on the back of her neck stood erect, and her face went slack. *Something's wrong.*

Jacob quickly replaced his glasses, and they turned their attention back to the house as the mood shifted to one of shared alarm. An uninvited presence crept toward the backyard fence, watching and waiting like them.

Marie scanned the fence for any movement, but didn't see anything. It was there, though, and it wasn't alone. Her body tensed. "I feel two...no, three of them. Do you?"

"Yes. They're in the alley, behind the fence." He closed his eyes for a moment, lines of concentration creasing his forehead.

She resumed searching for the intruders. What were they doing here? Why Parker's house? They'd never shown any interest in him or his family before. A brilliant flash of lightning, followed by a loud crack of thunder, illuminated the backyard in an eerie light. Her eyes darted along the fence. Several silhouetted figures lurked behind it.

Jacob opened his eyes. "Seth is near," he said, his voice taut with alarm.

Cold sweat broke out on her forehead, and she wiped it away with a clammy hand. Of all the names, that was the one no guardian wanted to hear. Ever. She swallowed and tried to keep her voice from trembling. "Seth? Are you sure?"

He didn't answer, but stared at the backyard fence. He interlocked his fingers and cracked his knuckles, his customary nervous habit. "When was your last fight?"

Although her preference was to avoid combat, confrontation always remained an option. Her last altercation had been a violent affair, but she had resolved long ago to do whatever it took to protect her charges, especially this one.

"Um, about twenty years ago. In Argentina." The melee during Carnival had been brutal. The colored lights of angel fire, agonizing screams, and the smell of burning flesh came back to her. An icy ball formed in the pit of her stomach, the landscape tilted and spun, and she placed an unsteady hand on the wet bark of the tree next to her.

"You'll be rusty if it's been that long. Remember, strike only when you have to and use quick, controlled bursts over as short a distance as possible."

His tone took on one of mock authority and bravado, but it wasn't convincing. She let the lecture slide for the moment. Seth's close proximity had Jacob rattled.

She looked back at the house. Parker and his family, asleep in their warm, cozy beds—they had no idea of the danger around them.

She clutched her chest, her breathing becoming labored. "They're moving closer to the house, aren't they?"

He jerked his head in an awkward nod. "Yeah." His eyes roamed the fence from behind wire-rimmed glasses. His forehead glistened. Was it from the precipitation…or fear?

A chill ran through her body and an army of goose

bumps formed on her arms. She crossed them over her chest and cast a wary gaze toward the backyard fence.

"'Something wicked this way comes,'" she muttered.

Jacob locked eyes with her and said, "C'mon. We have work to do."

They disappeared into the darkness and crept toward the alley.

CHAPTER 3

Water cascaded down his body in a torrent of rivers amidst clouds of roiling steam. Parker leaned his head against cold tiles and inhaled the warm vapor in measured breaths that soothed his lungs.

When the alarm went off at 6:45 a.m. with a blast of hip-hop, one breath was all it took to know that the storm hadn't just triggered a change in the weather. After eighteen years of wheezing and sucking down albuterol, he had learned one cold hard fact: asthma sucks.

After washing, he went back to his room and threw on some jeans and a forest green polo shirt. He combed his hair and checked himself in the mirror one last time before opening the door and walking down the hallway lined with family photographs.

The door to Abby's room was still closed, but the music and vocals of a girl's pop song blared from inside—as usual. He pounded on the door with his fist, provoking an immediate response.

"Quit it!"

That's my sister. He grinned and walked past the living room. Lamplight spilled from the corner where Mom sat next to the upright piano, dressed for work and reading her daily devotional.

"Riley Parker Austin, don't be mean to your sister."

"I wasn't." He entered the kitchen and sat down at the

breakfast table by the window. Cereal and a few thick slices of ham sufficed for a quick breakfast.

Water dripped from the saturated roof in a slow trickle of clear, tiny spheres falling in front of the bay window. His stomach did a somersault. If the ground was too wet, it would make the playing conditions difficult. A wet, heavy ball was impossible to throw, let alone catch. With the biggest game of the year on the line and the whole town there to see it, what if—

Black marks along the fence by the gate leading into the alley caught his attention. A large section of the red-painted wooden fence appeared charred. Bits of paint were cracked and crusted over with ash like a roasted marshmallow.

There goes tomorrow afternoon. Dad would definitely insist on help to repair it.

He stuffed the last bites of breakfast into his mouth, the salty ham mixing with the sweetness of honeycombs. Although concentrated around the section with the gate, the damage ran along the entire length of the fence. That was odd. Weren't lightning strikes usually in one place? And would lightning sprinkle the entire fence with burn marks? The wood planks looked as though drops of fire had rained from the sky.

High heels clacked against the kitchen floor. Mom came up from behind and kissed the top of his head. "Morning, Park. How're you feeling?"

"Fine." He swallowed the last mouthful. *Here comes the health check.*

"I heard it storming last night." She turned around and refilled her coffee cup. "How's your breathing?"

"Good."

"You used your inhaler?"

He rolled his eyes. "Yes."

"And steam from the shower?"

"Mom, I said I'm fine." He turned around to face her. Forest green clips and ribbons decorated her hair, and a gaudy shade of green that matched a heavy layer of eye shadow plastered her lips. She looked ready to attend a Mardi Gras parade. "Geez, I thought Halloween wasn't until tomorrow."

She gave a disapproving look and took a sip of coffee.

Three large, round buttons adorned her black blouse. One read, *Bobcat Mom*. The second one had *#12's MOM* on it, and the last one contained a picture of him posing in his uniform.

Seeing their names and images plastered over cheap trinkets adorning their houses and their parents' wardrobes was a rite of passage all teenagers in Briar Ridge had to endure. Mom obediently honored the tradition and even took it one step further by shoe-polishing her own car windows on game days, leaving no pane of glass untouched.

She poured the remainder of her coffee into a stainless steel thermos and then massaged her temples.

"Bad headache?"

She nodded, but managed a weak smile. "I'm fine, just the change in the weather, that's all."

"Weather? Really? What about all the coffee you drink?"

"A little coffee doesn't do any harm."

Parker laughed out loud. "A little? Mom, a dozen cups a day ain't a little. Nobody should be slurping down that much caffeine."

"*Isn't* a little. And besides, it's just a harmless habit from working the ER."

"Why don't you try decaf?"

Mom raised the mug to her lips. "Decaf is someone's idea of a sick joke." She took a sip and peered out the window over the kitchen sink. "What in the world?"

"Looks burned, doesn't it? Gotta be lightning."

"Did that happen last night?"

He nodded. "Yeah. Dad would've noticed if it had happened sooner. I didn't hear any lightning strikes last night though. Did you?"

"As loud as your father snores a freight train could pass by and I wouldn't hear it." She studied the fence again.

"Well, I'm sure your father will get right on it tomorrow."

Yep, there goes my weekend.

She turned and leaned on the granite countertop, facing him. "How you feeling about the game? You ready for tonight?"

He slid back in his chair and crossed his arms. "Oh, yeah. I throw a few touchdowns against Gatling, and I'll have my pick of schools and can punch my ticket outta here." The nightmare of living in this podunk town could end tonight with a stellar performance and a scholarship offer—the only dream worth dreaming the past three years since they'd moved to Briar Ridge.

His mother paused, but let the periodic remark of his disdain of living here slide. She grinned slightly. "Jeremiah 29:11. 'For I know the plans I have for you, says the Lord, plans to prosper you and not to harm you, plans to give you hope and a peace.'"

Whether the verse was in response to the game or to living in Briar Ridge wasn't clear. Regardless, Parker could've said his mother's favorite verse verbatim, as often as she'd quoted it over the years. The scripture was also on the bottom of a painting hanging in the living room depicting a small sailboat caught in a violent storm at night. From a dark shore, a lighthouse penetrated the gale with its beacon to lead the boat out of danger. Mom always liked to say that even in the darkest hour, God still provided enough light to navigate the storm.

She looked at her watch. "Go check on your sister for me."

"I'm coming, Mom," Abby called from the hallway. She hobbled into the kitchen, beaming. Forest green ribbons adorned her hair, and a big round button fastened to her white shirt read, *# 12's Lil Sis.*

Parker grabbed his thick letterman's jacket off the back of a kitchen chair. Football-shaped patches ran up and down both sleeves, indicating the numerous awards and recognitions he'd received over the years. He retrieved a package of strawberry Pop Tarts from the pantry and slid it into Abby's backpack.

"Thanks for letting me help on the sideline tonight, Park. I'm really excited to see the game from the field."

"No problem. It's the biggest game of the year, and I wanted you to see it from the best seat in the house."

Mom walked over and kissed Abby's forehead. "Bye, sweetie. I love you. Have a good day." She grabbed her purse off the kitchen counter and slipped it over her shoulder. "Park, don't forget I need you to stop by Gibson's Pharmacy on your way to school and pick up Abby's prescription."

"Got it, Mom."

Parker took Abby's backpack and escorted her into the garage where he shook his head at the shoe polish on his mother's car. Oh well, as long as he didn't have to be seen in it.

They stepped out into the cool morning air. Overcast skies blocked the morning sun and contained the first real hints that colder weather was coming. Last night's storm had definitely brought a change in the air. The chill carried by the breeze didn't seem like the temporary kind that would fade. No, this cold had a bite to it, and it wasn't going anywhere.

Parker and Abby crossed the damp driveway to the black Pontiac Firebird. Raindrops still beaded across the hood and on the windows. A few revs of the engine and the car backed out of the driveway and sped down Elliott Street. The pavement was still wet in most places, and the occasional splashing of puddles from potholes offered the only sound.

A black Dodge Charger appeared in the rearview mirror, following closely behind. Tailgating at 7:30 in the morning wasn't cool. Not that there was anywhere exciting to get to in Briar Ridge, but the guy didn't have to hug the bumper like a NASCAR driver.

They drove in silence while Abby ate her Pop Tarts. As

he neared Wabash Avenue, Abby finished her breakfast and asked to play some music.

He nodded and braced for more Taylor Swift.

A check of the mirror showed the black car had backed off a few car lengths, but it remained in the rear view down Elliott Street, onto Harding, and into Wabash Avenue, the main Briar Ridge thoroughfare.

Gibson's Pharmacy loomed ahead, just a few blocks down from the post office. Founded by the Gibson family and still family-owned, it was the oldest pharmacy in town and known for strong coffee and even stronger opinions thanks to the old-timers who gathered there in the early morning hours and gossiped like school girls.

Sitting close to the pharmacy counter, it was easy to learn who was sick, both physically and mentally, the latter of which always generated a good deal of talk. But no topic was more discussed than the Briar Ridge High School football team.

Parker pulled into the pharmacy parking lot. He sat for a moment, tapping his fingers against the steering wheel, and studied the rearview mirror. The Dodge Charger slowly turned into the asphalt lot and idled nearby. Abby seemed oblivious, leaning back with eyes closed, nodding her head to the beat of the music and mouthing the lyrics.

He got out, cupped his hands around his mouth, and blew warm air on them while surveying the Charger. Three people sat in the car, two in the front seat with one in the back, but the tinted windows prevented any identification.

Strange. Nobody who drove such a vehicle came to mind.

His body shook from a sudden chill, prompting him to hustle inside the pharmacy, where a strong aroma of coffee singed his nose and made him recoil.

How can anyone drink that stuff?

He snuck up to the pharmacy counter. A quiet murmur of conversation came from the old-timers. They hadn't noticed him yet, and if all went well, they never would.

Mr. Gibson was busy sorting pills. Parker drummed his fingertips on the white laminate, waiting to be noticed. The quiet chatter behind him continued.

Finally, the pharmacist finished counting and looked up. "Hey, Parker! How's it going, Mr. Quarterback?"

The chatting switched off like someone hit the power button. "I'm fine, Mr. Gibson. I'm on my way to school and just need to pick up Abby's prescription."

Gary Don Gibson, Sr., a heavyset man who was never in a hurry even when he meant to be, ambled forward, leaned against the counter in front of Parker, and casually asked about his family as if he had all the time in the world.

"They're fine, sir." Parker's foot tapped against the linoleum floor. "Um, how's yours?"

Mr. Gibson crossed thick arms over his chest and shook his head, jiggling his round, chubby cheeks. "Gary Don, Jr.'s back home with us now. Been here a couple of weeks since flunking out of community college. Honestly, that boy's drug problems since high school have cost him everything. He's got no shot at getting into pharmacy school now. I don't know what we're going to do with him." His shoulders sagged for a moment, but then his head jerked up and his brown eyes brightened.

"On the other hand, Joe Willie's graduating from pharmacy school, and he'll be starting with us in January. At least one of my boys can keep the family business going."

Yeah, I really don't care. "Um, Mr. Gibson, could—"

"Say, how about the Gatling game tonight? How are we looking?"

The pharmacy grew as quiet as a tomb.

"We'll have our hands full for sure, Mr. Gibson, but I've got no doubt we'll win. Um, if you don't mind, sir, can you get Abby's prescription so we're not late for school?"

As he turned to retrieve the medicine, the crowd behind Parker peppered him with questions. He turned around to face the old men. There were nine of them, gray-haired and wrinkled, scattered around the booths with coffee.

"So, y'all gonna run the ball at all tonight?" one of them asked. Without waiting for a response, the man continued, "That's how we did it back in my day." Everyone nodded. "Back in '57, we ran the Oklahoma Split-T…"

Here come the war stories. Parker rolled his eyes. *Thanks, Mom.*

An old man sitting alone in the far corner caught Parker's attention. Pale, sick-looking, his eyes were such a light brown color they looked almost yellow. The ghastly old man stared at him intently, leaning forward, both hands clenched so tightly around his coffee cup they began to shake.

"Well, are y'all just gonna throw the ball all night?" one old-timer asked.

Again, before he could give any response, another man spoke up. "Only soft teams throw the ball. Why are y'all so soft? Afraid of gettin' hit?"

One old man turned to another. "Why would they get bit?"

"No, Earl. He said, 'hit.' Why are they afraid to get hit?"

Earl nodded, finally understanding the question.

A man and a little girl, walking hand-in-hand, turned the corner and stopped at the next aisle. The man examined a jar of children's vitamins. The young girl smiled at Parker and then looked around the store in an absentminded fashion.

Where was Mr. Gibson with Abby's prescription? He'd already found it in the pick-up bin and was just listening to the conversation. Parker raised an eyebrow at him, and he slowly stepped forward to ring up the pills on the register.

Parker shot a quick glance at the old, sick-looking man in the corner. The unpleasant look on his face morphed into an awful scowl, but it was aimed at the man and little girl in the aisle across from him.

What's this guy's problem?

"Hey, Mr. Gibson. Who's the guy in the corner over there?"

The pharmacist gave a slight shrug. "Don't know. He's not one of my regulars. He came in a little while ago and said he was waiting for someone."

"Whether you run the ball or throw the ball, it don't mean nothing if y'all don't beat Gatling," said another coffee drinker, leaning in Parker's direction as if to emphasize his point.

At the mention of Gatling, Parker returned his attention back to the old timers as sounds of utter contempt emanated from the coffee area. Gatling was Briar Ridge's archrival and sister city thirty-five miles to the north along Highway 44. It was larger, more affluent, and proud of it. A bunch of snobs, really.

An old man slapped his palm onto the table. "How long have you been here, son?"

Parker glanced at his watch. "I'd say a little over two minutes." Mr. Gibson laughed.

Confusion spread across the old man's face. Clearly that was an unexpected answer. He frowned. "No, I meant how long have you lived here."

"Three years, sir."

"Then *you* don't know what this game really means to *us*." There it was. Another jab at his outsider status.

"Gatling's the rich folk—the oil men, the ranchers, their rich bankers and lawyers. But we're the roughnecks and ranch hands. We do all the hard, honest work. And this is the one time a year when we get to stick it to those people who always look down on us. You ain't playing for your school, you're playing for this town—for all of us."

Earl leaned over. "A bus? What bus?"

The man sitting next to him grumbled, "No, Earl. Nobody said anything about a bus. Check your hearing aid battery. I think it's running low."

Earl shook with disapproval and crossed his arms. "I don't sew. Mabel does. It's her hobby."

"For cryin' out loud," one man muttered into his cup.

Mr. Gibson rang up the bill for Abby's prescription. Parker handed over the money and took the change and Abby's medicine.

He spun around and bolted out of the pharmacy. A quick scan of the parking lot showed no sign of the Charger. He opened the car door and sat down only to be greeted by more screeching from a teen pop star.

Turning down the music prompted Abby to open her eyes. "Hey, I like that song."

He sped out of the parking lot and onto Wabash Avenue, heading east and merging with morning traffic. "Sorry. My car, my rules. Why don't you listen to that mess on your iPod instead?"

"It sounds better out here."

"Then pick something else. I don't like that song."

Abby grinned and hit one of the buttons on the console while he turned south onto Harper, which dead-ended in front of Sycamore Elementary School. An all-girl teenage pop band wailed about boyfriends and bubble gum.

Parker sighed, but couldn't suppress his amusement. "You know I hate that stuff." His eyebrows arched and the corners of his mouth turned up in a smile.

Abby chuckled. "Just messing with you." She ejected the CD and put it into her backpack.

He swerved out of traffic and pulled into the first available parking space in front of the school. The noise of idling car engines and children's laughter filled the air as he got out and helped Abby into her walker. Although her legs were getting stronger from years of physical therapy, she still needed her trusty walker for the time being, though she talked constantly of getting rid of it for good.

He slung her backpack over his shoulder and accompanied her up the damp sidewalk.

Abby grunted. "For the millionth time, you don't have to walk me to the door. I can do it myself."

"I know you can, but for the millionth time, I'm gonna walk with you anyway."

She rolled her eyes. "No one's gonna mess with me,

Park. It's been three years since that thing with Billy and Brian McGonagill and nothing's happened. I'm okay."

Parker's mouth creased into a smirk. "Yeah, nobody's messed with you because they all saw what happens to anyone who does. Anyone who bullies my little sister is gonna get taken out."

She shook her head. "But you didn't have to beat them up. Principal Traylor was going to handle it."

He kicked a small rock across the sidewalk. "Please. You sound like Mom."

"And you're just like Dad—always doing stuff without thinking." She stopped and stared into him. "Really, Park. What would've happened if they'd recognized you? That family is crazy."

"You really are Mom's kid. You worry just like her." He placed a hand on her walker and grinned. "Look, Billy and Brian's dad is a drunk truck driver who is never around. I mean, he basically doesn't exist. And their older brother, Bobby, is locked up in juvie somewhere. Besides, it was three years ago. If anything was going to happen to me, it would've happened already."

The snail's pace procession resumed for a moment but stopped as several kids skipped past them. Abby watched her schoolmates bounce down the sidewalk, ponytails swaying back and forth. A look of melancholy rested on her face.

"Don't worry. Pretty soon, you'll be able to skip as fast as them."

She shook her head and looked down at her legs. "No, I won't."

His jaw dropped. "Hey, what kind of talk is—"

"I'm going to go faster!" she interrupted, her blue eyes beaming at him.

He laughed out loud. "Now that's my little sis." He rubbed the top of her head lightly, careful not to disturb the ribbons in her hair. She always did have that can-do spirit. Despite her mild cerebral palsy, she never expressed any frustration in her effort to live as fully as possible.

They continued their trek toward the front of the building. When they arrived, he held open the glass door. "See you at the game."

He went back down the sidewalk, smiling at the little kids whose eyes lit up with recognition of the high school's quarterback. His grin faded though when the black Dodge Charger cruised past him.

CHAPTER 4

Parker slammed his car door shut at exactly 8:00 as the school bell rang. He hustled toward the bobcat statue in front of the school building where Summer Hayes met him every morning. She was already there, chatting with a friend while eyeing his approach. She wore her cheerleading uniform and thick letter jacket. Her blonde hair flowed like golden streamers in the cool morning breeze.

"Hey, handsome," she said as he reached for her. She buried her head in his chest, and he kissed the top of her head. The sweet aroma of strawberry-scented shampoo wafted into his nose.

She looked up at him. "Where've you been?"

"Had to stop by Gibson's to pick up some medicine for Abby."

"Gibson's? Hanging with the grumpy old men?" They turned and walked up the steps, holding hands.

"Yeah. There was this one creepy-looking guy in there who I'm pretty sure wanted to take a swing at me. It was weird."

They nodded quick hellos to friends on the way into the building and squeezed their way through the crowded senior corridor. Trashy lockers, bleak, narrow hallways—the whole building was a joke. If dilapidated ever became cool, BRHS would be the coolest place on Earth.

Each let go of the other's hand as Summer stopped at her locker and Parker proceeded to his, which was hard to miss. Summer had decorated the rusty, paint-chipped locker from top to bottom with white flowers, forest green ribbons and bows, and other small trinkets of school spirit. The only part still visible was the small latch used to open it. He popped open the locker and riffled through the disorganized stack of textbooks and folders. After a few moments, he located his government textbook, grabbed the first notepad he found, and started off to first period.

The last one into his government class, he sat down at his desk on the far side of the room next to the row of dirty windows that even an all-night rain shower couldn't wash.

Most of the students were getting out their materials, sending out last-second texts to friends, or engaging in idle conversation. A few had their heads on their desks or were slumped in their chairs, still holding onto the last precious moments of thoughtlessness.

Parker slouched in his chair and glanced out the window. It was still overcast, but the wind had stopped. The dirt, dust, and grime on the pane of glass gave everything a brownish-yellow hue, kind of like that old man's eyes at Gibson's. His mind wandered back to the strange old man. Who was that guy? Why was he so angry?

The Dodge Charger pulled into the parking lot and cruised down the rows of parked vehicles. Parker bolted upright in his chair. The car paused behind Parker's Fire-bird, the exhaust pipe spitting out small puffs of smoke as the engine idled, and then continued through the lot and out of sight.

No Briar Ridge student had a car like that, so who was in the car? What were they doing here? Were they following him?

Thoughts of the mysterious car preoccupied him until the bell rang and the mad dash to second period began.

He walked into the crowded hallway and found Summer waiting for him at his locker. He slid both arms around her waist and their lips met. His mouth watered at the taste of the cherry-flavored lip-gloss. Yum. The kiss lingered, and Parker slid his hands past her lower back.

She grinned. "Later," she whispered.

He uttered a low growl, smiled, and opened his locker.

"So, what do you want to do after the game tonight?" she asked as he searched for his English literature book.

"I don't know. Who's hosting the party?"

"Tasha, I think."

He grimaced. An evening with the obnoxious fire hydrant? No way. "Tasha's? That's where you want to go tonight?"

"Yeah. She's added a karaoke machine to their upstairs game room. Should be fun." She peered into his locker. She reached in and pulled out the English textbook. "Here you go, Sherlock."

"Thanks." He took the book from her. "Hey, do you know anyone that drives a black Dodge Charger?"

"No. Why?"

He shrugged. "Forget it."

He told her he'd see her later and headed to Mr. Ellis's English class while trying to put the black car out of his mind.

He walked into the classroom and sat down at his desk just as the bell rang.

Mr. Ellis stepped inside, pulling the classroom door closed behind him. He stormed to his desk with a look of great annoyance and bellowed in his thick, raspy voice, "Sit down and shut your stinking mouths. We have miles to go today."

It didn't matter that everyone was already seated and not a word was being spoken. Each class period began with the same stern admonition. Nothing was allowed to disrupt him. He once forbade the class from leaving during a fire drill since it would've interrupted his lesson on William Faulkner's *Intruder in the Dust*.

"All right, people, yesterday we discussed the background of John Milton in preparation for reading *Paradise Lost*. Now that you've finished the poem, let's dive into it." He scanned the room. "Alarcon, why does Milton open by invoking a muse?"

Stacie Alarcon was an honor student, baton twirler, and front-runner for valedictorian. She sat ramrod straight, everything on her desk neat and orderly.

She spoke with confidence. "Milton addresses the muse because it was typical of epic poems amongst the ancient Greek poets to invoke a muse for inspiration, much like Homer's *Iliad* and *Odyssey*. Milton's poem is an epic in that style and tradition, hence, the inclusion of the muse."

"Good," Mr. Ellis said, picking at something on his shirt. He looked up and glanced around the room.

"Austin. Start us off with the story."

Great. Here we go. "The story opens with Satan and his followers in Hell. They're depressed and trying to figure out what to do. They'd just—"

"Wait a second. Who exactly were Satan's followers?"

"They were some of God's angels, like Satan was, before they rebelled."

Mr. Ellis nodded. "And do they notice anything different about themselves now?"

"What do you mean? Like their appearance?"

"You tell me, Austin."

"Yes." Parker remembered. "They're no longer beautiful like they once were when God made them. Because they rebelled against God, they were transformed into ugly, evil things. Kind of like devils or demons, I guess."

Mr. Ellis leaned back and clasped both hands behind his head. "All right, keep going."

"They'd just rebelled against God and God had beaten them and banished them to Hell. Some of Satan's followers are depressed, so he tries to rally them. He creates his palace, 'Pandemonium.' And they discuss what to do next." Parker stopped and looked at Mr. Ellis to see if he should continue.

Mr. Ellis was looking up at the ceiling, eyes half-closed. "I didn't say stop."

Parker sighed. "Satan tells everyone how they can get back at God. He tells them that by corrupting God's favorite creature, Man, they can have their revenge."

"And what does Satan think is worse than Hell?"

Parker thought for a moment. "Serving in Heaven."

"What's the exact line?"

"'Better to reign in Hell, than to serve in Heaven.'" *Take that, Alarcon!*

"Then what?"

"Satan gets two of his followers, Sin and Death, to help him sneak his way to Earth, where he corrupts Adam and Eve."

Mr. Ellis unclasped his hands from behind his head, took his feet off his desk, and sat up. He leaned forward and put his elbows on the desk. "Good," he replied with a thin smile. "Enough of the Austin show. Let's move on to someone else. Let's see...Welles!" Adrian Welles jumped in his seat. "Your turn at bat. Pick up where Austin left off."

After nearly an hour of reviewing and discussing the poem, the bell finally rang. Parker made his way through the school, then out to the bobcat statue—the only thing kept in pristine condition on the campus. It sat on a giant block of granite and depicted a bobcat in a crouching position, ready to pounce. It even had its own spotlight so it could be illuminated at night. A fresh coat of green paint was applied to it every year, mainly because the student body believed rubbing its nose would bring good luck. Naturally, on game days and on days in which a test was administered, the statue received a good deal of rubbing.

He rubbed the mascot's cold nose and waited for Summer.

She emerged from the front doors chatting with Tasha, and the two made their way down the steps to him. When they got to the statue, he smiled at Summer and ignored Tasha, though her fiery red hair, freckles, and fake tan begged for ridicule. Although her family was loaded due to her father losing a leg in a freak oil drilling accident, the money couldn't buy her any maturity or intelligence—just a big mouth that never closed. Ever.

Tasha smirked. "Geez, Parker, you look terrible. Afraid you're gonna choke in the big game?"

"Nope. Afraid a dog is going to mistake you for a fire hydrant?"

Tasha sneered. "Why don't you go back to Houston where you belong?"

"That's enough, you two." Summer grabbed Parker's hand and dragged him to his car before the situation got heated.

"Still don't know why you put up with her." He opened the door for her. Tasha never missed a chance to remind him of his outsider status.

"Because she's been my friend my whole life, that's why. She's actually pretty artistic and a good writer too. She's working on a book right now."

"What's it called? *Fifty Shades of Crazy*?"

"All right, Park. Just drop it."

Whatever. He shut the door and climbed in.

As usual, she did most of the talking during lunch as she shared the latest rumors of the day, including the one about Action 9 News coming to tonight's game.

On the way back to campus, the Dodge Charger appeared in the rearview mirror again, just a few car lengths behind him. It copied his lane changes and speed adjustments, trailing him all the way back to the school parking lot. Definitely not a coincidence.

Parker parked his car and jumped out to confront the driver, but the mysterious car sped down the street and disappeared around the corner. Whoever was in the car sure didn't want to be seen.

Summer flipped open her compact and studied her appearance. "What was that about?"

Were they really following him or was this a case of pre-game paranoia? Better to keep quiet and figure it out later. "Nothing. Forget it."

The bell rang and he walked her to her locker. He kissed her goodbye, strolled to the end of the senior corridor, and entered the auditorium for drama class.

Like everything else at the high school, the auditorium reeked of neglect. The carpet was stained and moldy, and none of its wooden chairs were cushioned. Parker made his way down the left aisle toward the front where the class gathered. Stopping at the third row, he sank into a stiff, wooden chair and tried to relax. A few students rehearsed a song from *Camelot*, the school's fall musical set to be performed in two weeks and in which he had been cast as Lancelot and Skylar Reece as Guinevere—a casting decision Summer had been griping about for weeks.

Skylar was a hardcore swimmer and had a body that could melt most guys' earwax. She'd also been Summer's rival for Parker when he'd first moved to Briar Ridge. Even now Summer still gripped his hand more tightly whenever Skylar passed them in the hallway.

And with good reason. Skylar loved flirting with Parker, just to agitate Summer. And during rehearsal today she held nothing back while on stage with him. Seductive grins. Mischievous winks. She'd even leaned in like she was about to kiss him at one point.

By next period, word would've gone around the entire school that the two of them had engaged in dirty dancing on the stage together. It'd send Summer through the roof. He cringed.

The bell was a welcome release and Parker made his way through the side exit of the auditorium, careful to keep his distance from Skylar. He walked upstairs to Mrs. Calvin's classroom.

Mrs. Calvin taught Business Applications, an introductory course to the world of business and finance. He'd hoped that the class would help prepare him to be a business major next year in college. Big mistake.

Mrs. Calvin's class consisted of busy work and occasional episodes of crazy when she conversed with imaginary friends or animals. She'd suffered a mental collapse after her divorce four years before and never returned to normal.

A quick study of the business problems on the dry erase board revealed they were the exact same problems from yesterday, and no one had the slightest interest in calling her attention to that fact. Instead, everyone pecked away at the buttons on their calculators and wrote down the same answers as yesterday while Mrs. Calvin sat at her desk, staring into space.

It was a mind-numbing exercise, but at least it kept him busy for an hour. When the bell finally rang, he rushed to turn in his work but managed to knock over the stack of books on the corner of Mrs. Calvin's desk. He stooped to gather them from the floor. The other students filed out.

"God's a comedian, Parker."

His head jerked up. "Ma'am?"

She smiled. She never smiled. "God's laughing. He's laughing." Her voice was soft and dreamy.

The hairs on the back of his neck stood up. "Mrs. Calvin, are you okay?"

"Can't you hear them, Parker? Can't you hear them?"

She's not playing with a full deck.

He glanced around the room. "Um, I don't hear anyone." He put the last book on the stack.

"Yes," she whispered. Her eerie smile stayed in place, and she nodded. "Yes, I agree. It would be better that way."

Nope. Not one card.

He edged to the door.

"Parker." Despite the smile that seemed frozen in place, cold, lifeless eyes stared into his. "Goodbye."

He hurried out of the room and didn't slow down until he reached his Spanish class. The vibration of his cell phone broke him free from thoughts of Mrs. Calvin as he sat down at his desk. A text from Summer. It read: *WHAT HAPPENED IN DRAMA???*

He sighed. No response would cool her down, so he slid the phone back into his pocket and tried to conjugate verbs for an hour.

When class ended, he joined the throng of students heading to the pep rally. He shuffled through the glass doors and toward the side of the non-air-conditioned gym, where the football team sat in a solitary row of folding chairs facing the student body. Summer stood with Tasha and the rest of the cheerleading squad, her back to the crowd, scanning the gym's entrance. As soon as they made eye contact, she headed straight for him, leaving a scowling Tasha and a gossipy cheerleading squad behind her. He put his hands in his jacket pockets and braced for the storm.

She marched across the basketball court, her eyes never leaving him. "What happened in the theater with Skylar?"

"Nothing."

"Was she flirting with you again? Was she coming on to you? Did she touch you?"

He paused. At least the marching band was making so much noise that nobody could hear what they were saying, although Summer's body language clearly indicated trouble in paradise.

"Well?"

"No, she didn't touch me. She was just messing with me during rehearsal, you know, trying to break my concentration, that's all. It was nothing."

Summer's eyes widened. "Nothing? That's not what I heard!" She had yet to break eye contact. "I heard she was all over you. And if that tramp thinks she's going to bump and grind on my boyfriend, then she's finally going to get it." She jabbed a finger into his chest, her sharpened, manicured nail, almost drawing blood. "And don't even try to stop me this time, Park. Only one person gets to touch you, and that's me!"

She spun around to rejoin a leering Tasha and the rest of the squad. He took an open seat with his teammates. Even though it was cool outside, the stuffy gym warmed quickly as the entire student body crowded inside. Parker took off his letter jacket and draped it across the back of his chair.

Tyler Maxwell sat next to him, eating a small bag of Doritos. He leaned over and grinned. "Havin' fun?"

Parker scowled. "Always."

With his hands in his pockets, he slid back in his chair and brooded throughout the pep rally. Skylar's stunt and the trouble it'd now caused weren't cool. With the biggest game of the year only four hours away, he didn't need any additional drama if he was to have the best performance of his life tonight.

When the pep rally ended, he exited the gym with the masses and made his way to his car.

A piece of white paper, folded in half underneath a windshield wiper, caught his attention. He grabbed the note and opened it. Large, red letters read: *You're dead!*

Parker glanced around, but nothing seemed unusual or out of place. With a smirk, he folded the note and stuck it into the pocket of his letter jacket. Had to be Gatling fans. Arriving in town early and already talking trash.

He got into his car and left the school behind. Five minutes later he turned into the parking lot of the Briar Ridge Methodist Church, where his family worshiped every Sunday. He got out of the car and went inside, passing the church office on the way to the sanctuary. If the secretary noticed him, she made no effort to look up from her issue of *Redbook*.

Light shone through the stained glass above the choir loft, bathing him in colors on the second-row pew. Briar Ridge Methodist provided a quiet spot to clear the mind and focus on game days. It was even a decent place to be on Sundays. "Pastor Jim" was pretty cool—huge football fan.

Parker glanced at his watch. He had to get all this junk out of his head. The entire day had been bizarre—the burnt fence, the strange old man in Gibson's, the Dodge Charger, Mrs. Calvin, and the note. Something really weird was going on. But what?

His right knee bounced with nervous energy. He leaned forward against the back of the pew in front of him, clasped his hands together, and bowed his head to pray.

CHAPTER 5

Marie sat in the top row of the balcony and watched Parker pray. Of all places, the peaceful sanctuary should have comforted her, but not even the tranquility of this place could stop the waves of concern sweeping through her. Even Jacob had been surprised by the others' brazen display of aggression during the night. She'd dared to poke and prod for an explanation even though he seemed impatient about the entire situation.

"C'mon, Jacob. Tell me. Why are they acting this way?"

His eyes had clouded with concern. "Because they can feel the impending doom, the approaching darkness. Sensing it's so close, they're getting all the more hungry for it, craving to feast on death and destruction—even wanting to take part in it."

At least the thunderstorm had masked their intervention, but the damaged fence offered proof of the fight that had occurred.

The others withdrew from the house, but they didn't go away. She sensed them wandering around the area throughout the night, but they kept their distance. Why were they interested in Parker?

The strange events throughout the day pointed to something big about to go down. The black Dodge Charger, the enemy in the pharmacy, Mrs. Calvin, the note on his car. Was he being targeted?

And what about the crazy rumor that Yaris had been killed in human form?

She frowned. The stigma of her outsider status often prevented the free flow of information to her, though Jacob would share if she pestered him enough.

She pressed her lips together tightly and shook her head. The lack of full inclusion by her colleagues might jeopardize her charge. If Parker was being targeted, she needed to know. She'd tell one of them if she knew one of their charges was in jeopardy. So why not do the same for her? Unless…they wanted her to fail. Would they really sacrifice a charge just to get rid of her? No way. Surely their petty feelings didn't run that deep.

She glanced down at Parker. He hadn't moved from his praying position. *My sweet Parker.* What would happen if she cleared her throat in an exaggerated manner? Would he look up? Would he see her? What if she walked down the stairs and waited for him in the narthex on his way out? A smile stretched across her face as she imagined the possibilities and thought of speaking to him in a regular conversation. Would he like the sound of her voice? Would he like her?

Soft footfalls on the stairway behind her diverted her attention. A chill raced through her and she shivered. Why hadn't she sensed the presence sooner? Her heart thumped in her chest as she turned toward the dark stairwell.

Slowly, with each careful tread, his silhouette came into view as he neared the top of the stairs. He paused in the shadows for a moment, watching her, as if enjoying her anxiety. She swallowed and kept her eyes glued to the shadowy figure as he finally emerged from the darkness and crept toward her. He stopped at her pew, towering over her. He motioned toward the vacant seat next to her.

"May I?"

It couldn't be. Speechless, she slowly nodded.

He sat down beside her. His black leather jacket crackled against the wooden pew. Smooth, black boots, waxed and buffed to a high sheen, propped up on the back of the pew in front of him. He leaned back and clasped his hands behind his thick head of black hair.

She continued to watch him, still unable to speak. His fiendish yellow eyes and the pale ghastliness of his skin stood out even in the dimly lit balcony.

He turned his head toward her, grinned, and whispered, "Forzieri."

She blinked and tried to concentrate. What had he said? Forza what?

"The jacket. It's Forzieri. Only the finest in leather fashions. I find their product line quite superior to Armani." He held out his arm to her. "Go ahead, feel it. You'll notice the quality."

The bogeyman was here, speaking to her in person for the first time, and he wanted to talk about fashion? She held his cocky gaze, but found it difficult to find words. She hadn't been expecting to be confronted like this, not by *him*. And certainly not about fashion.

After a long, awkward silence, he smiled, put out a thin, sinewy hand. "My apologies, that was awfully forward of me. Allow me to introduce myself. I'm—"

"I know who you are," she quietly interrupted him and studied his white, translucent face. His hollow, yellow eyes seemed to glow in the darkened sanctuary, making him look even more otherworldly. "You're Seth," she whispered. "Disciple of the fallen angels who took the names 'Sin' and 'Death.' Any guardian who doesn't know who you are would be sent to the mailroom."

"I'm flattered." He withdrew his hand. His yellow eyes sized her up. "Nice suede. Ralph Lauren?"

She ran her fingers along the inside seam of her jacket. "Um…yeah."

He nodded in approval. "It's nice. Trendy and hip, yet not too chic." He surveyed her again with a cool air bordering on arrogance. "I thought I knew most of the old guard. What's your name?"

"Marie," she replied softly. "My name is Marie."

His eyes locked onto hers.

She sensed him probing for something, a weakness most likely. Conversation might break his concentration. "So what are you doing here?" she asked, careful to keep her voice down.

Seth shrugged. "Why not? I've had a very busy day so far, and this place looks as good as any to relax." He looked around the sanctuary in a disinterested fashion. "Besides, you know there's no place that's off-limits to us. We go where we please."

Her mind raced. What was he up to? She checked on Parker. He was still praying. Good. She exhaled deeply, her shoulders lowering and her muscles relaxing. She looked back at Seth. Was her concern obvious? What else could he sense? She needed to put up a front, keep up her guard, but would she give herself away if she overplayed it?

He tilted his head to one side and raised a thin eyebrow. "Why have you appeared? I mean, why appear just to watch him?"

He senses something. Better to avoid his question, lest it give him an area to exploit. She set her jaw. "I could ask you the same thing."

He paused before answering, obviously mulling something over in his deceitful mind. Empty, soulless eyes stared back at her. "Give it up, Marie. You can't stop what's coming." He turned and settled himself deeper into the pew as if he were about to take a nap. "None of you can."

"You're delusional."

"The war is coming to Briar Ridge tonight. Cling to your sad, tattered shreds of hope all you want," he said, his eyes closed. "You're the one who's delusional if you think it's going to make any difference."

"Hope, faith—they always make a difference. That's what you and your kind can never understand. And you never will."

He sneered. "Poor Marie." He slowly opened his eyes

and swiveled his head in her direction. "So *naïve,* just like all the rest. Be honest. Do you really think your boss cares about that kid down there or anyone else in this backwater town? You watch. He's not going to do a thing to stop us tonight." A sinister grin spread across his face.

"We'll see about that."

"You're in way over your head, and it's already showing."

"What do you mean?"

He sat up. "Look at you. You've appeared just to watch your charge." He turned and motioned down at Parker. "That's not standard operating procedure for guardians. In fact, it's *discouraged.* And yet you've deliberately chosen to do it anyway when it's completely unnecessary, and I've got the feeling it's not the first time you've done so. Is it?"

"S—s—so?" Marie stammered.

He faced her. "So, that can only mean one thing." He paused and the clear implication lingered between them. "And if you're not careful, it'll cloud your judgment." His grin widened and his eyes flashed. "But I suspect it already has."

She rubbed her sweaty palms on her jeans.

"After it all goes down, they'll come to you. Usually it's someone you know, someone you trust. They'll approach you like they're just checking in on you, as if they're concerned for your well-being. That's how it starts."

"How what starts?

"How you get replaced, of course."

Those words sucked the air out of her lungs. Having a charge revoked was the ultimate loss, a humiliating blow that always resulted in the loss of guardian status.

What would she do if she couldn't see him anymore? How could she go on without ever hearing his voice or being in his presence? She wiped her brow with the back of her hand and tried to pull herself together, but couldn't escape the fear of losing him.

"How many charges have you had, if you don't mind my asking?"

Was it ten or eleven? "Eleven," she replied slowly, still trying to overcome the thought of losing Parker. "He's my eleventh charge."

"So that means you've only been doing this for…what, five hundred years, give or take a decade?"

She nodded. "Something like that."

He shook his head, his mouth turned down in mock pity. "*Extrarium*." The word had been muttered, but every syllable stung just as painfully as if he'd shouted at her.

"Outsider—that's what the *real* guardians call you, isn't it? Maybe not to your face, but it's always on their minds whenever you're around. It's an example of the hypocrisy that's been going on for millennia, and another reason why you should leave."

Outsider. A lump formed in her throat. She'd been so excited when she joined the Protectorate, to be a guardian and make a difference.

Five centuries of being looked down upon and treated as less than equal were taking a toll. Still, the thought of leaving never crossed her mind.

She swallowed past the lump. "Leave and follow you? Never this side of Hell."

He placed his hands on the back of the pew in front of him and pressed himself up.

"Fine. Continue to be treated as second-class. But, know this—you're definitely in over your head. The war's coming here tonight no matter what, and there's nothing you and your colleagues can do except stand around and watch—like you did last night outside that kid's house." He exited the pew and walked toward the stairs.

Her stomach churned, and she wiped tiny beads of perspiration from her forehead.

Descending the stairs, he whispered, "See you later, Marie—if you're still around."

She turned and stared at the stained glass-window. Moist

palms pressed together. Lips moved in prayer. Maybe, just maybe tonight could be stopped.

CHAPTER 6

Parker got out of his car and headed across the practice field. That the team was allowed to practice here was criminal. Like dangerous landmines, ant piles sprouted in small mounds. The field, infested with fire ants, gave the football players more issues than injuries during the season.

Still, the ants paled in comparison to the pump jack. How it came to be built there had never been clearly explained, but a Gatling-owned oil pump jack sat on one half of the field. It creaked and groaned, bobbing up and down, pumping out oil, despite all the cuts and scrapes players received from crashing into its protective chain-link barrier every day. Injuries to the roughnecks' kids in Briar Ridge meant nothing to their boss in Gatling, so the pump jack would never be moved. It made beating the snot out of Gatling all the more sweet.

Parker crunched across the withered grass, passed through the propped-open rusty doors of the field house, and entered the varsity locker room. The familiar scent of body odor, mildew, and cheap cologne greeted him inside the large square-shaped room lined with open metal locker stalls. Several of his teammates were already busy getting dressed.

Black game pants and jerseys hung in everyone's locker. *Awesome.* The black jerseys were the team's favorite. Always reserved for the most important games, the all-black look made them feel intimidating, and if there ever was a good time to wear them, it was tonight.

He undressed, slid into his football pants, and slipped on the gray T-shirt emblazoned with the scripture from Colossians 3:23, *Whatever you do, work at it with all your heart, as working for the Lord...* Mom and Dad had gotten him the shirt three years ago when he'd become the starting quarterback. They'd said it was a reminder that no matter what you do, do it with everything you've got. Total commitment.

"No half-assing," Dad had said in his usual direct way.

Parker had worn the shirt under his shoulder pads during every game the past three years. And with such an important game, not the slightest deviation from tradition or ritual could be tolerated.

He grabbed his iPod and walked barefoot across the cold, concrete hall and into the training room to get his ankles taped. He leaned against the cool cinderblock wall and let the Christian rock music of Kutless and TFK wash over him as he waited his turn.

An athletic trainer motioned for him. Parker got on the table and dangled his bare feet off the front end. The athletic trainer sat on a stool in front of him. With a flurry of precise movements, the trainer wrapped his ankles in white athletic tape.

Abby stood in her walker near the large ice machine at the other end of the room. She concentrated on scooping ice cubes into the large orange Gatorade coolers on the floor. The large scoops were heavy, and her face twisted with the effort.

His chest swelled. She worked so hard at the "menial" tasks everyone else took for granted. She never quit or told anyone she couldn't do the work—no matter how difficult it was or how long it took her to get the job done.

The athletic trainer tapped him on his left knee. Parker took out one of the earphones and the trainer asked if the taping felt tight enough. He wiggled his feet around. Tight, but not too uncomfortable, with the prospect of only a minimal loss of leg hair upon removal. Not bad. He nodded, hopped off the table, and walked over to Abby.

She had filled one cooler and started dumping ice into another one. Two student trainers came by and picked up the first cooler and hauled it off. Parker stopped his iPod and took out the other earphone. Abby was too busy concentrating on lifting the heavy scoop to notice him. He waited until she emptied it and then spoke up.

"Hey, sis. How you doing?"

She looked up. "Fine," she said with a smile. "Just filling the coolers with ice."

"How long have you been here?"

"Um, Mom dropped me off a few minutes ago."

"How was she?"

"Nervous, like she always is before your games. She kept saying she wished she could be here. She wouldn't stop talking about it."

That figured. Mom always talked a lot when she was nervous. "You ready for tonight?"

Abby's eyes widened and her face brightened. "Oh, yeah, I'm ready! It's going to be a great game."

Parker grinned.

The small training room swelled with teammates needing to get taped, and student trainers weaved in and out, grabbing water bottles, cups, first aid supplies, and other equipment. Loud, crowded, and hectic, it was a difficult place to hold a conversation. Still, the urge to linger with Abby kept him rooted to the floor.

"So how many touchdowns you want me to throw tonight?"

She scrunched her face in concentration. "Um...seven."

"Seven? That's an awful lot. Why seven?"

"Because that's my favorite number."

He laughed. "All right, sis. I'll see what I can do."

One of the assistant coaches announced the call for pregame warm-ups.

"Well, I gotta go. I'll see you out there." He hurried back to the emptying locker room to put on his shoulder pads and shoes. As he tied his cleats, Tyler walked up to him, finishing a Snickers bar.

He stood to grab his green helmet off the top shelf of his locker. "Ty, did you find a note from Gatling fans on your car after school today?"

Tyler wadded up the candy wrapper and tossed it in the general direction of the trashcan. "Nope."

"Know anybody that drives a black Dodge Charger?"

Tyler shook his head. "Why?"

"Some stupid Gatling fans left a note on my car that said I'm dead. I just figured they were talking trash. It was pretty lame."

Tyler's eyes narrowed for a moment. "I didn't get anything on my car, and I haven't heard of anyone else getting any notes, either."

Parker paused, shrugged his shoulders, and put on his helmet.

They exited the locker room into the concrete hallway lined with team pictures of previous Briar Ridge football teams. They walked in silence, the only noise a clacking from their cleats striking the floor.

"How'd they know it was your car?"

"Huh?" Parker replied.

"Did you doze off? The note, dude. How did Gatling fans know it was your car?"

"I don't know." Parker dismissed the question with a shrug and tried to focus on the game. They passed the coaches' office and exited the main doors of the field house to Bobcat Stadium.

Tyler inhaled deeply and grinned. "Ah, the sweet smell of cow manure. Smells like victory, doesn't it?"

Bobcat Stadium was as plain and uninspiring as the rest of the campus. The facility had been built on a cow pasture behind the high school about a million years ago and very little had changed ever since. Even the smell of cow manure somehow seemed to remain. The walk from field house to stadium was only one hundred feet, and cheering fans lined the sidewalk as Parker and Tyler walked past.

Parker nodded in acknowledgement to the encouraging comments, and paused to make sure he gently slapped every child's palm within reach. Seeing their little eyes light up and their smiles stretch from ear to ear after a high five was priceless.

As they approached the main gate, three uniformed police officers held back the crowd so the players could pass through. As Parker stepped onto the field, he glanced around the stadium. Fans poured into the bleachers on both sides, the Gatling students announcing their presence with a banner hanging from their side of the stadium that read: Cash versus Trash.

An ominous black was overtaking the dreary gray skies. A chill hung in the air, and a slight breeze blew across the field.

The Action 9 News television van from Fort Worth was parked on Azalea Drive, which bordered the north end zone. The news crew huddled around their equipment and surveyed the stadium. *So the rumors were true after all.*

A student trainer brought a bag of footballs and emptied it in front of Parker and his backup, Hayden Hyghtower. He reached down and grabbed a ball. The tight leather felt good gripped in his hands.

Coach Sinclair stood close by, watched him throw for a few minutes, and asked how he felt.

"Good," Parker replied, trying to clamp down the pre-game nausea swirling in his stomach.

"Are you loose?"

"Yes, sir."

Parker liked Coach "Sinc." He never cursed, which definitely set him apart from most other coaches.

"Any questions about the first series? Gatling's coverage, adjustments—anything?"

"No, sir."

"Good. Let's get the offense together and run a few plays."

The bleachers on both sides filled to capacity—and kickoff wasn't for another thirty minutes. Students from Gatling hoisted a banner that read, "Cash vs. Trash." As if there was any doubt how they felt. The feeling from beating those jerks just couldn't be measured.

The Briar Ridge marching band assembled at the stadium's north end and was warming up. He spied Abby standing behind the benches, filling small paper cups with Gatorade and putting them on the table in neat little rows. In her own little world, she seemed as happy and content as ever.

Behind her the cheerleaders were putting their pom-poms and megaphones in the correct positions. God forbid they get misplaced. Otherwise, chaos would reign. Tasha was busy holding court, probably telling everyone about her latest expensive purchase. She'd curled her red hair and applied heavy makeup to her face, turning herself into a circus clown. Parker shook his head and looked for Summer. She stood at the foot of the bleachers, talking with her mother at the railing on the front row.

After warm-ups, Coach Sinc hollered for everyone to head to the field house. The players jogged to the south end zone and made their way through the main gate where the three officers cleared a path for them again. The crowd lining the sidewalk was much thicker now. The fans were rowdy, some of them already liquored up, anticipating a beatdown of the rich snobs from Gatling.

Once inside the field house, Coach Sinc launched into his motivational pep talk and soon had everyone foaming at the mouth, ready to hit anyone in Gatling colors. They put their helmets on and charged out of the field house.

With the sky now completely black, the only light came from the four giant stands of stadium lights illuminating the field. The air was cold, the temperature dropping. Fans cheered themselves hoarse. The smell of chili, nachos, and popcorn from the concession stand wafted through the air—almost strong enough to mask the manure.

As the team entered the stadium, the marching band played the school fight song—one of the few tunes they played that could be recognized. The Briar Ridge fans rose to their feet, screaming at the top of their lungs.

Abby, standing behind the benches in her walker, gave Parker a 'thumbs up' sign. He smiled and returned the gesture.

"I've Got a Feeling" by the Black Eyed Peas blared from the stadium's speakers, the student section singing along to the song. He turned to see them tossing around an inflated beach ball. The mood and atmosphere in the stands seemed incredibly festive, almost carnival-like.

In a few moments, Gatling kicked off to Briar Ridge, which returned the ball to its own twenty-seven-yard line. "Let's go to work, Park," Coach Sinc said, slapping Parker on his back.

This was it. The dreams and expectations of an entire town rested on his shoulders. And a means of escaping Briar Ridge came down to this one night. His chest tightened, his palms grew sweaty, and he tried to swallow, but the dryness in his mouth wouldn't allow it.

In a flurry of hand and arm movements, Coach Sinc signaled the first play. The taunting from Gatling players commenced. "Comin' after you, Austin. Gonna be in your face all night long, baby."

Whatever, dude.

Parker signaled for the snap. The ball came to him, he took a step forward, and threw the first pass of the night. *Thwack!* As soon as the ball left his hand, someone slapped his left shoulder from behind. Tyler Maxwell caught the pass and turned up field for a gain of nine yards.

A Gatling player gloated, "Almost got you that time, oil trash."

Yeah, keep talking, rich boy.

Parker watched the sidelines for the next play. On second down he handed the ball to the running back, Royce Brown, who plunged forward for a quick gain of three yards and a first down at the Briar Ridge thirty-nine-yard line before being leveled by a gang of Gatling players.

On the next play, Zach Douglas came open, but before Parker could throw the ball someone crashed into him from behind. His head snapped backward from the impact, almost knocking the wind out of him, and sent him flying to the cold, hard ground.

Getting sacked was not going to look good to the college scouts. *That can't happen again tonight or else the chance to get out of this place might slip away.* Parker slapped the dry grass with the palm of his hand and propped himself on his knee.

The stadium tilted like a seesaw, and the stabbing pain in his back was almost unbearable. Grimacing, he slowly got to his feet, the Gatling crowd roaring with delight. Jubilant, cocky Gatling players pointed at him. "Yeah, we've gotta lot of that for you tonight, trailer trash!"

Joe Bob Swain apologized profusely for letting the Gatling player get by him, but Parker waved him off. *Save the apologies. Just shut up and do your job.* He tried to block out the dizziness and the pain in his back as he concentrated on the next wave of signals.

On second down, he threw a quick pass to an open receiver for a six-yard gain as Gatling players came within inches of hitting him again.

"We're still coming, redneck. Every play." Their mouths were getting old. Fast.

On third and eight, Parker took the snap, faked a handoff to Royce Brown, and spun around and sprinted as fast as he could in the opposite direction. He raced up field, the Briar Ridge fans on their feet, erupting in a deafening roar as he flew past Gatling defenders.

He ran about twenty-five yards before a white blur appeared and knocked him out of bounds at the Gatling thirty-yard line. The long run electrified him. Every hair on his body stood erect. He leaped to his feet, fully energized, adrenaline coursing through him. "Yeah, baby! Woo-hoo!"

Abby stood not far away, grinning from ear to ear, cheering. Teammates on the sideline swarmed him as the Briar Ridge band struck up the song "Ironman."

As he came back onto the field, he looked for the nearest Gatling player. Something needed to be said. He jogged up close to the guy and said, "Take that, you arrogant prick."

"Shut up, oil trash. We still ran you down."

Parker snorted, still glaring at him. "Yeah, but not before I ran for thirty."

The Briar Ridge fans chanted, "Bobcats, Bobcats, Bobcats." The noise from the stadium was at a fever pitch, sending chills through his body. He felt it now—the competition, the rush of playing the game he loved. God, was there any better feeling?

Coach Sinc was yelling and waving, trying to get his attention. He frantically signaled the next play and yelled at everyone to hurry. A surge of adrenaline coursed through Parker again, his heart racing. He wiped sweat from above his eyes and took a deep breath.

He turned to Royce and told him to switch sides.

Royce took out his mouthpiece. "What?"

Parker raised his voice over the din. "You heard me. Line up over here."

Uncertainty spread over Royce's face.

"Just do it. I promise Gatling's gonna blitz from this side. Just go right at them!" Parker reached over and grabbed Royce, who stood to his left, and pulled him over to the other side so he'd have a better shot at the Gatling defenders.

As soon as he got the ball, Royce took off like a missile, heading right for the blitz Parker had anticipated. Tyler Maxwell raced up the middle of the field, no one near him, and Parker threw a perfect pass. Tyler caught it and crossed the goal line directly in front of a camera from Action 9 News.

The Briar Ridge side erupted, and the band struck up the school's fight song.

Parker and several teammates ran to the north end zone to congratulate Tyler. As Gatling players passed by, he lofted another barb. "Yeah, I'll be doing that all night long, rich boys." *Take that, Gatling!*

He got to the end zone amidst the sound of firecrackers. Not exactly fireworks and the theme song from *The Natural*, but the added touch was nice. He raised his hand to give Tyler a high five, only Tyler didn't respond. Instead, his teammate's mouth fell open and his face went slack as the pitch and tone from the crowd changed into something wild and frenzied. High-pitched screams carried across the stadium, and the crackling sound of gunfire—not firecrackers—filled the air.

CHAPTER 7

Suzy Austin escorted Marjorie Brandt out of her office and closed the door behind her. She turned and leaned back against the wood-grained door. Her head throbbed and her palms were sweaty. Why did confrontation have to be so difficult? Marjorie was a big woman with a big attitude, and even though the disciplinary action was more than justified, having to deal with it still created stress. Hopefully, Marjorie got the message that insubordination wouldn't be tolerated and that her fat mouth was quickly talking its way to the unemployment line.

Suzy went back to her desk, quietly jotted down her notes from the meeting, and placed the file folder in the over-stuffed filing cabinet. She slumped in her office chair that leaned too far back, sipping coffee and filling out never-ending paperwork. Long hours spent squinting at the computer screen were taking a toll. Her eyes hurt from the strain, and Tylenol had long ago ceased its usefulness.

She kept putting off the decision to get reading glasses. At forty-two, her auburn hair had begun to show its first signs of gray, and she was sensitive about it. So what would the addition of reading glasses do? Certainly not make her look or feel younger.

Taking a break from reading the memo in front of her, she massaged the inside corners of her eyes, taking care not to smear her eye shadow. Her desk, usually very organized, remained buried under manila file folders and stacks of paper, though she'd been sorting and filing for hours.

These days it took a Herculean effort just to prevent the slush piles on her desk from getting any higher. She sighed at the sight of them. She'd come to loathe administrative work despite knowing it was part of the job when she took over as Director of Nursing at Wheeler Memorial Hospital. She glanced at the clock on the wall. Just a few minutes shy of six. Time for the next shift change.

After firing one of her nurses last month, she had to help with the coverage until a replacement could be hired. None of the other available nurses wanted to cover the Friday night shift, so she was stuck with it, preventing her from attending Parker's game with Kenneth and Abby.

She looked at the framed picture of her family sitting on a stack of file folders on her desk. Kenneth, and her two children posed around her, smiling. It'd been such a hot, dry, August day at the portrait studio in Abilene. Too many years had passed since the entire family had posed for a formal portrait together, and she'd insisted they sit for one.

She'd been the only one who wanted to be there that day. Kenneth wanted to get back home to watch a baseball game on television. Parker kept complaining this was his last Saturday before football practice started and he wanted to spend it with Summer. Abby desperately wanted to shop for new school clothes. Still, they'd all managed to humor her for a few minutes and smile for the camera.

A knock at the door, and Theresa Mott stuck her head inside. "Hey boss, ready for change of shift report?"

Suzy nodded. Theresa entered, sat down in the chair previously occupied by Marjorie, and handed over the charts of the three patients in the south wing. They discussed them for a few minutes. Pretty minor stuff, though the patient in 109 had a serious staph infection that needed to be monitored. Should be a fairly simple shift overall.

Theresa glanced at her watch and stood to leave. "Is Parker excited about the game?"

"Yeah. He usually doesn't say much on game days, but I think he's looking forward to it. Are you going?"

"It's Gatling. I wouldn't miss it for the world." Theresa turned and headed for the door. "See ya Monday," she said over her shoulder. "Go Bobcats!"

"Go Bobcats!" Suzy repeated.

Suzy shut her office door and changed into her dark blue scrubs. She made her way to the nurses' station down the hall. The Friday night shift had arrived and was making its rounds. With the exception of a few orderlies delivering and retrieving dinner trays, the hospital corridors were quiet.

Heather Callum, a nurse's assistant, sat behind the desk sifting through a stack of paperwork. Betty Crane stood behind her, leaning against the counter reviewing charts.

Like Suzy, Betty was an advanced practice nurse, with more education and a higher degree of authority than RNs, and had worked at a large urban hospital prior to coming to Briar Ridge. Aloof didn't come close to describing her, but it was nice to have an experienced nurse on staff.

"Has everybody checked in and completed their change of shift reports?" Suzy asked.

Both Betty and Heather nodded.

"And is Beck really the on-duty doc tonight?"

"Yes," Betty said quietly, not looking up from her charts.

Suzy rolled her eyes. *Great. I get to spend my evening with Doctor God-Complex.* "Who's on-call?"

Heather turned around. "Dr. Farmer is on-call tonight, ma'am."

"Thanks, Heather. I'm off to make rounds."

Wheeler Memorial was the only hospital in Joe Wheeler County and the only source of medical care in a thirty-five-mile radius. The entire facility fit on one floor and contained just forty-eight beds, but it did have some amenities that most small hospitals did not. It boasted a surgery department capable of providing modest surgical procedures, an ICU, a maternity ward, a radiology department, and was certified as a Level IV trauma center.

It seemed a far cry from Methodist Hospital in Houston where Suzy had spent the majority of her career in the fast-paced, frenzied atmosphere of the emergency room for the nine-hundred-bed facility. For years she'd lived on a diet of nerves, adrenaline, and coffee, but at this stage of her life, the slower pace of Wheeler Memorial provided a pleasant contrast.

Suzy checked on her three patients and returned to the nurses' station. She walked up to the front of the counter and entered her notes while listening to the conversation of the other nurses who'd gathered there.

By the time she'd finished with the second chart, the talk turned to football.

"So how's Parker doing? Is he ready for tonight?" Sherry Prater asked.

"Oh, I think he's fine. He gets a little nervous on game days, but I know he's really looking forward to it," Suzy said with a smile.

"My husband said he's been playing really well this year and that several schools are recruiting him. Does he know which college he's going to pick?"

Suzy shrugged. "I'm not sure, Sherry." She finished writing her last comment in the chart and slapped it shut. "He's received interest from a few schools, but to be honest, I really don't care which one he picks as long as the scholarship will cover his tuition."

Sherry rolled her eyes. "I know what you mean. Frank and I just got this semester's tuition bill for Cindy, and it just about gave us both a heart attack. I couldn't believe how much it was."

"Did Cindy come home this weekend for the game?"

"Of course. It's Gatling. She's up there now with Frank, probably yelling herself hoarse before the game even starts."

Suzy glanced down at her watch. "Hey, speaking of the game, has anybody got it on?"

Heather, who sat at her computer station, waved her

hand. "I'm about to." She made a few clicks of the mouse, and in a few seconds, the southern, country drawl of JR Tooley, the self-described "voice of the Bobcats," came across in mid-sentence.

"...seven thousand fans jam-packed into Bobcat Stadium tonight for the annual installment of the Briar Ridge-Gatling rivalry, one of the more storied and tradition-rich rivalries in the history of high school football. We're just seconds away from kickoff of this highly anticipated match-up of these archrivals, and I, JR Tooley, the voice of the Bobcats, will be bringing it to you live, right here on KCAT."

"Let's go 'Cats!" Heather said. She adjusted the speaker to the maximum level.

JR Tooley would be a character in any small town. When not broadcasting Bobcat football games, he worked as a disc jockey for the local radio station and made homemade beer and wine for local customers. His apricot brandy wasn't too bad.

Heather straightened up in her chair. "Hey, they're about to kick off!"

Suzy leaned against the counter, her palms damp with sweat, heart racing. She mumbled a quick prayer and wiped her palms on her pants.

Tooley gushed about the size of some of the Gatling players. "They're as big as a brick house and look stronger than nine acres of garlic." He followed this comment with a loud belch that he tried, rather unsuccessfully, to hide under his breath.

"Good grief. Is that old coot drinking his own stuff on the air again?" Catherine asked.

"Sounds like it," Heather said over her shoulder.

Tooley pardoned himself and continued with the coverage. The teams were lining up and music blared in the background. Tooley described the kickoff and then talked about how the teams were lining up for the first play.

"C'mon, Park, you can do it," Suzy whispered. Tooley narrated Parker completing his first pass of the game. Good.

Completing his first pass was usually a good omen that he would play well. She took a deep breath and tried to relax.

"First and ten, Bobcats, on their own thirty-nine yard line," Tooley announced. "Two receivers right, two receivers left, Brown in the backfield with Austin. Austin sends Douglas in motion across the formation. There's the snap, Austin looking to his left, wants to throw, steps up and— whoa! Sweet Georgia pickles! Austin is leveled from behind by a bevy of Gatling players! Wow, what a hit they put on Parker Austin! They was all over him like a duck on a June bug!"

Suzy cringed. No matter how many times Parker had been hit over the years, it never got any easier. She breathed a sigh of relief when Tooley said Parker had made it to his feet, albeit slowly. Her cell phone vibrated. She pulled it out of her pocket and read the text.

Kenneth: *Parker on his feet. He's okay.*

She stepped away from the counter and paced in front of the nurses' station, fidgeting with her hands as Parker completed his next pass for a short gain.

Tooley's narration rolled into the next play. His voice broke into a shrill of excitement. "Austin turns the corner and heads up field, blockers in front of him! He makes a move to his left, dodges one tackler, and is in open space!" The crowd roared in the background as he continued. "Crosses midfield to the Gatling forty-five, the forty, the thirty-five, and is knocked out of bounds at the Gatling thirty-yard line. Holy guacamole! On third and nine, Coach Sinc puts the ball in the hands of his best player and the result is a gain of twenty-nine yards and a first down!" The nurses broke out into a chorus of applause.

"And Austin had some choice words for a Gatling player afterward. These two teams have been exchanging pleasantries after every play," Tooley stated.

All the nurses grinned, but Suzy shook her head. *Parker, don't do that. Just play the game.* She paced as the action continued.

"The Bobcats line up quickly. Three receivers to the right, one to the left, Brown in the backfield with Austin. Austin and Brown chatting about something...now Austin grabs Brown and moves him over to his right...Austin waiting for the snap...he's got it. Gatling blitzes, it's picked up by Brown! Austin in the pocket, steps up and fires one deep over the middle of the field...and he's got a man wide open! Tyler Maxwell catches it at the five-yard line and waltzes in for the score! Touchdown *Bobcaaaaats!*"

Cheers erupted at the nurses' station. Heather jumped out of her chair and yelled, "Yes!" as she fist-pumped the air. Suzy stopped pacing, closed her eyes, and breathed a deep sigh of relief. Her phone vibrated.

Kenneth: *TOUCHDOWN!*

She smiled and returned the phone to her pocket again. All the nurses, even Betty, were beaming.

"It's going to be a good night for the Bobcats," Catherine said.

Suzy nodded. "Yep, we're off to a good start. We just need our defense to—"

"Shush! Shush! Be quiet!" Heather exclaimed, holding up her hands. Her brow wrinkled and her eyes narrowed as she listened to Tooley's voice. "I think something's happening," she said quietly.

In the silence of the nurses' station, Tooley's voice cried out. "He's shooting! He's shooting! Oh, my God!"

Marjorie exchanged confused glances with the others. "What did he say?"

The nurses crowded around Heather's chair, getting as close to the speaker as possible. Suzy folded her arms on the countertop and leaned in to listen.

Against the chilling background noise of frantic screams, Tooley struggled to find words. "I don't...I just can't...he's shooting people. Everybody's running," He spoke as if trying to wake from a bad dream. He paused, tried to clear his throat. "There's a guy in front of the bleachers, shooting into the crowd. No, there's another one! There's two of 'em.

Run! Run!" Panic drenched his voice. "Run, daggummit, run!"

Sherry put her hands over her mouth as she gasped. Everyone looked shocked. Tooley yelled for someone to call nine-one-one. The nurses stood in complete silence, his descriptions of the carnage growing desperate.

"This—this can't be happening," Heather said, her voice trembling.

Suzy tried to concentrate, but everything seemed fuzzy. A white noise buzzed in her ears. *Kenneth? The kids?* Her knees wobbled, her body numb.

Betty's voice prodded her. She was telling Suzy to initiate "Code Black," the hospital's designation for mass casualties.

Think! Think! Snap out of it! "Yes." Suzy slowly nodded. She turned to look at everyone. "Yes. 'Code Black' everyone. Let's go."

They scrambled out of the nurses' station toward the emergency room, just a short walk up the east wing. Everyone had their cell phones, quickly texting their families at the stadium. Suzy sent a short text to Kenneth asking if the kids were safe.

A staff member made the "Code Black" announcement over the hospital intercom and instructed the trauma team to mobilize.

The on-duty physician, Dr. Beck, hustled into the emergency room. "What's the Code Black about?"

"There's been a shooting at the stadium," Suzy answered.

"What?"

"It's kinda sketchy right now, but dispatch says two ambulances en route with teenage patients, both with multiple gunshot wounds, and to prepare to receive more casualties."

"Call every physician in town and get every off-duty nurse up here now. Orderlies too. And tell the hospitals in Gatling and Eastmoor to stand by to receive patients as needed."

His god-complex aside, it was nice to have a decisive doctor around who knew what he was doing. "Word's gone out to all staff, and we've already given the other facilities a heads-up."

"Good. What about medevac? How long does it take for the helicopters to get here from Fort Worth?"

"About forty minutes."

"Call Harris and tell 'em I want those birds prepped and ready to fly at a moment's notice. Same with Memorial in Abilene." Beck turned and dashed to the nearby doctors' lounge to change into his scrubs. No sooner had he disappeared than Heather came into the emergency room, rubbing her hands together, her eyes wide with fright and worry.

"Mrs. Austin…"

"What is it, Heather?"

A few nurses darted by.

Heather cleared her throat and tried to speak.

"Heather, we don't have much time. What's wrong?" Suzy spied the nurse anesthetist and radiology technician darting into the ER.

"Ma'am, I can't stay here. I gotta see if my family is okay. I gotta check on 'em." Her eyes watered and her voice cracked.

"Heather, all of us have family at the stadium, but we're also nurses and we all have jobs to do right now. People's lives are at stake, and we're the ones that can save them." Heather's eyes darted down at the floor. "Heather, look at me. I need everyone on our staff right here, doing their job. I need you to help with dispatch and coordinate intake and transfers to other hospitals. Got it?"

Heather nodded. "Yes, ma'am."

"Good. Let's get to work." Suzy turned Heather around and nudged her toward the door while Betty, Catherine, and Sherry threw on their emergency room gowns and gloves. Suzy watched Heather make her way back to the nurses' station and then raced back into the emergency room.

A quick glance at her phone showed Kenneth hadn't replied to her text. A small, cold knot formed in her chest. She donned a gown and gloves with trembling hands. *Focus.* She clasped her hands together and took a deep breath.

Beck hustled into the emergency room fully prepped as a nurse announced the ambulances had arrived. The trauma team launched into action with the critical care of the two gunshot victims. Beck assessed the more severely injured patient, a fifteen-year-old girl suffering from gunshot wounds to her chest and abdomen, determining that she would need to be evacuated to a larger trauma facility. He immediately ordered the medevac helicopters from Fort Worth to come transport the patient.

More and more patients arrived, overwhelming the hospital staff. Every licensed physician and off-duty nurse in Briar Ridge were now in the ER, and they rushed around, trying to triage and stabilize the wounded as quickly as the ambulances and other vehicles brought them in.

Amid the frenzied noise and confusion of the ER, Dr. Beck conferred with Suzy while they treated a patient. "We can't take any more trauma patients—we're beyond full capacity. They're gonna have to be diverted to either Gatling or Eastmoor."

The chaos surrounding her confirmed they were on the brink of losing control. "I agree. I'll pass the word."

Suzy dashed out of the ER, slipping on the blood-soaked floor and nearly losing her footing. She shot past busy hospital traffic to the nurses' station and relayed the information to Heather.

"Dispatch says EMS units from both Gatling and Eastmoor are already en route!" Heather stood and yelled above the din. "ETA six minutes!"

Suzy hurried back to the ER and on to another blood-covered patient who was wheeled into the room on a gurney. Her attention was diverted from the patient by Marjorie. "There's too many of them! There's too many of them!" Marjorie shouted.

She'd been trying to stabilize a patient with Dr. Farmer but had backed away, eyes wide open, her face ashen.

Uh-oh. She's losing it.

Dr. Farmer snapped at Marjorie to help with the patient, but she didn't respond. A pair of EMTs hit her from behind with a gurney as they wheeled in another gunshot victim and yelled at her to get out of the way.

Beck yelled, "Somebody get her the hell out of here!"

Suzy darted toward Marjorie, grabbed her by the elbow, and led her out of the ER. When they were finally clear, she spun around and pushed Marjorie up against the wall.

"Marjorie, snap out of it and pull yourself together. I can't have you losing it in there. I need every nurse I've got right now!" She took a deep breath to collect herself, then calmly said, "Marjorie, you've got thirty seconds, and then I want you back in there." Suzy headed back down the hallway. A quick check of the cell phone revealed no messages. It'd been over an hour since she'd texted Kenneth. He should've responded by now. Her heart nearly leaped into her throat and she couldn't breathe. *Something's wrong.*

She quickly sent a message to Parker's cell phone, *Is everyone safe?* She pocketed the phone, re-entered the ER, and tried to quell her rising panic.

Dr. Spradlin, an old family physician nearing retirement, called out for assistance. He struggled trying to intubate a convulsing patient, and he couldn't immobilize the child to insert the tube. Betty rushed to assist and called for the anesthetist.

Suzy spent the next fifteen to twenty minutes tending to various patients and yelling instructions to her nurses in a desperate attempt to maintain control and to prevent a complete breakdown in emergency services. The majority of the trauma patients were teenagers, and it took all Suzy had to force thoughts of Parker and Abby away. Still, she couldn't help checking to see if each new patient was one of her own children. *Something's wrong!* Kenneth or Parker would've gotten word to her by now that they were safe.

She refocused as Dr. Farmer called for assistance when his patient suddenly flat-lined. "I need the crash cart! I need the crash cart!"

Suzy raced across the crowded ER and wheeled the cart to Dr. Farmer, who charged the paddles.

He stared at the monitor, his face tense. "C'mon, c'mon." The machine emitted the signal to provide the requisite shock to the teenage girl's heart. "Clear!" He placed the paddles on the girl's chest and administered the first shock.

The small blip continued its horizontal path across the screen. "Nothing," Suzy reported.

Dr. Farmer charged the paddles again and repeated the procedure, but the patient continued to flat-line. The tending staff worked on reviving the girl for another ten minutes, but to no avail.

Dr. Farmer's shoulders sagged, his face drawn, hands falling to his sides. "All right. I'm calling it." The flat, monotonous tone of his voice indicated it was no sudden pronouncement he was making, merely a formality in stating the obvious. For they'd all known for some time now that the girl was lost.

Still, it was hard giving up on a patient, especially a child. Dr. Farmer shook his head and looked up at the digital clock on the wall. "Time of death, eight fifty-three." He moved on to another patient and immediately went back to work, leaving Suzy the grim task of removing the girl's bloodied body.

She was just one more to add to the total. Another casualty, another statistic to be catalogued. But this wasn't an elderly grandmother succumbing to a bout of pneumonia or a ninety-year-old whose heart had finally stopped after a long, rich life.

The young girl's lifeless eyes stared at the ceiling tiles. This was someone's child whose last moments on Earth had been witness to a nightmare, an unimaginable horror.

How many other parents had lost a child tonight? Would

she be included in that group? Her stomach rolled over, triggering a brief urge to vomit.

Suzy forced the thought from her mind and left the ER to grab an orderly to remove the girl's body. As she scanned the busy corridor, Heather ran to stand in front of her. "Suzy, your husband's been admitted with a closed head injury. He's in radiology awaiting a CT scan."

Suzy thanked her and dashed down the crowded hallway past hospital staff, patients, and people looking for injured loved ones. She ran into the darkened radiology lobby. Kenneth slumped in a wheelchair, alone.

Suzy knelt next to her husband. His eyes were half-open, and he appeared dazed and unable to focus. She grabbed his hand and called his name. He turned his head slightly in her direction. A faint expression of recognition flickered across his face.

"Honey, are the kids okay? Are they safe? Where are they?"

He mumbled and dropped his head.

She repeated the question, but he didn't move.

"Ken?" She placed her hand on his arm and squeezed. "C'mon, sweetie. Listen."

Kenneth lifted his head and looked at her under half-opened eyelids.

"Where are the kids? Have you seen them since the shooting?"

He shook his head from to side to side.

"No?" Her voice quivered with panic. *Oh, God. Please, no.* "Honey," she finally brought herself to ask, "did you see the kids get shot?" He shook his head in the negative. She exhaled. *At least there's that.* "Do you know where they are?" Again, he shook his head.

A radiology technician entered the room. "It's his turn."

She stood, leaned over, and kissed the top of her husband's head. "I love you, honey. I'll be back to check on you when you get assigned a room."

The radiology technician wheeled Kenneth around and

pulled him through the door leading into the lab. Exhaustion enveloped her, but knew she had to get back to work.

She walked out of the radiology lobby and made her way toward the ER when her phone vibrated. "Oh, thank God," she blurted out as Parker's name flashed across the tiny screen. She kept walking, opened the text, and read the message.

She abruptly stopped and her mouth opened. Her heart stopped, and she gasped for air, her hands trembling. Tears blurred her eyes as she shook her head. "No, no, no, no, no!" She ran for the privacy of the nearby nurses' lounge.

Tears streamed down her cheeks as she elbowed and shouldered her way down the hall. She burst through the door and into the empty nurses' lounge, and a loud, anguished cry escaped from deep inside her. Her legs buckled and she dropped to her knees, wailing and screaming. She bent over and caught herself on her hands, face down toward the floor, tears falling onto the cold, white floor tiles beneath her. She tried desperately to catch her breath, to slow down, to get back some control, but couldn't.

Pictures of Abby flashed through her mind—smiling, laughing images of her precious daughter. Guilt and shame overwhelmed her. She should've been there. To hold her. To protect her like a mother's supposed to do. The agony and heartbreak swelled in her chest.

I should've been there. She crawled to the bench in front of the small row of lockers and spent the next several minutes collapsed upon it while trying to regain her composure. The tears slowed to a trickle, and she was able to stand. She walked unsteadily to the mirror over the sink, pulled out a paper towel from the wall-mounted dispenser and tried to clean herself up. Streaks of green eye shadow ran down her cheeks. Her hands shook and her lips quivered. She blew her nose a few times and then staggered to the door on wobbly legs.

The Earth still seemed to move underneath her, and a dull buzzing sound filled her ears.

She straightened her scrubs, took a few deep breaths, and pulled the door open.

The hallway swarmed with frenzied activity. The intercom announced a 'Code Blue' in ICU, followed by a page for her assistance in the OR. Both announcements could wait. She headed to the nurses' station to see what room her husband had been assigned and prepared herself for the most difficult conversation of her life.

CHAPTER 8

Parker shut his cell phone and laid it beside him. The words just wouldn't come. Besides, she probably wouldn't have been able to talk on the phone anyway, let alone hear it ring since it had to be crazy at the hospital right now. So, he sent her a text and would find the words later.

Parker slouched in his stall. His black pants and jersey helped camouflage the dried blood on them, but the caked crimson on his hands stood out. The police had already questioned him for over an hour and would've continued had he not begged them to at least let him pass the word to his mother about Abby and clean himself up.

Like a robot, he got undressed and walked across the locker room to the showers.

He turned on the nearest showerhead and stepped into the downpour. As he leaned against the cold tile, the hot water cascaded down his tired body. For several minutes he closed his eyes, trying to comprehend all that had transpired over the last two hours, but a mental numbness enveloped him.

He turned until his back flattened against the cold tile wall. Weakened legs gave way, and he slid down until he sat on his bottom, his legs straight and receiving the brunt of the shower's spray.

Parker stared at a spot on the tile floor, his mind completely fogged as the images of the shooting flashed through his mind.

Abby. Tears pooled in his eyes again. He slowly pulled his knees up to his chest and wrapped his arms around his legs. The sound of gunfire, Abby screaming for help—they kept replaying in his mind. Holding her in his arms, her blood spilling onto him—

"Parker—Parker." Even at the sound of his own name, he couldn't bring himself to turn and look. Someone walked over, turned off the shower, and squatted next to him.

"Parker." The voice was calm, steady. A hand rested on his left shoulder. Coach Ricky Connor spoke to him. "Parker? Parker, you okay?" Coach Connor jiggled Parker's shoulder. "C'mon, Park. Let me help you up so you can dry yourself off." He took Parker by the left hand and helped him to his feet. He gave him a towel and Parker wiped his face with it.

"You need to get to the hospital and check on your dad. I'm sure your mom would like to see you, too."

Parker nodded. *Mom.* That wasn't a conversation to look forward to. He dried off, noticing blood on Coach Connor's shirt and pants as he turned to leave. The noise of confusion and chaos outside interrupted the silence of the locker room as the door swung open and shut.

Alone in the room, he walked to his stall and pulled on his jeans. A messy display of uniforms, equipment, and athletic tape littered the floor, trappings quickly discarded as his teammates had scrambled to get dressed and leave for the hospital.

The black and white nameplates at the top of each stall stood out in the soft fluorescent glow. How many of them were dead or wounded? The only other fatality he knew of was Joe Bob Swain, who had fallen on him when he was shot.

Joe Bob's stall was four stalls down. His large jeans, game day shirt, and massive letter jacket hung from hooks inside the metal stall. His boots were at the bottom, stuffed with his socks. A coiled belt, along with its near hubcap-sized belt buckle, sat on the top shelf of the locker with other small personal items. Simple, everyday things really, but now they seemed tainted, almost haunted, because they belonged to a guy who'd been murdered.

Parker dressed and stuffed his personal effects into his pockets as he headed out the door. People still rushed about, some in the hallway, others going back and forth into the training room for ice, bandages, towels, and anything else that could be used to help treat the remaining injured. Parker passed the coaches' office where several people talked on their cell phones, none of whom he recognized. Opening the front doors of the field house, he stepped out into the cold night air.

The stadium and its immediate vicinity were awash in the flashing lights of emergency vehicles. Several helicopters hovered over the scene. Emergency responders swarmed about like ants, still attending to the less seriously injured, who seemed to be many. Briar Ridge police and Joe Wheeler County sheriff's deputies sealed off certain areas with yellow crime scene tape, took pictures, and marked certain spots with evidence tags. Several bodies, covered with white sheets, lay on the ground just inside the gate.

He walked across the gravel drive and up the sidewalk toward the stadium. He squinted against the constant flashing of red, blue, and yellow lights. He put up his hand to shield his eyes. A vehicle spun its tires in the gravel as it left in a hurry. A hand grasped his shoulder as he neared the gate.

"Parker, you okay?"

The smooth, tenor voice belonged to Wesley Boddicker, his face illuminated by the flashing blue lights of a police car. The only detective in the Briar Ridge police department, he'd already questioned Parker about the shooting. He stood at least six-foot-two-inches tall, but when wearing his cowboy hat like he was now, he seemed even taller. Bowlegged and thin as a rail, he looked like Ichabod Crane.

"Just checking to see if they've moved my sister."

"What?" Boddicker shifted his toothpick from one side of his mouth to the other as he cupped his ear.

Parker leaned closer to the detective and repeated his reply over the sounds of the hovering helicopters.

Boddicker shook his head. "Can't do that, Parker, I'm sorry. We've already sealed off the field since it's a crime scene. We can't allow folks to walk through there. Stay right here and I'll check for you, okay?"

Parker nodded and stuck his hands into the front pockets of his jeans. Boddicker turned and ducked under the yellow tape and entered the stadium. Parker looked around and took in the scene. Law enforcement officers busied themselves taking pictures, videotaping certain areas, and interviewing witnesses. Others assisted with some of the lightly wounded that still remained. The more seriously injured had already been evacuated. People milled outside the stadium, some of them crying. A few looked dazed and seemed to wander aimlessly. Several television crews had gathered near the gym, filming interviews and live reports. He looked down at his shoes and kicked aside a pebble. His shoulders sagged with emotional fatigue. He closed his eyes and wished everything would just go away.

Boddicker's voice pried open his eyes. "Your sister will be moved to the morgue at the hospital in a few minutes."

"Thanks."

"Parker, I know this is tough, son, but we're going to have to visit with you again about what happened. We've just got to get all the details ironed out. All right?"

Parker looked at the ground, but nodded.

"I'd give you a ride to the hospital myself, but I've got a few more things to take care of here. I'll meet you up there and we'll talk some more. And Parker, a lot of other people are going to want to talk to you about tonight—friends, the media, whatever. Be prepared for them to call you and drop by your house even. Just remember, you don't have to talk to them if you don't want to. Okay?"

Parker nodded and turned, making his way down the gravel drive toward the field house. He walked through the front doors and down the concrete hallway. He opened the back doors and stepped out onto the practice field where he'd spent countless hours in the scorching heat and frigid cold perfecting his craft as a quarterback.

He crossed the field, not caring about ants this time. The pump jack bobbed up and down in the darkness, oblivious to everything taking place around it. He headed for his car, one of the few that still remained, and noticed Joe Bob's Chevy pickup sitting alone—an eerie reminder.

His last memory of his teammate was of him lying on the ground, a massive bullet wound in his neck that had sent blood spurting in all directions. Parker had rolled over on top of him and had thrust his own hands down onto his teammate's throat in an attempt to staunch the flow of blood, but it didn't make a difference. Joe Bob's wide-open eyes stared back at him, confusion and disbelief on his face as his brain struggled to comprehend what had just happened. He'd tried to say something to Parker, but blood gurgled in his throat and he died a few seconds later.

Parker shook his head and climbed into his car. He slammed the door shut and cranked the ignition. The Firebird roared to life, and he sped down a deserted Pecan Street. He drove in silence, not paying attention to where he was, but vaguely aware he was moving. *What do I say to Mom? How do I even begin?* A strange, numbing sensation took over. None of this could be real. The nightmare would end any minute now. *Please let it be just a nightmare.*

The headlights of cars on Wabash Avenue got his attention. Rows of parked vehicles lined the street a few blocks ahead of him. He wouldn't find a parking space if he crossed over toward the hospital, so he pulled over and parked on the side of the street in front of a small, gray house with crooked shutters.

The cold night air had a bite to it. He put his hands into his jeans pockets to keep them warm and jogged toward the town's main thoroughfare. Cars lined both sides of the avenue for many blocks. He waited for a break in the traffic, but after a few minutes, he grew impatient and darted into the first crease he found, causing agitated motorists to blare their horns. Crossing the four lanes of traffic, he walked toward Wheeler Memorial.

Parked cars and trucks surrounded the entire block around the hospital. A massive crowd and several news crews stood outside the hospital's east wing, which housed the emergency room. The ER lobby having already been swamped past capacity, the overflow crowd spilled outside where hundreds huddled in groups, talking and crying. Several ambulances sat in the emergency room driveway, their lights flashing. A medical helicopter perched on the small, concrete tarmac next to the emergency room driveway, its rotary propellers spinning and its engine running.

A woman burst through the emergency rooms doors, screaming and crying, a man following close behind her. She stopped, collapsed onto the ground, and went into hysterics. The man caught up to her, knelt down, and tried to calm her.

Everyone's attention turned toward the tarmac when the helicopter revved its engines. It eased into the air, lights flashing, rotating propellers kicking up strong waves of cold wind. Parker stopped and watched it rise, and the wind whipped through his hair. *Who is getting transported? How many have already been flown outta here?*

A girl's face in the crowd diverted his attention. She stood out because she wasn't looking at the helicopter like everyone else. Her back was to the chopper and she stared at Parker. He squinted to get a better look at her as lights of nearby emergency vehicles illuminated a face he'd never seen before. She stood perfectly still, with a forlorn expression, her eyes locked onto him. Before he looked away, she smiled at him. It wasn't a big, broad smile, but one that contained hints of sadness—or concern.

The helicopter hovered overhead for a moment, then ascended into the cold, dark sky and flew into the distance, the roar of its engines growing softer with each passing second.

He weaved his way through the masses again. He hadn't gone very far when a passerby bumped into his shoulder rather roughly, almost seeming intentional. He stopped and turned to see who had run into him. He nearly did a double-take. A man in a black leather jacket with bleached blond hair looked over his shoulder. The same haunting, yellow eyes as the old man at Gibson's that morning stared back at him. The man smirked and then disappeared into the crowd.

Parker tried to follow but someone grabbed him by the arm.

"Parker Austin?"

He nodded. "Yes, ma'am."

The unknown woman's face lit up. Even in the darkness, her eyes widened into large pools of white.

"Oh, Parker. Parker, thank you. Thank you for what you did." She drew herself close and wrapped both arms around him in an embrace. She buried her face into his shoulder and mumbled "Thank you" into the folds of his letter jacket.

He hesitated. The only words that came to mind were, "It's okay." He repeated them to her while she sobbed, and he patted the back of her head.

At least she wasn't very loud. The chances of her causing a scene and drawing attention were low, but they'd increase the longer this continued. He glanced around to make sure no one else was approaching, then leaned into her ear and said he needed to get inside to find his mother. The woman looked up, wiped away a few tears, and let him go. She looked at him again, smiled, and said, "Thank you." She turned and disappeared into the crowd.

He reversed course, heading toward the street and away from the hospital, careful to avoid being recognized. He proceeded a block south, past more vehicles and groups of distraught people. The hospital's main entrance was an option, but a large crowd probably gathered there as well. Instead, he ducked into the service delivery drive and covered the twenty yards of concrete in quick strides until he came to the loading dock. He sprang up the short flight of stairs, opened a rusty door, and entered the confusion and chaos of the hospital.

CHAPTER 9

Raised voices and intercom pages echoed in the fluo-
rescent-lit hallway. Parker paused to get his bearings, then turned to the intersection of the main
north-south corridor. Hospital staff rushed in all directions.
Some pushed patients on gurneys or in wheelchairs, while
others dashed to other parts of the hospital. The occasional
shouts of doctors and other hospital staff reverberated down
the hall.

Parker leaned against the wall, careful to stay out of the
way. He wasn't sure where either of his parents might be,
but of the two, Dad had to be the most accessible. He headed toward the nurses' station. Noise and frantic commotion
increased with each step. Hallway traffic thickened, making
it impossible to continue without turning or twisting sideways as blue-scrubbed hospital staff rushed by. A beehive
of frenzied activity surrounded the station. Nurses, doctors,
and orderlies swarmed from every direction shouting orders
and questions over one another as they tended to patients.
The chaotic tension in the air was sharp enough to cut glass.

This was definitely not the place to be right now. No
way would anyone stop what they were doing just to look
up a patient's room number. Instead of interrupting someone, Parker headed down the west wing toward the hospital's main entrance to the visitor information desk. The
main lobby loomed ahead, full of people. A large group

clustered around the information kiosk, overwhelming the old retiree who volunteered there on the weekends.

The nurses' station had been a bad idea, and the information kiosk was inaccessible. So now what?

Summer waved at him from the lobby area. Still in her cheerleader uniform but wearing her letter jacket over it, she rushed toward him, a rumpled tissue clutched in her hand.

He opened his arms as she thrust herself into his chest, wrapping herself around him in a tight embrace that nearly squeezed the air out of his lungs. Her head bobbed up and down just below his chin as she sobbed. He let her cry on him for a few moments while he stared into space, still reliving all that had happened at the stadium. Finally, she lifted her head. Tears rained down from bloodshot eyes. She sniffed and wiped her nose with the tissue. He wanted to comfort her, reassure her, but the words couldn't get past his throat.

Her lips parted, and she let out a huge breath. "I'm so glad you're safe."

Parker wiped a tear running down her cheek.

She took hold of both of his hands. "Park, I'm sorry about Abby. Are you okay? Have you—"

"No." He shook his head. Numb with fatigue and shock, he had no strength to talk about Abby at the moment. "Not now, okay?"

She nodded.

"Who else? Have you heard?" he asked.

She cleared her throat and took a deep breath. "Yeah, but they're still trying to sort everything out. Amy Zimmer, Tracie Mortenson, and Stacie Alarcon are dead. So are Danny Brooks and Kelly Don Wright..." She paused, trying to recall more names. "Andrea Krummer, Callie Cox, Paul Peirson...and Joe Bob Swain, too. Plus a couple of freshmen I didn't know. And all six of the cops who were there. Those are the only ones I know about for sure, besides Abby. But there's probably a lot more."

"Geez," Parker said softly as the scope and magnitude of

the shooting sank in. Time slowed down. Mental pictures of his classmates flashed through his mind, and he staggered against the wall. "I saw a helicopter take off when I got here. Who was in it?"

"I don't know. Several helicopters have been in and out since I got here. But lots of people have been shot. They've had to send some to the hospitals in Gatling and Eastmoor. And I think the helicopters took some to Fort Worth and Abilene." She paused again. "But that's not all. Actually, this wasn't the only shooting tonight."

"What are you talking about?"

"I just heard about it, but Mrs. Calvin shot herself in her home after school today. She's dead. I guess she finally snapped."

Crazy Mrs. Calvin. Parker recalled the strange comments she'd said to him earlier in her classroom. He reached up and rubbed his eyes.

"Was one of the shooters really Bobby McGonagill?" Summer asked. "Was that the one you—"

"Yes." Parker's teeth ground together, and the muscles in his face tightened. *Scumbag.*

Her jaw dropped. "Wow. What was he doing back here?"

He shrugged his shoulders. "How should I know?"

"Do you know who the other one was? No one else seems to know."

He shook his head. "No, I don't know."

"Everyone's been talking about it, about what you did, and calling you a hero. They're saying that—"

"I don't care what people are saying," he snapped. His body tensed. "I'm not a hero, understand?" He shot an icy glare at her. "I did what I did and that's it."

"Okay." She broke eye contact and let go of his hand, looking back toward the crowded lobby. "I should probably get back. I—I don't want to keep you."

His muscles relaxed and his body sagged. "I'm sorry. I didn't mean to snap at you like that." He grabbed her hand.

"Hey, I'm just really tired, and I need to check on my dad and talk to my mom. I'll call you later, okay?"

She nodded. "I love you."

"Love you too." He turned without another word and went back down the hall.

A few minutes later he found an orderly who knew where his father was and headed down the south wing to see him, careful to stay out of the traffic as much as possible.

He found room 227, the name "Austin, Kenneth" on the small, dry-erase board outside the door. Before he knocked, someone called out to him.

He turned to see a nurse in dark blue scrubs, standing in the doorway of a room a few doors down. Her face seemed familiar, but fatigue prevented him from recalling her name.

"Parker." She shut the door behind her and walked over to him. "Parker, you okay?" Her voice was tired, but delicate, as if her words might shatter something fragile.

Why do people keep asking me this? Of course I'm not okay, you idiot! He took a deep breath and tried to relax and not shoot daggers at her from his eyes. "Yeah, I'm okay," he replied as calmly as he could.

She looked as though she fully expected him to burst into tears and collapse onto the floor at any second. She nodded at his father's door. "Your father's got a pretty bad closed-head injury, a very serious concussion. We're waiting on the results of the CT scan right now."

"Can I go in and see him?"

"Just for a minute. And when you go in, don't turn on the light. Leave the room dark."

He glanced up and down the crowded hallways. "Have you seen my mom?"

"She's been in the ER most of the night, but I'll let her know you're here. When you're done with your father, you can wait for your mom in her office."

"Thanks."

He knocked on the door, cracked it open, and stuck his head inside. No light illuminated the dark room except for a small lamp on the nightstand next to the window on the far side. The curtains were closed, the television turned off. Dad rested in the bed, his eyes closed and his hands at his side. The monitor next to the bed beeped softly as it tracked his heart rate, blood pressure, and oxygen levels.

"Dad?" Parker whispered. "Dad, can you hear me?"

Getting no response, he stepped inside and shut the door. He took a few steps closer to the bed and called him again. His father turned slightly in Parker's direction, eyelids rising. He managed a weak smile.

Parker went to his father's side. His ashen face drooped, and he had the sheets pulled to his chin as if they could somehow insulate him from the emotional devastation of what had happened. He looked broken.

"How's your head, Dad?" His father continued to lie quiet and still, eyes closed, the sheets slowly rising and falling with each breath.

"Fine," he whispered.

"How long have you been in here?"

His father paused before answering. "Not long."

Does he know? Parker hesitated, his chest tightening. "Has Mom been to see you?"

Getting no response, he stepped as close as he could to the bed and leaned over. He swallowed. "Dad, has Mom talked to you?"

His father opened his hand, and Parker took hold of it.

"Glad you're safe, son." His voice cracked, and he turned away, lips pressed tightly together, eyes blinking away the gathering tears.

The realization struck him like lightning, nearly knocking him over. *He knows.* Parker's eyes grew wet. He stood in the semi-dark room, unable to do anything more than simply hold his father's hand.

Only minutes passed, but it seemed far more like eternity. The periodic beeping of the bedside monitor provided the only sound in the room. At least Dad wasn't in a condition to ask about Abby—that would take a heavy toll. Mom, on the other hand, would want to know everything, and there would be no getting around it.

"Dad, I gotta go see Mom. I haven't talked to her yet. Get some rest, okay?"

His father didn't respond.

Parker took a deep breath and exhaled slowly. "I love you, Dad."

A feeble squeeze of his hand was the only reply. It wasn't the firm, overpowering grip he was accustomed to. There was nothing there, really. Just the shattered pieces of what had always seemed unbreakable. The pillar, the rock that weathered every storm with a quiet, unmatched strength, had been broken. He gripped his father's hand, lingered for a moment, then let go and walked out of the room.

He gently closed the door behind him and made his way through the crowd to his mother's office, eager to be alone for a few minutes. As he placed his hand on the nickel-brushed doorknob, a familiar voice called to him from down the hall. Detective Boddicker walked toward him, his bowleggedness more apparent than ever.

Parker greeted him with a murmur, not enthused to continue discussing the events at the stadium. Boddicker assured him the conversation wouldn't last long, and they stepped inside the office to finish the interview.

They sat in the cushioned chairs opposite his mother's desk and faced one another. The detective removed his black felt cowboy hat and placed it on a stack of manila file folders on the desk in front of him, ran a hand through his thinning gray hair, and exhaled deeply. For someone wanting to continue questioning a witness, the guy didn't seem all that eager to talk. Maybe this was his first quiet moment away from all the madness.

Parker looked down at his own hands. Dried blood that hadn't washed out remained under his fingernails.

Boddicker retrieved a small notepad from inside his coat pocket, tapped it against his leg for a few moments, and then flipped it open. He riffled through the pages of his handwritten notes, and Parker glanced out the window behind his mother's desk at the fountain in the courtyard with the cascading water.

The orange and blue lights inside the cement fountain's pool gave the water a surreal look.

Boddicker took a ballpoint pen from his shirt pocket, clicked it open. "Again, this ain't gonna take long, Parker. I just need to ask a few more questions, okay?"

Parker continued to gaze at the fountain.

"We've got pretty much everything nailed down as far as your actions at the stadium, but one of the areas we're hoping you might help us with is motive, specifically the McGonagill kid."

Parker remained motionless and continued to watch the illuminated water.

"Parker?" Boddicker paused and when he got no response, he tried again. "Parker? This has been a rough night for all of us, son, I'm dang tired, and I've got a lot of work to do, so I'd appreciate it if you could—"

"Did you know them?" Parker asked, still looking out the window.

Boddicker blinked. "Did I know who?"

"The cops who got killed tonight. Did you know them?"

The detective leaned back in his chair. He reached up and pulled the toothpick from his mouth. "Yeah. Of course I knew 'em. They were my friends."

"Were you there tonight? At the game?"

"No," the detective said quietly. "I was called to the scene of another shooting, along with two other officers, who normally would've been at the game as additional security. If that lady hadn't shot herself, we would've been there and this might have been prevented, or at least not turned out as bad." Boddicker paused again and cleared his throat. "And that's why I need your help. You were there, and I need you to help me make sense of what happened tonight."

Parker blew a sarcastic huff out the side of his mouth. He

was just one of seven thousand eyewitnesses. "How could I make sense of this?"

"Well, for one thing, did Bobby McGonagill know it was you who beat up his two little brothers a few years ago?"

Parker snapped out of his trance with the colorful water and turned his head toward the detective. Where had that question come from? His lips parted, and his mouth went dry. What did the detective know? What was he getting at?

Boddicker held up his palms. "It's all right, son. You're not in trouble."

There could be only one reason why the detective was asking about that incident. The implication hit Parker like a truck. "Are you—" His pulse thundered in his brain, and his throat seemed to constrict, making it difficult to get the words out. "Are you saying—*I* caused this?"

CHAPTER 10

The memories of three years ago came back to Parker in a flash. How could he forget? Finding Abby in her room, curled up on her bed and crying into her pillow, was tough. Hearing how the McGonagill boys found her alone in the hallway and kicked the walker out her hands so she wobbled and fell to the ground was tougher, but the ugly bruises on her legs told him something besides complaining to the principal had to be done.

Sure, his parents wanted apologies for the assault, assurances for Abby's safety, and appropriate punishment for the McGonagills, but none of that would keep Abby safe.

No, the only thing that would work was payback. He lay in wait behind the fence on Wheeler Street as they made their way home, grabbed them, and threw them into the vacant lot behind it. And then beat the hell out of them. It had worked like a charm. It also provided the opportunity to take back Abby's iPod.

Although he was disguised in a John Deere cap, which every male in Briar Ridge owned, who cared if they recognized him? So what if he'd been spotted? The message was sent—no harassment of Abby would be tolerated or go unanswered.

It didn't matter what anyone else thought, even Mom and Dad. For weeks afterward they'd watched him in silence, their lingering stares inviting a confession, an admission confirming their doubts of his "non-involvement."

But he'd refused the bait, although Abby's recovered iPod should've removed all doubt. They never asked how he got her device back, but he sensed they knew he was responsible for the attack on the McGonagills. Mom seemed distraught at the thought of it, but he didn't care. All that mattered was Abby's safety.

"Parker—Parker."

The detective's voice jarred him back to the present. Parker blinked. "What did you say?" He pressed his hand to his chest, fingers splayed out like a fan. His breathing became labored.

"I said I'm just looking at all the angles regarding motive." He sighed and toyed with his toothpick. "Son, we'll probably never really know why these SOBs did what they did tonight, but I have to try and figure it out anyway. And this happens to be the angle that fits best. That's all."

The wheezing intensified, the burning sensation spreading like wildfire across his chest. A sudden gasp jerked him upright. He took out his inhaler and sucked in two quick puffs of the albuterol. Stupid asthma.

Parker slumped in his chair when relief came and put his hands inside the pockets of his letter jacket. His fingers caressed the folded note he'd found on his car. *This didn't come from a Gatling fan.* His eyes drifted to the floor. "What do you want to know?" he asked quietly.

Boddicker sat up, placed the toothpick back into the side of his mouth, and put the pen to the small notepad. "Well, first of all, was it you that beat up the younger McGonagill boys?"

"Yes."

"And did their older brother know it was you?"

"I don't know."

"At the time, there was speculation that it might have been you because of the earlier attack on your sister, if I recall correctly, but since neither of them boys got a good look at their assailant, no positive ID could be made."

Parker sat still and didn't respond. *I killed my sister.* His stomach roiled with cold nausea. the room tilted and spun like a carnival ride. "I think I'm going to be sick." He leaned forward, resting his elbows on his knees. Maybe a few deep breaths would help keep from vomiting.

Boddicker looked up from his notepad. "You're really pale. You okay?"

Parker didn't say a word but continued to take slow, measured breaths until the queasiness passed.

The detective stood up and walked behind the desk. "Well, did you ever tell anyone that you beat up the McGonagill boys?" He stepped forward and set a small trash can in front of Parker.

Saliva built in his mouth, and Parker spit into the plastic receptacle. "No." Memories of that day came roaring back, the sensations easy to recall. A racing heart as he hid behind the fence. Bruised knuckles. The sound of cracking bones. Wrath coursing through him to the point his eyes had flooded with angry tears.

Boddicker sat back down across from Parker. "To the best of your knowledge," he began, his voice dropping an octave, "you've never said a word to anyone that might have given them the impression you were responsible?"

Parker let out a slow breath, trying to put a mental distance between then and now. "No, I've never said a word to anyone." He cast a quick, sideways glance at the detective.

Without looking up, Boddicker asked, "And over the years, do you recall the McGonagill boys ever telling anyone they thought it was you?"

"No."

"Did anyone ever approach you about it or ask you about it?"

Parker turned toward the detective and shrugged. "Honestly, I don't remember. But even if someone had asked me about it, I would've lied." Boddicker scribbled a few more notes. "Why are you asking me about McGonagill?"

The lanky detective reached down next to his boots and

pulled onto his lap a crumpled, brown paper bag that Parker hadn't noticed until now. With the subject of the policeman's questioning, there was no telling what it held. Parker sat up and craned his neck as Boddicker opened it and stuck his hand inside. The blood-stained, black football jersey Parker had worn just a few hours earlier emerged.

Boddicker tossed the paper bag onto the floor. He unfurled the jersey, held it up, and inserted his pen through a small hole in one of the sleeves. The top of the pen appeared through the other side of the crimson-smeared uniform.

"I've counted four of these," Boddicker said as he inserted his pen through each of the bullet holes.

Parker's eyes followed the detective's pen to each bullet hole. Boddicker dropped the jersey back into his lap and looked at Parker. "You don't recall being shot at?"

Parker stared at the jersey, but it wasn't the bullet holes he thought of. After a few moments, he shook his head. "No." He pulled out the folded note from the front pocket of his letter jacket and held it out to Boddicker. "Here," he said quietly, his voice choking.

"What's that?" The detective's eyes glimmered underneath a furrowed brow, but he didn't make the slightest move to take it from Parker's hand.

"It's a note. I think it's from Bobby McGonagill."

"Unfold it and lay it on the desk," Boddicker instructed, his tone rising with anticipation.

Parker unfolded the paper and laid it on a stack of folders. Boddicker scooted to the edge of his chair, leaned toward the desk, and read the message. Parker slumped into his chair and looked out the window while Boddicker studied the large, red letters. After a moment, he said, "Fold it over a couple of times for me."

Parker blew out past his lips, sat up, and folded the note.

Boddicker took out his pen, stuck it through one of the three notebook holes of the paper, and lifted it into the air. He carefully brought it over and dropped it into a small, sandwich-sized Ziploc bag he retrieved from his coat pocket.

"Who else have you shown this to? Has anybody else seen this?"

"No, nobody else has seen it."

"What makes you think this is from Bobby McGonagill?"

"Because someone followed me all day today."

"What do you mean, 'followed?'"

An enormous wave of nausea hit Parker, and he leaned forward over the small trash can. He took a few more deep breaths until his stomach calmed down. "A black Dodge Charger followed me to Gibson's this morning. It followed me to school and followed me during lunch. I tried to see who was in it, but I couldn't. There were three of them, I think."

Boddicker scribbled in his notepad with intensity. "Did you get a license plate number?"

"No."

"Anything else that might help describe the vehicle? Bumper stickers, dents, scratches, anything?"

"No."

Boddicker finished writing and then sat back in his chair, massaging his forehead.

After a few moments of silence, the detective spoke up. "I've already seen the footage from Action 9 News. After Bobby McGonagill shot the three officers at the visitors' gate, he made a beeline for you in the end zone. You were the one he had in his sights. And you didn't realize someone was shooting at you?"

Parker shook his head again. "No. Like I told you earlier, I was standing at the goal line when I first heard the gunfire, but wasn't sure where it came from. When I thought it might be coming from behind me, I turned around, and that's when Joe Bob Swain got hit and fell on top of me."

"Frankly, son, I'm shocked. With the weapon he had and at that range, it's a miracle that you didn't get hit." Boddicker shifted his toothpick to the other side. "I guess some-one was looking out for you."

Parker grunted. "Yeah, lucky me."

"Did Bobby McGonagill say anything to you when he walked by? While you were on the ground underneath Joe Bob?"

"If he did I didn't hear him."

Boddicker reached for his notebook, flipped it open, and entered more notes. "Did you recognize him when he passed you?"

"I don't think I saw him. Joe Bob was on top of me, and I was struggling to get out from underneath him. He's one of our biggest linemen." Parker turned and resumed his mindless trance with the colored waterfall outside.

"Did you recognize McGonagill when you were beating him?"

Parker took a deep breath, struggling to keep open heavy eyelids as exhaustion washed over him. "Not at first. He had his back to me when I went after him." He shook his head. "I really didn't know Bobby. I mean, I'd only seen him a couple times at the city pool the summer I moved here and then he got shipped off when school started." Parker paused, tried to think, but found it difficult. "What was he doing back here?"

Boddicker looked up from his notepad. "You mean why wasn't he locked up in Brownwood?" He shrugged his shoulders. "I don't know. We weren't aware that he'd been released." He looked back down and jotted more notes. "But could you positively identify him in a courtroom as one of the shooters?"

Parker frowned. "Yes." A trial would mean having to take center stage and relive everything all over again. "Seriously? A trial?"

"Maybe. Depends on whether the DA offers a deal, but that's unlikely. This is Texas. We'll stick anybody with the needle." Boddicker chuckled. "Provided they're in any shape to execute."

The insinuation of the severe beating Parker had administered prompted no reaction. Still, curiosity was hard to resist. "How bad is he?"

"He'll be taking meals through a tube for the rest of his life, if you know what I mean. He was flown out of here to one of the hospitals in Fort Worth. Which is a good thing too, because I don't think we could've kept him safe here."

Should've beaten him harder.

With a yawn, Boddicker stretched and slowly rolled his head, neck muscles popping. "Word's already out he's one of the shooters, and that family ain't the most popular in Briar Ridge. We've already had to post a black-and-white at their house, just in case. Speaking of, I probably need to check on that unit to make sure they don't take matters into their own hands either."

The McGonagill house vandalized and the entire family dragged outside and lynched didn't seem like a bad thing at the moment. That clan was nothing but trash anyway. Would anyone really care if it actually happened?

Parker's thoughts were interrupted when the office door swung open.

A glance over his shoulder revealed his mother standing a few feet inside the doorway, looking from him to Detective Boddicker, clearly puzzled over the presence of Ichabod Crane.

With some effort, Detective Boddicker grabbed the paper bag off the floor and stood. He placed Parker's bloodied jersey into it and then retrieved his hat off the desk.

She came forward in short steps, apparently unsure of the conference taking place in her office. Boddicker stepped toward her with his hat over his chest. "Mrs. Austin, I'm very sorry about your daughter. You have my sincerest condolences, ma'am." He pursed his thin lips and shifted his weight. "If there is anything I can do, please don't hesitate to let Margaret or me know, okay?"

Parker's mother nodded. "Where is she? Has she been moved yet?" Exhaustion dripped from every syllable.

"Yes, ma'am. She should be arriving in the morgue any minute."

She gave a fleeting smile. "Thank you, Detective."

His mother's eyes found him again, but he turned and slumped in his chair, his hands slipping into his jacket pockets.

"Is there something wrong with Parker that I need to know about?"

"Not at all, ma'am. I just needed to ask him a few more questions about tonight, that's all." The detective's boots shuffled along the linoleum floor. "Thanks for chatting with me, Parker. I'll let y'all know if I need anything else." The door opened, letting in the sounds of nervous activity. "Ma'am, you've got a damn fine son, there. There's no telling how many people he saved tonight."

Parker squirmed slightly in his chair, dreading any more attention. There'd been only one life he'd wanted to save.

When the door closed and silence prevailed again, his mother walked over and squatted next to him. She threw her arms around him and laid her head on his shoulder, hugging as tightly as she could. He wanted to return the embrace, but couldn't find the strength or the will to do so. Guilt ate at his insides, weighing him down. He closed his eyes as his mother's sobs filled the room.

She wept for a few moments but finally collected herself. Wiping the tears from her eyes, she sniffed and took a Kleenex from her pocket. She rubbed her nose a few times with the tissue and then looked at Parker. She placed a gentle hand on his arm. "I just thank God you're safe, Park, that you're okay." Her voice was hoarse, strained.

Parker said nothing, but continued to stare out the window at the fountain. Guilt, like acid, continued spreading, burning his insides. He fought it as best he could, but the effort to resist only drained him further. Mom's continuous stare didn't help either, and he sank deeper into his chair, unable to return her gaze.

"I saw Dad. What do the doctors say?" he asked quietly.

The question would buy some time from the inevitable, but only a moment.

The query was dismissed in a quick, monotone response. "Pretty bad concussion, but he'll be all right." She cocked her head to the side and paused, an obvious invitation for him to speak, but he wasn't ready.

She took a deep breath and exhaled, patting his arm. "I saw Summer in the lobby. I'm glad she's okay."

If that was an attempt to soften things up, get him to relax and start talking, it failed. Summer was the least of his concerns at the moment. He continued to sit motionless, staring out the window. Moments of awkward silence ensued.

"What was Detective Boddicker talking about when he said you saved lives tonight?"

Mom was probing now, trying to find an opening. He shrugged it off, but there was no escaping telling her what happened to Abby. He looked out the window, longing to be anywhere else at the moment. The moon, like a baleful eye, cast the courtyard in silvery light.

"Park—please, what happened?" The tenderness of her plea gripped his heart.

Here we go. He shook his head, unable to speak. How could he tell her Abby was murdered right in front of him and that it had been his fault? No reprieve would come from her, so he wasn't surprised when she confronted him.

She stood up and walked a few steps to the front of her desk and leaned against it, displacing a few file folders and blocking his view of the fountain. With a firm voice, she repeated her request. "Parker, what happened?"

A lump formed in the back of his throat and water pooled in his eyes. He leaned forward, propped his elbows on his knees, and rested his head in his hands.

A few moments passed, and when the words still wouldn't come, Mom issued a stern command. "Riley Parker Austin, I need to know what happened to Abby. Tell me."

There was no more delaying. He slowly nodded and sat up, tears running down his cheeks again. He sniffed, cleared his throat, and started the painful narrative.

CHAPTER 11

Marie sat on one of the benches next to the fountain in the hospital's inner courtyard, the colored water cascading into the churning pool. Like Parker, she found it entertaining, but not quite to the same level. She kept her hands in the pockets of her brown suede jacket and rested her chin on her thick wool scarf. Her legs stretched out into the path of crushed gravel that circled the fountain, the toes of her boots touching its stone base.

The cold night air no longer contained the possibility of precipitation, and the first twinkling of stars appeared overhead. It was a pretty nighttime sky, all things considered—even the wind had died down to a trace. She looked up and admired the starlit heavens. God's perfect universe still went on despite the tragedy that had just occurred. There was comfort in the thought that no matter how much heartache and devastation might take place, God was always present to shine through the darkness.

The falling water danced in the colored lights. A somber mood tugged at the periphery of her emotions, but the fact that Parker had escaped the carnage unscathed prevented it from taking hold. Unfortunately, the damage that had been done was entirely internal, and a possibility existed that he might never recover. Hopefully, he would listen to her through the emotional clutter of the next several days and weeks.

She sank her chin deeper into her scarf and reflected on everything that had transpired that evening. Seth and his cohorts had pulled off the massacre brilliantly. It was now obvious why the others had targeted Mrs. Calvin. Her suicide siphoned off resources that normally would've been at the game. With only six officers present, the two shooters ambushed and made easy work of the unsuspecting policemen. How different would this night have been had those additional officers been at the stadium instead of Mrs. Calvin's home?

Her thoughts drifted back to Parker. She peered through the fountain and watched him through the water. He was talking to his mother about his sister, and it was killing him to do it. His broken heart and the enormous weight of guilt that now descended upon him consumed her. She bowed her head and prayed for him, hoping he could find the strength to get through this nightmare.

While finishing her intercessory plea, she felt a familiar presence near her, and smiled. She glanced toward the courtyard's entrance. A figure stood under the covered, unlit walkway, leaning against one of the columns in the darkness. Concern radiated from him.

"Well, Markus, are you going to sit with me or not?"

He stepped forward from the walkway and onto the path, the crushed gravel making a soft grinding noise with every step. As he drew closer to the lights of the fountain, he came into view. He'd packed on some additional weight since last she saw him. He wore black corduroy pants, and a striped gray and forest green Briar Ridge sweatshirt stretched tightly over his round belly. A Bobcat baseball cap sat atop a mound of unkempt gray hair. He crossed in front of her and sat his hefty frame down next to her on the bench.

"Why have you appeared, Marie?" he asked in hushed tones.

"It's good to see you, Markus," she replied softly. Of all of the guardians, Markus was the one to whom she felt the closest. Not only had he served as a mentor over the years, but he was also a close friend. "Nice outfit. You blend in nicely."

"Well, you know what we used to say back in the day, 'when in Rome...'" He looked around the courtyard, then back at her. "Again, why are you out here?"

She didn't really feel like defending her actions at the moment, but she'd known Markus for so long he at least deserved a response. "It's quiet back here, peaceful." She shrugged her shoulders. "Besides, what's the harm if someone comes along?"

"It would depend on how you handled it, of course. You know that, Marie."

"I think I'd be just fine. I've been around enough to handle those situations. I've done it before."

Markus sighed. "But you haven't been around as long as I have, my dear. And that's my point. You never truly know how our interaction with people will go, which is why we don't appear. There are too many risks. But if you want to appear, at least do it in the confines of a sanctuary. We've got one set up here already."

"You've appeared human many times before, so don't act like what I'm doing is so wrong. Besides, I'm not all that welcome in sanctuaries, so what's the point in going?"

"Hey, relax." A warm smile stretched his flabby cheeks. "I was just curious as to why you've appeared, that's all." He surveyed the courtyard again and settled into the bench. "But don't discount using the sanctuary. I mean it, Marie. It can be useful. It's a safe haven to be with other guardians, to draw on each other's strength for hope and encouragement."

"Spare me the sales pitch, all right? The last time I stepped into a sanctuary—the one in Vancouver, remember?—conversation stopped and everyone cleared out."

Markus nodded. "I was briefed on it. Again, I think you're exaggerating things a bit."

Marie shot him a cold stare. *Exaggerating? Really?*

"Okay." He patted her on the leg. "Forget I brought it

up." He leaned back and put his hands behind his head. "This is a lovely place."

"I thought it would be a good place to watch him."

Markus leaned over. With a quiet, gentle tone, he said, "But you don't have to appear to watch him, do you? That's my point. You can watch him any time you please."

Marie didn't say anything and returned her attention to the window where Parker continued to struggle with telling his mother how Abby died. If only she could take away his pain. It was like standing before a dam that was cracking with small streams of water shooting out of tiny fissures. With each passing minute, more cracks appeared, letting more water spill out. The cracks needed to be sealed, to keep him from breaking wide open and being overcome by the flood.

They sat in silence, watching him, the only noise coming from the gurgling fountain. Without turning to Markus, she said softly, "You were sent, weren't you?"

"Yes," he replied, his voice tender, delicate. He slid his arm around her and she drew close to him. Why he'd decided to put on the extra weight she didn't know, but it came in handy, for his extra padding served as a nice cushion. They sat quietly, appearing for all intents and purposes like a middle-aged father consoling his daughter.

"My heart breaks for him," she whispered.

"I know it does. I know it does."

"You should hear his thoughts right now. He's so devastated. He's hurting, and he feels so guilty." She watched Parker as he finished telling his mother what had happened. His mother stepped away from the wall, walked up to him, bent over, and gently kissed the top of his head.

No matter how many horrendous, heartbreaking, gut-wrenching things she'd seen over the years, it never got easier. Tears welled in her eyes.

"I remember the last time I cried over him. He'd almost died then, as a scared, helpless four-year-old boy isolated in an intensive care ward. I appeared to him and comforted him, helped him ease the pain, loneliness, and fear." She sniffed. "And I want so desperately to do it again now."

Markus gave her a gentle squeeze.

"'Let us sit upon the ground and tell sad stories of the death of kings.'" Her voice cracked and a tear rolled down her left cheek. "Shakespeare had never penned a sadder line."

"King Richard II. Act three, scene two, if I remember correctly."

"Yes, that's right." She dabbed her eyes. "I feel so sad, overwhelmed." She sniffed again. "Parker's not like any of my other charges. He's so different."

"Different how?" His voice was subdued, the tone bordering on concern.

"His spirit is stronger than any I've ever come across. It's so genuine, so raw." Memories of the past eighteen years flooded her mind. Marie sat up and smiled through the tears. "In the seventh grade, a new kid moved to his middle school. The kid's family was poor, unlike Parker and his friends, and he didn't wear the right clothes or accessories. Nobody would eat with him or even talk to him during lunch in the cafeteria. Until Parker did. After two weeks of watching the kid eat by himself, Parker just got up, walked over, and sat down next to him. Oh, Markus." Marie shut her eyes and relived the moment. "You should've seen that kid's face when he did that. It was—it was as if he saved him. Saved him from becoming something he wasn't meant to be."

Her eyes slowly opened. "And then there's my favorite—when he was on his church's mission trip two years ago down on the border helping paint and roof houses. He took that homeless man living under the bridge across the street to McDonald's and fed him. Parker spent every dollar he had to feed him. And when he got back to the church and the kids asked him why he did it, do you know what he said? He shrugged it off like it was no big deal and said, 'Why not?'"

She turned and her gaze drifted to the fountain again. "I want him to always be that person, Markus, but sometimes I feel like I may not be good enough to protect him, to make sure he stays that way." She raked her teeth across her bottom lip and sighed. "I don't know. Maybe promoting me was a mistake. Maybe I shouldn't be here." Then again if that were the case, she never would've come to know Parker. Never would've gotten lost in him, or experienced the thrill of his voice, or felt the excitement of physically being in his presence.

My sweet, beautiful Parker. Her heart fluttered, hot internal steam warmed her cheeks.

"I was sent to check on you, to be here for you if you needed anything. And it looks like you do."

She snapped out of her thoughts and wiped her hand across her face. Surely he didn't see her blushing, did he? "Yes. Thanks for coming." She patted him on the leg. "It's good to have a friend with me right now." A calm washed over her with the realization that Markus had been sent to comfort and provide support. Incredible. Throughout the tragedy and amidst the chaos and heartache of all these people, *she* had been thought of as well.

"Two things, Marie. First, your charge made it through, he's alive. Hurt and devastation leaves him vulnerable, so he needs you now more than ever. That's job number one. Got it?"

She nodded. "And the second?"

"Second, I'm crashing this pity party of yours. I know Uriel and some of the other guardians haven't exactly made you feel like you belong, but you wouldn't be here if I didn't think you could handle it. I recruited you. I believe in you. 'So turn out the lights. The party's over.'"

She smiled at her friend. "You're quoting Willie Nelson?"

"Hey, I know he's not your beloved Shakespeare." Markus straightened, lifted his hand as though it held poor Yorick's skull, and spoke with a thick English accent as the bard's name rolled off his tongue. "But country music has some merit, believe it or not."

Markus in a honky-tonk? She couldn't help but chuckle at the image. Good. The humor helped. Her confidence rose. Perhaps laughter really was the best medicine after all.

The levity of the moment vanished when another presence from the covered walkway alerted her. She jerked her head in that direction. A man stood quietly at the entrance of the courtyard, watching them. He stepped onto the path of crushed gravel and walked at a slow and casual pace in their direction.

As he neared, Markus whispered, "Stay calm. Relax."

She nodded.

As the man drew closer, a small yellow flame from a cigarette lighter illuminated his face. The blond hair was new, but his yellow eyes looked as feverish and haunting as always. He sauntered toward the fountain, took a long drag on the cigarette, and exhaled a huge cloud of billowy smoke. He stopped near the bench where Marie and Markus sat watching him with intense, taut eyes.

"Hello, Marie." Seth let out a low, long whistle. "Nice scarf. Hermès?"

Not this again. "Yes, but it's one of their lower-end scarves."

Seth smiled. "Oh, I'm not going to let that take away from your sense of style. It's an excellent choice. Another line of scarves you might like is Burberry, if you prefer something more modest."

"Did you really stop by to talk scarves?"

"Hardly. Did Markus stop by to check on you?"

She cast a quick, nervous glance at Markus, who ignored the question and avoided her quizzical gaze.

"What are you doing here, Seth?" Markus asked.

Again, the cigarette lit up as Seth took another long drag. He exhaled slowly, the smoke hanging in the air between them. He eyed Markus with disinterest.

"I could ask you the same thing, pork chop. Are you here to check on Marie's well-being or are you trying to figure out what to do next now that it's happened?" Seth stared at Marie, who quickly averted her gaze. "Oh, come on, Markus, you know I like to rub it in a little when we win."

"You must be pretty proud of yourselves," Markus replied dryly.

"Proud? No. Getting that crazy old woman to off herself and those two crackheads to shoot up the stadium was easy. They were low-hanging fruit. Just needed a little nudge in the right direction, nothing more." Seth suddenly went rigid, his face contorted as if a foul odor wafted into his nose. "Okay, this can no longer be ignored. Markus—" Bitter disgust laced Seth's voice. "—what on Earth are you wearing?"

Markus glanced down at his clothes. "It's a sweatshirt."

"No, it's an eyesore. My eyes are hurting just looking at it." Seth squinted and rubbed his eyes. "Did you buy that off the rack in a convenience store? Seriously, have I not taught you anything? Horizontal stripes *accentuate* an expansive waistline and make you look even wider. If you're going to go with the fluffy look, then you need to sport a solid V-neck top, no stripes or patterns, light in color, and dark pants."

Markus rolled his eyes and pursed his lips. He leaned toward Marie. "Annoying, isn't it? I've been putting up with this drivel for millennia."

Turning his attention back to Seth, Markus said, "But what's really an eyesore is you clothing yourself in the finest human garments possible in a forlorn attempt to hide the ugliness you've become. And no matter how stylish or flashy your clothes, you know deep down it was your own vanity that cost you your beauty."

Seth flicked his hand in a dismissive manner. "Spare me your psychobabble nonsense. You might as well tutor a young protégé in order to silence the screams of all the charges you've lost, thinking maybe if you can produce a really good guardian it will somehow make up for all of your other failings."

Markus shifted his weight on the bench. "Whatever. Let's get back to the matter at hand. Why don't you get out of here and leave these people alone?"

Seth smirked. "Our work here isn't finished, that's why." He nodded at the window of Suzy's office.

"What?" Marie hissed.

"Take it easy," Markus reminded her.

"You heard me. We're not done yet," Seth replied. "I've got my eye on that one."

Marie's jaw dropped. Fear and anger swirled through her, and she gripped the edge of the cold iron bench to keep from shaking uncontrollably. "Stay away from him, Seth," she spat out in a desperate attempt to keep him away from Parker.

But she knew full well that he wouldn't.

"Or you'll do what? Please, give me a break. This game is too big for you." He turned toward the window. "I can already feel him breaking." Seth closed his eyes and took a slow, deep breath. "I can feel his anger, his *doubt*."

Marie watched Parker follow his mother out of her office.

Seth opened his eyes and grinned as he faced her. "He's already slipping away from you."

The contemptuous look on his pale face was enough. She shot up off the bench and stepped toward him, stopping just inches from him. "Wipe that smirk off your face," she said through gritted teeth. "You will not have him, I swear it!" Her pulse raced, her body trembled. A bright blue aura emanated from the balled fist of her right hand. Nothing seemed more appealing at the moment than seeing the quick flash of blue light escape from her hand and strike Seth, hear him cry out in agony as the angel fire burned his demonic flesh.

Markus stood. "Not here, Marie. Not now. There'll be another time, another place to fight."

Seth snickered. "Itchy trigger finger you've got there. Overreact much?" He took a long drag on his cigarette and blew the smoke into her face, causing her to cough. "Well, I guess five centuries of ridicule by your own colleagues has made you a little sensitive. I mean, it must not be easy constantly feeling unappreciated, irrelevant, and alone."

Marie shifted her weight under the thoughts of the past five hundred years. Why wasn't Markus coming to her defense? He just stood there, cool, calm, and measured as always. Just once it'd be nice to see him show a flicker of intensity, a spark of defiance. She cleared her throat, set her jaw, and locked eyes with Seth. "Yeah, you ought to know all about feeling irrelevant and alone."

"You must have a very short memory, my dear. Remember, when we left, a third of all Heaven went with us, and our ranks have been multiplying ever since. On the contrary, I'm anything but alone."

"And you have an interesting spin on history. You didn't just leave—you rebelled and lost, got kicked out and received exactly what you deserved."

Seth laughed. "I like you, Marie. You've got a lot of fire in you. It's too bad you're on the wrong side. I can show you a freedom you've never imagined." He opened his hands, palms up. "Think about it. Freely accepted as yourself, without being judged, and nobody to make you feel like you don't belong. Just imagine how that would feel."

"I like where I am just fine," Marie replied, holding Seth's gaze. "Besides, I'm not the one on borrowed time."

"Yeah, right. You keep believing those lies and see where it'll get you." Seth smiled at Marie and Markus. "Well—" He took a final puff on his cigarette. "—I've got more work to do." He exhaled another vaporous smoke cloud and tossed the cigarette into the fountain. "Adios." He turned and strolled out of the courtyard, spitefully whistling the tune to the old church hymn "A Mighty Fortress Is Our God."

As Seth disappeared around the corner, Markus said, "You can breathe now."

She exhaled and tried to relax. "I might need that sanctuary after all."

CHAPTER 12

Suzy's heart thudded against her chest, her stomach twisted in knots as Parker narrated the events at the stadium. Gunfire after the touchdown, a teammate killed, mass chaos and panic. Abby killed. The words came fast, Parker's voice flat and monotone. Reluctance, even evasiveness, oozed from her son with mock coolness as he sped through the story. Parker, she assumed, to spare her from any more pain, was attempting to keep it brief and matter-of-fact.

So protective, just like his father.

However, she'd seen and dealt with tragic losses from acute trauma over the years, and this incident dealt directly with her own daughter. "Parker," she interrupted, "Stop it. It's okay. Go ahead and tell me everything, no matter how much it might hurt me. I have to know."

He only nodded in response, but still kept things simple, even detached. It'd been a futile effort on his part, for when he told her about seeing the look on Abby's face when she screamed for him to help her, he lost all control and broke down. Suzy stood against the wall, staring into nothingness, listening to the description of Abby's final moments. How frightened she must have been. And helpless.

Her heart ached hearing Parker's voice waver and crack. His painful wailing when he finished his narrative tugged at her instincts, breaking her out of her trance. Pure, unadulterated emotion overwhelmed him. He sat on the edge of the chair, rocking back and forth, his arms crossed. Parker avoided her eyes and bowed his head, tears streaming down his face from swollen, bloodshot eyes.

"I was too slow," he stammered, his face red and contorted. "I couldn't get to her—I—I was too slow."

Parker sobbed uncontrollably as she took the tissue box from her desk and handed him a Kleenex. He grabbed it, wiped his nose, and the crying slowed.

A heaviness weighed her down, and a sickness washed through her stomach. It wasn't easy watching her own son break down like this.

But she had to know. They had to press on.

She let him recover for a moment, but this wasn't over yet. One last question needed to be asked. "Park, did Abby say anything to you, at the end?"

The question opened the floodgates again and he lost it, burying his face in his hands. His shoulders rose and fell with each heavy sob. She paused to give him time to catch his breath and get back some control, but he seemed unable to stop. No reply was forthcoming. No words, no hints—nothing that even remotely indicated he was about to answer her.

Something was different this time. The crying was intense, but an indescribable rawness accompanied his grief. A cry that could only come from the depths of the soul, buried under remnants of a broken heart and a shattered spirit, emanated from him. What could Abby have said to produce such a reaction?

She leaned against the edge of her desk facing him and folded her hands in her lap. "Park, what did she say?" Her voice was soft, caring, and delicate. The words navigated through his sensitive emotions to carefully extract an answer in the least disruptive manner.

He raised his head, his face flushed and wet. Puffy, glassy blue eyes met hers, and Suzy held her breath, her heart racing.

Her son sat up, recited Abby's last words, and then collapsed into his chair.

Air shot out of her lungs, and her body sagged. Her knees buckled, and she staggered from the desk. Only a hand against the wall to steady herself kept her upright.

Breathe, just breathe.

She clutched her tightening chest and tried to control the tiny gasps for air. Her eyes watered and her vision blurred. Tears slid down her cheeks, and an audible cry escaped past her lips.

She leaned against the wall, bumping into framed diplomas and licenses, and thought of Abby lying in Parker's arms, speaking those last words to him with her dying breath. She repeated the two brief sentences to herself. Both a profound sadness and a blessed assurance flooded over her.

Suzy wept into her tissue while Parker sat slumped in his chair. He stared at the courtyard fountain in silence, his cheeks stained from a river of tears.

Guilt had to be eating him, just like his father. And, if he took guilt to the same extent as Kenneth, then he'd beat himself up as a result, hold himself personally responsible for everything. Ridiculous, of course, but Kenneth and Parker had been present at the massacre—Parker literally at ground zero. So, maybe they were entitled to a little self-loathing. It was okay to grieve, but it couldn't give way to drifting, to doubt, or worse.

There would be time enough to address this, but not now. Regaining some of her motherly composure, she walked over to Parker, leaned over, and whispered, "It wasn't your fault." She kissed the top of his head and turned to leave.

She crept toward the door, wiping her eyes, barely conscious of moving at all. It still felt unreal, like a dream she didn't believe was actually happening. The only thing that did register was to continue to plod ahead as well as possible, take things one moment at a time.

After all, what else was there to do?

Taking a deep breath, she opened the door and turned left toward the east wing. The hallway traffic remained busy, though not quite as frantic as it'd been earlier. A few hospital staff rushed here and there, but for the most part order was regaining a foothold at Wheeler Memorial. However, before resuming nursing duties, she had to tend to one last personal matter.

"Mom, where are you going?" Parker called from behind her.

The words nearly died in her throat, but she managed to get them out. "I'm going to see Abby."

The intercom broadcast a page for one of her colleagues. She focused on putting one foot in front of the other and getting to the morgue.

Parker dashed by. He turned and stood in her path, a look of uncertainty on his face. Dr. Beck and Betty Crane walked hurriedly by him, brushing against Parker's shoulder as they hustled down the hall. Suzy stopped and watched her son.

"What is it, Park?"

He shook his head. His eyes remained watery and bloodshot. "Mom, it's just…um…I don't think…" he mumbled, eyes darting to the floor.

Suzy stepped closer. "Look at me, Park." Eventually he lifted his head and looked her in the eyes. "What is it?" she asked.

"It's just—I don't think that's such a good idea." He took a deep breath. "Her body got really messed up by the gunfire. And I don't know if you—"

Suzy managed a weak smile. "I appreciate what you're doing, Park. I really do." She placed both hands on his shoulders. "But this is something I have to do. I have to see my baby. It doesn't matter what condition her body is in, I have to see her and hold her." The thought of holding Abby for the last time made her lips quiver again as a lump formed in her throat. "When you have children of your own someday, you'll understand."

She skirted past Parker, who made no effort to stop her. She made her way down the east wing and turned into the smaller, quieter hallway. Pausing at the double doors leading to the county morgue, she used her identification badge to buzz them open.

She stepped into the large, cool room lined with small, stainless steel doors on the far side of the wall. An employee busily filled out a mountain of paperwork at a small desk near the door. The county coroner, Arturo Ortega, stood at the end of the room, visiting with the Wheeler County sheriff, Billy Clyde Maddox. Both men abruptly turned and looked at Suzy as soon as she entered.

She stepped past the registration desk, where the morgue attendant kept his head down and continued filling in blanks and checking little boxes. She continued toward the far side of the room, glancing at the storage bays out of the corner of her eye. Which one held Abby?

Both Arturo and Sheriff Maddox came forward and met Suzy in the middle of the large, white-tile-floored room. She was mindful of the cold. The tiny hairs on her arms stood erect. In fact she'd often wondered how anyone could work in there for any length of time, but now the temperature didn't seem to bother her as much.

"Suze, I'm so sorry about Abby." Billy Clyde offered his giant hand.

"Thanks, Billy." She looked at his droopy red face. Genuine sympathy greeted her from large brown eyes.

"If there's anything, I mean anything, Sarah and I can do for you, don't hesitate to let us know," he said as he cupped her hand in both of his. "In fact, I'm gonna have Sarah bring over some food for you and Kenny. Sarah's baking all the time, and it's the least we can do for y'all."

"Thanks."

"No problem at all, Suze." He squeezed her hand and let go. Arturo stepped forward and also offered his condolences. She gave the obligatory thanks and then paused, unsure how to proceed.

After all these years working in hospitals, the majority of which had been spent in the emergency room, she'd always been the one to accompany the doctor, or go it alone when the doctor chickened out, to inform families that their loved ones had died. She knew all the right words and expressions to use when conveying such a sad and somber message, and she'd seen every conceivable human reaction to it hundreds of times over. Now, finding herself on the opposite side, she had no idea how to respond when someone else offered condolences to her.

"Gentlemen, I just want to...um...have a moment with my daughter." She bit her lip to keep from crying. The morgue was foreign territory. So was its protocol. Hopefully, the professional intimacy of working in such a small hospital could override any formal procedures.

"Of course, Suze." Sheriff Maddox turned to Arturo. "You've got no objection, do you, Art?"

Arturo shifted his weight from one foot to the other and wiped the back of his neck with his hand. "Well, uh, no. I guess not. But, Suzy please understand that your daughter hasn't been prepped, okay? That will take place at the funeral home, which I'm assuming will be Tealman's?"

Funeral home? Burial? She hadn't thought of where to place Abby. Here or in Houston? The question brought her to a standstill.

She slowly pulled her fingers down her cheeks and gazed about the room in a search for answers that wouldn't come.

"Never mind," he said. "Just pull the sheet down so you can only see her face, all right?"

Suzy's head flinched back slightly, and she blinked several times until she broke free from her mental fog. She nodded. Arturo stepped aside and called out to his attendant at the front desk to identify Abby's storage bay. The young man turned around and only then seemed cognizant of Suzy's presence. He turned back to his computer, made a few clicks of the mouse, and called out, "C-2."

Suzy followed Arturo over to the wall lined with small,

stainless steel doors. Three rows of storage bays, all looking identical to each other, reflected the soft fluorescent lighting of the room. He crossed to the middle row and opened a door. Streams of cold air billowed out as Arturo reached in and slid out the table that held Abby's sheet-covered body.

Arturo stepped back and waited. She seemed unable to move and found herself planted to the floor. Her feet and legs were heavy, as if cement blocks weighed them down. She stared at the form under the sheet, wondering how her daughter would look and if she could actually go through with this.

No, I have to see her, I have to hold her. "She's my baby," she said, her voice no more than a painful moan. She took a deep breath and walked over to Abby's side. Frigid air escaped from the storage bay next to her.

"Take as much time as you need, Suzy." Arturo walked over to the registration desk and told his attendant to take a break from the paperwork and get a cup of coffee.

"A hot cup of joe sounds good right now. I think I'll join him," Sheriff Maddox said. "Besides, I need to check on a few deputies and prepare for a press conference."

Arturo sat down at the registration desk, his back to Suzy as the attendant and Billy Clyde left the room. She looked down and studied the contour of the white sheet and how it outlined Abby's body.

Her forehead, nose, chin, and shoulders were clearly distinguishable. It reminded her of when Abby was a toddler and how the two of them played peek-a-boo with Abby's bed sheets every night as a way to help Abby with her motor skills. Abby and Suzy would take turns holding the covers over each other's faces and saying, "Where's Abby?" and then drop them to say, "Peek-a-boo!" Every time they played, Abby would laugh that sweet, genuine, innocent laugh only a small, loving child can make that is music to a mother's ears.

Suzy closed her eyes and heard that laugh now, like it'd happened only a moment ago, and it brought a faint smile to her face. With both hands she gently took hold of the white sheet and brought it down past Abby's face, stopping at her chin. "Peek-a-boo," she said softly, her lips quivering, and then burst into tears.

Abby looked ashen, but peaceful, as though in a deep sleep. Her lips were blue. "My baby," Suzy said as she caressed Abby's cold, pale cheek. Her nose began to run and she sniffled a few times. She stroked the top of Abby's head with her hand, feeling the stiffness already setting in.

She remembered doing Abby's hair in the mornings, putting cute little ribbons, clips, and bows in her hair and styling it in a variety of adorable looks. Each morning before taking Abby to day care or to school, she would spend up to twenty minutes working on her daughter's hair. Kenneth had asked why she spent so much time meticulously working on Abby's hair since it usually made her late for work. She replied she wanted everyone who saw Abby to know she was loved and cared for, that she was precious to someone.

Abby still looked precious, even now, and the thought of living without her seemed unfathomable. This was her only daughter, and now she was gone. Gone, too, were all of the hopes, dreams, and aspirations she'd harbored for Abby since she'd been in her womb and had felt her kick for the first time. She'd longed for many things for Abby, despite her physical struggles. She wanted to share the experience of helping pick out her first prom dress, watching her glow as she made her way down the wedding aisle, and sharing with her the joys and trials of becoming a mother herself someday.

But the small, daily things in life so often taken for granted were also gone. Never again would she wake up in the morning to music coming from Abby's bedroom, never again hang her artwork or report cards on the refrigerator, nor would she ever hold her and tell her how much she loved being her mommy.

Those had been her last words to her, she recalled, when

she'd dropped Abby off at the stadium late that afternoon. She'd helped her into her walker, and, standing next to her and admiring how cute she looked in her game day attire, she'd said, "I sure am proud to be your mommy, kiddo." Abby flashed a smile and winked in return and said, "Love you too, Mom." For those to have been the last words spoken between the two of them, Suzy couldn't have been more thankful. There would be none of the guilt or grief had their last words been something of anger, contempt, or just meaningless, idle conversation. Instead, she was left with the best words the two could've ever said to one another.

She wrapped her arms around Abby for the last time, though the cold, stainless steel table made it difficult. Clinging to her, she didn't want to let go. She wanted to keep her, hold her forever, but she couldn't. Abby and a cherished, longed-for future were already gone.

Quiet tears streamed down her face. "I love you." She repeated it several times, kissed Abby gently on her cold forehead, and stood. She carefully replaced the sheet. She pressed her fingertips to her lips, gave them a kiss, and then placed them on Abby's covered forehead. She smiled through the tears and then quickly walked past Arturo and through the double doors.

CHAPTER 13

Time to go home. The emotional catharsis of describing how Abby had died left Parker drained and exhausted. Even breathing required too much effort. A jackhammer assaulted his temples and forehead, and his eyes were tender from crying. Although his emotional reservoir had dried up and surpassed his capacity for shedding more tears, seeing Abby in the morgue was out of the question. So when his mother turned and walked past him in the hall, he made no attempt to follow her.

All that mattered was finding the nearest exit and getting home. He headed toward the hospital's main entrance in a trance, his mind numb, and only vaguely aware he moved at all. The large crowd in the main lobby soon appeared, but he trudged on, ignoring the vibrations of his cell phone in his front pocket.

The lobby remained full of people, though not quite as loud and emotional as they had been earlier. Mr. Gibson was setting up two large pots of coffee on a card table. It was going to be a long night for many people.

A few heads turned in Parker's direction. His shoulders sagged at the sound of his name, but he couldn't help but glance in the direction from which he was being called. A few of his teammates stood in a corner, accompanied by their girlfriends.

What he needed was a quick exit, not more conversation,

but Tyler and his girlfriend, Angela, came over and prevented any escape from the building.

"Glad you're safe, man." Tyler took a bite out of a Big Mac.

Parker nodded. Although he hadn't eaten in almost eight hours, the sight and smell of food didn't prompt the least bit of interest. "You, too. Your family okay?"

Tyler chewed for a moment. "Yeah. Scared to death, but they made it out all right."

Parker's eyes shifted toward the doors. "Good for them."

"Park, I'm real sorry about Abby. She, uh…"

"I know. Thanks, Ty."

Tyler looked back at Parker and shrugged. "Anything I can do for you?"

Parker shook his head. "No. I just need to get out of here, get some rest." His phone vibrated again in his pocket. He ignored it.

"Yeah, I think I'm going to go home soon, too. Not much can be done at this point. I've just been hanging out, trying to find out about everyone." Tyler wrapped his arm around Angela and took another bite of his hamburger.

"What's the latest?"

"Oh, man, it's bad," Tyler's cheeks bulged like a chipmunk's. He chewed quickly, then swallowed. "The last numbers I heard were like twenty-nine dead, about 100 wounded. Probably would've been a lot higher had you not gone after McGonagill, but it's been hard to get an actual number since so many had to be sent to other hospitals."

The high numbers meant nothing. Only one casualty mattered at the moment.

"Hey, speaking of which, one that got sent to another hospital was Coach Sinc."

Parker's mind flashed to his last image of his head coach signaling the play on which they scored. He envisioned Coach Sinc standing a few yards out onto the field, as was his custom when excited, signaling the play he knew would work. Parker thought about the play, and naturally, what immediately followed. He tried to block it out, but couldn't. He was vaguely aware of staring into space, unable to respond to Tyler, but couldn't snap out of it. Abby's screams filled his mind.

"Park? Park?" Tyler asked, pulling on the sleeve of his jacket.

"Huh?"

"I asked if you heard about Coach Sinc."

Parker sighed. *Why can't people stop asking me that?* "No. Is he going to be okay?"

Tyler shrugged. "I guess so. I heard it wasn't too bad." Tyler looked at Parker and seemed to study his face. "Dude, you look seriously tired. Why don't you get out of here and get some rest? You need me to drive?"

"No, I'm okay. But, thanks. I'll see you later."

Parker headed for the door, his head down. A throng of people waited outside the front entrance, just like the large crowd outside the emergency room entrance. People huddled together, their jackets buttoned or zipped to the top, hands gloved or in pockets. A few were crying. More news crews had arrived and were reporting or conducting interviews.

The lights from the front entrance illuminated the wide sidewalk in front of him and he quickly got his bearings. As he made his way through the masses, the light of a nearby camera shone like a supernova in the dark to highlight the reporter and the interviewee. Tasha stood in front of the camera dressed in her letter jacket, displaying a gaudy amount of jewelry. Parker paused and watched the interview for a moment. *This might be interesting.*

"My name's Tasha." She looked directly into the camera and spoke slowly as though she were speaking to the learning impaired. "Tasha Turner. T-U-R—"

"Yes, we've got your name," said the female reporter, interrupting Tasha. "Can you describe the shooting? Tell us what you saw."

Tasha grabbed the reporter's microphone to bring it

closer. The reporter resisted the intrusion, and a brief tug-of-war ensued in front of the camera. Tasha smiled under the strain of trying to pry loose the mic and answered the question.

"Well, I was cheering on the sidelines. I'm on the varsity cheer squad, been on it for four years now." Tasha whipped her red hair back out of her eyes and flashed a toothy smile for the camera as if this were a photo shoot. "Leading cheers for an entire town is a very big deal, and—"

"That's great, Tasha, but what about the shooting? What was it like?"

Without missing a beat, Tasha's eyes widened and her mouth opened. "Oh, it was terrible. Just terrible. Lots of people were shot." She looked at the reporter and nodded as if to confirm the seriousness of her comment.

If anyone had ever doubted Tasha's place on the ladder of intellect, here was proof positive that she stood on the bottom rung.

"Right," the reporter said, sliding the word out slowly and looking unsure of Tasha's ability to answer further questions.

"I mean it was so bad," Tasha continued, "I just know I'm gonna need years of therapy to get over what I saw."

Damn right you need therapy.

She shut her eyes and frowned as if she were trying to hold back tears. A quick wave of the hand brushed her red bangs out of her face and she began to sob. Parker took a step closer but saw no actual tears. In fact, her eyes didn't appear wet at all.

"You've got to be kidding me," he said, quickly following it with the words, "oil trash."

Tasha's eyes popped open and she sneered in the direction of the comments that had interrupted her on-camera moment. Parker stalked away and weaved through the crowd.

He pulled out his cell phone and scrolled through the recent text messages and voicemails. All of them from curious classmates, many of whom didn't run in his circle of acquaintances. He stuffed the phone back into his pocket with a scowl. The small-town gossip machine would have to be fed by someone else.

He walked as briskly as he could through the cold air, but lethargy tugged at his limbs. He had to concentrate on just keeping his feet and legs moving.

His nose numb and ears stinging from the cold, he made his way to his car. He got in, cranked the engine, and set the heater on the highest setting. While waiting for the air to warm, he rubbed his hands together and put them up to his lips to blow on them.

The illuminated numbers of the dashboard clock seemed to taunt him, teasing with the wish that he could turn them back by several hours to a time when there was nothing to worry about except a stupid football game.

He leaned back in his seat and thought about his conversation with Detective Boddicker. *If I hadn't beaten up the McGonagill boys, this wouldn't have happened—if I hadn't arranged for Abby to help on the sidelines, she never would've been down there—if I'd only been faster, I could've saved her.* The thoughts repeated over and over again, without letting up. He shook his head. *It's all my fault.*

Grief gave way to anger. *Why did this happen? Why did Abby get killed? Why did the bullets miss me but not her?* He punched the middle of his steering wheel, and the car horn sounded. He slammed the gear shift into drive and sped off on screeching tires, his hands gripping the wheel so tightly his knuckles turned white.

He turned onto Wabash without yielding to traffic, forcing a few angry motorists to swerve and honk. He continued down the main drag of the town, a town in which time seemed to stand still, resistant to change of any kind, but which now had been irrevocably changed forever.

If only we hadn't moved here.

Yeah, the move here had sucked. The economy tanked

and Dad's mobile home company laid people off left and right. It was Enron all over again, but instead of being laid off, Dad got the option of taking a lower-paying transfer to the company's exterior design center in Briar Ridge—a podunk town in the middle of nowhere. He should've opted for unemployment instead.

"The country, we're going to the country! There'll be horses and ponies, Park!" Abby had gushed. She couldn't pack her things fast enough.

But the news crushed Parker. Houston had been the only home he'd ever known, the only neighborhood where he'd played. He'd learned to throw a football in their backyard, learned to ride his bike down their street. Houston was home.

Moving to a hick town miles from nowhere? Culture shock. He'd been born and raised in the giant concrete and asphalt jungle of Houston and had been indoctrinated into urban living. Starbucks? There're seventeen of them around the corner. Shopping? Take your pick of a dozen upscale malls. Want to go the movies? Domestic, foreign, or indie— they're all here. Restaurants? Any kind for any taste— Houston had them all, even the celebrity chefs on TV.

What did Briar Ridge offer? Aside from riding pump jacks, cow tipping, and swimming in a dirty lake—nothing. Starbucks? Never heard of it, though this had been more of an adjustment for Mom than anyone else in the family. Shopping? Closest mall was in Abilene—sixty miles away. Movies? Gatling had a three-screen theater, but that place was off-limits—nobody from Briar Ridge would dare spend a dime to help Gatling's economy. Restaurants? Fast food all the way, baby.

Still, he'd been eager to fit in and make new friends, but the kids his age considered him a curious novelty, like a new species of bug that needed to be gawked over and poked. And it didn't help matters when the local boys learned he didn't like to hunt or fish, the two most popular recreational activities in Joe Wheeler County and prerequisites for establishing manhood. *Hunting dove or deer? Why? Are they attacking us? And, no, hunting is not a sport if one side doesn't even know they're playing. Fishing? Getting sunburned and drinking beer in a tiny boat all day while trying to outsmart a little catfish ranked right up there with watching paint dry.* His disdain for the outdoors resulted in being tagged a "metrosexual," a term he was surprised that anyone from Briar Ridge even knew. But once they saw what he could do on the football field all the teasing stopped.

The one good thing about the move was that the curiosity prompted two of the more attractive girls at school, Summer and Skylar, to take an interest in him. Really, what guy would mind two hot girls gawking over him? That certainly helped with the transition.

Over the next three years, his athletic talents and academic performance, coupled with dating Summer Hayes, made living in Briar Ridge bearable.

Yet, only a second-class citizenship could be granted to outsiders in this barren, isolated town. Accepted on the outside, but never truly considered one of them since he hadn't been born and raised there like everyone else. This feeling usually manifested itself whenever someone made a casual reference to an episode from their childhood together in Briar Ridge. Everyone would laugh and make comments in reply, but he'd always felt like the one person in the room who didn't get the joke. Whenever he inquired, he'd always get the same dismissive response: "Forget about it, it was before your time."

There were the physical indicators as well. The subtle hints of body language detected now and then. The cold stare before an answer, the occasional hesitancy before a greeting, the lack of eye contact to acknowledge his presence in a room—they were all periodic reminders that despite every attempt at assimilation, he'd always be viewed as an outsider. Never fully embraced or included, just tolerated.

"I hate this town." His grip on the steering wheel tightened, his muscles tensed, and his foot pressed down on the accelerator. The more he thought about Briar Ridge, the angrier he got and the faster he drove. He sped down Wabash Avenue, weaving in and out of traffic, his mind swirling with images of Abby getting shot.

It didn't take long before he pulled into his driveway, the headlights illuminating the giant "B" and "R" that Summer and the cheerleaders had painted in his driveway before the season had started. The first week in August had been scorching hot, humidity laying thick like a blanket over everything. Summer had worn a pair of Daisy Dukes and a bikini top, sweat glistening on her bronze body while she painted and flirted with a shirtless Parker, who had lain in the dry grass waiting for Summer to finish so the two of them could go swimming in the lake and make out.

The memory faded as he parked by the basketball goal, got out, and slammed the door shut. He shuffled through the open garage and through the door leading to the back hallway. Turning on the hallway light, he walked into the kitchen and tossed his letter jacket onto the breakfast table. A small growl emanated from his stomach when he passed the refrigerator, but eating didn't hold much interest.

Though his body sagged from exhaustion, sleeping held no interest either. He paused at the foot of the hallway leading to his and Abby's rooms. This was their corner of the house, their shared world—a safe harbor where the rest of the world couldn't enter and disturb, but now seemed invaded, dark, and lifeless.

Parker proceeded down the hallway lined with family photographs and tried not to look at them, but sneaked a peek at Abby's door out of the corner of his eye. How many times had he pounded on her door just to tease her? How often had music blared from inside?

He made it to his room and stepped inside without bothering to turn on the light. He flopped onto his bed, fully clothed, and buried his head under a pillow.

CHAPTER 14

Every time Parker's eyes closed, the haunting sounds and images of Abby and the others getting shot came roaring back. Try as he might, he couldn't relax long enough to fall asleep. So, he went to the medicine cabinet in his bathroom and took a heavy dose of cold medicine, hoping it would knock him out.

His last glance at the clock radio showed eighteen minutes past two. The next time, it was half past seven. The cold medicine had finally done the trick, but it had left a groggy hangover.

The ringtone of Imagine Dragons' "Radioactive" echoed down the hall as he stepped out of the shower. He wrapped a towel around his waist, dripping water on the floor as he walked back to his room, and studied the phone on the nightstand. The number was unfamiliar.

"Parker Austin?" He couldn't place the voice, but it definitely sounded like an adult.

He paused. "Who's calling?"

"Parker, this is Tam Schulster calling from Instant Cable News, and we'd love to visit with you on the air about your heroic action last night. We can put you on the air in a few minutes, okay?"

"Um…what?"

"I apologize that it's early, but our viewers are really interested in hearing about how you saved a lot of people last night. It's not every day that someone is a hero."

"I'm—I'm not a hero. Look, I really don't want to talk to anyone right now. Besides, how'd you get my number?" Go on live television and discuss last night with a smarmy, fake-tanned, bleached-hair, dim-witted, phony television journalist who had just invaded his privacy? No freaking way.

"Look, Parker, I know exactly how you feel."

Parker's head jerked. *Oh, really? You know how I feel?*

"I can imagine it's tough being thrown into the spotlight and being in the middle of a great big story. I mean, you're from a small town and not much ever goes on out there, so I can appreciate that you feel overwhelmed, but you've got to understand that you're a hero. You saved a lot of lives last night. And your story needs to be told."

While the reporter continued, Parker turned on his television and flipped to the Instant Cable News channel. Footage of the shooting, courtesy of Action 9 News, was on full display. With a camera crew positioned directly behind the end zone where Parker had been standing when the shooting started, a large chunk of the event was filmed from up close. ICN flashed a disclaimer at the bottom of the screen warning that some viewers might find the video disturbing.

The camera followed Bobby McGonagill as soon as he stepped onto the field and started shooting. It zoomed back to take in as much of the scene as possible while still keeping McGonagill in focus. Parker watched everyone in the visitor stands scatter in a mad stampede or dive to the ground as the Gatling players either hugged the grass or ran away to the visitor's locker room.

The camera continued to follow McGonagill as he walked past a pinned Parker, struggling to get out from underneath Joe Bob Swain.

The camera focused on McGonagill as he raised his automatic weapon and fired dozens and dozens of rounds into the packed bleachers, panic-stricken people running, scattering, hiding, even jumping off the bleachers to the concrete and asphalt below—anything to avoid the devastating gun-fire.

The television reporter continued to yammer about being a "hero" and the need to speak to millions of devastated viewers. Apparently grieving at the massive loss of life, the reporter claimed they needed to see some ray of hope in this tragedy.

He couldn't respond. Instead, his eyes remained fixed on the television screen as the camera followed McGonagill on his path of destruction. Suddenly, McGonagill turned to his left, raised his weapon, and began firing again. Parker knew exactly who he was firing at. The cell phone lowered from his ear as the events unfolded on the screen.

He gazed almost in disbelief as he saw himself enter the screen, in his football uniform and pads, and sprint at top speed at Bobby McGonagill. He watched himself lower his helmet and crash head-first like a pulverizing battering ram into Bobby's back. The shooter, having turned his attention back to the crowded stands, never saw Parker coming.

Bobby's head snapped backward from the crushing impact and the assault rifle flew from his hands. He watched himself scramble on top of Bobby and begin beating him quickly and ferociously, over and over again with his fists. He lifted Bobby up by his shirt collar while he ripped off his helmet and sent it crashing down into Bobby's face as hard as he could.

After the fourth or fifth blow, the shooter's body went limp, but the helmet bashing continued. After what appeared to be a dozen crushing blows, Parker rolled off him. He sprinted away and the camera bounced and jolted trying to follow him through the chaos. By the time it found him, it showed Parker on his knees, his back to the camera, clearly holding someone in his arms.

A new graphic flashed at the bottom of the screen: "Hero saves lives, but loses little sister." An icy ball formed in the pit of his stomach as a picture of a smiling Abby, the most recent school picture of hers from Sycamore Elementary, appeared in the top corner. One of the cable news anchors began discussing the issue of gun control.

"No," Parker said softly as tears welled in his eyes. He gripped the phone tightly in his hand and raised it to his ear. "Leave me alone!" He hung up, turned off the phone, and threw it down onto his bed.

Dazed, he stood as still as a statue, his mind whirling with a kaleidoscope of horrific images. He shut his eyes and shook his head, but no matter what, he couldn't shake Abby's terror-stricken face and desperate cries for her big brother to save her.

A lump formed in his throat as he tried to hold back the tears. "No!" He punched the wall with his fist. The impact and the instant pain in his hand snapped him out of his downward trajectory. He turned off the television and leaned back against the wall while massaging his throbbing hand.

His eyes locked onto the mounted corkboard on the far side of his room. Photos of him in his football uniform, team pictures, snapshots of him from games, and newspaper clippings of his football accolades were displayed. Interspersed were pictures of him and Summer smiling and laughing together, movie and concert ticket stubs from their dates, and boutonnieres from past homecomings Summer had given him.

The world depicted on the corkboard no longer existed—its thin, fragile protective covering shattered into a million little pieces. It tormented him as he looked at what had been and what would never be again. And it had all been his fault.

He marched to the corkboard and hastily ripped every item. Thumbtacks rained onto the carpeted floor as he jerked everything down and tossed them aside. "I hate this place," he said repeatedly until nothing remained on the wall.

He threw on a pair of jeans and a T-shirt, stormed out of his room, and went to the kitchen. The refrigerator motor almost lulled him to sleep as he stood in the open door, staring at leftovers. In the pantry, the shelves were even less appealing. A granola bar required little effort and he forced one down with some tap water out of the kitchen sink.

Escaping the house was possible, but as he stared out the kitchen window, the bleak, overcast skies only compounded the melancholy, and subdued any idea of stepping outside. Besides, where was there to go?

Not to Summer's house—Tasha would probably be there. One word from her and fists would fly. Not to Tyler or anyone else's—they'd only badger and gossip about the shooting.

Eventually, he turned his cell phone back on, and it continued to ring all morning, but he let most of the calls go straight to voicemail. The only people he talked to were Mom, who called to give updates on Dad, and Tyler and Summer, both of whom said reporters were calling them and anyone else in town that could help them get in touch with Parker.

Heavy feet dragged him into the darkened family room where he sank into the cushions of the couch and let the soft, blue glow from the television screen wash over him. Anything that was a distraction was more than welcome. Since it was football season, he tuned in to ESPN, but soon discovered it was off-limits.

The network anchors talked of nothing but last night's events without pause, and SportsCenter showed video clips of the shooting, promising to bring the viewing audience a live interview with the voice of the Briar Ridge Bobcats.

Parker had no desire to watch Tooley embarrass himself on national television, and finally settled on watching a *Big Bang Theory* marathon.

Mom came home in the afternoon after having been at the hospital around the clock since the first nine-one-one call had been received. She stopped in the family room. Her shoulders sagged, her face devoid of any life. She looked as though she'd aged ten years in the past twelve hours.

"Make sure you eat something," she said as though the simple act of speaking took every ounce of energy she had remaining.

Parker gave a slight nod and shifted his eyes back to Sheldon Cooper, but noticed in his peripheral vision that Mom didn't move. She stood for a minute, staring at something but apparently seeing nothing then slowly shuffled out of the room and down the hall.

The reruns occupied him until dinner time, when Sarah Maddox, the county sheriff's wife, delivered a few casseroles. The warm, rich aromas of homemade cooking made Parker's stomach rumble and growl like never before. As Mom came out of her room to thank Mrs. Maddox, Parker took the casserole dishes to the kitchen table and grabbed a small plate. He scooped up some of the sausage, egg, and cheese dish, but after a few bites his stomach tightened up and he lost his appetite. He put the casseroles into the refrigerator and walked to the front door where his mother was saying goodbye to Mrs. Maddox.

The sheriff's wife turned to leave, and two more cars pulled up in front of the house. Familiar faces from church got out and walked up the sidewalk to the front door, some carrying covered dishes of food as well. Included in the group were Pastor Jim and his wife, both of whom looked very tired.

Although Mom welcomed them into the house and invited them into the living room, Parker had no interest in talking and quickly excused himself to the family room.

When "thank you" and "goodbye" echoed from the entryway an hour later, he shuffled back to the living room. Mom sat in her favorite chair where she read her daily devotional every morning. An open bible splayed across her lap, her head bowed and her eyes closed.

Parker waited. He looked at the painting of the little sailboat boat caught in the storm, read the scripture at the bottom of it, and shook his head. *What a load of crap.*

He looked at his mother, still praying silently. With an

obvious trace of annoyance he said, "You're wasting your time."

She said nothing until she'd finished praying. She opened her misty eyes. "Even if that were true, Park, I still find that praying is good for my soul. Like Anthony Hopkins said in *Shadowlands*, 'I don't pray to change God, I pray because it changes me.'"

"Whatever," Parker mumbled. "When's Dad coming home?"

"He'll be discharged in the morning, and I'll bring him home. Afterwards, I need to get back to work since all our beds are full. So you'll need to stay around the house in case he needs anything."

"Fine." He turned to walk back to the family room, but stopped when his mother called to him. He faced her, leaned against the doorway between the two rooms, and crossed his arms over his chest.

"Park, I know you're hurting right now. I am, too. And it's okay to hurt and to be angry. But please don't let that change what you know is true."

Parker shook his head. "You have no idea what I know to be true."

She surveyed him for a moment, eyes narrowing with suspicion. "What's that supposed to mean?"

Before Parker could answer, the doorbell rang. A sigh escaped from his mother's lips and she got up to answer the door. When she opened it, the faint voices of children greeted her with, "Trick or treat." She called for him to get the bag of candy from the pantry.

He retrieved the large bag containing mini-bites of various candy bars and found a small pirate and a Disney fairy standing on the front porch.

Parker tried to smile at the little kids, whose eyes lit up when they saw the generous portions dumped into their open brown paper bags, but found it difficult. They each said "thank you," and their parents hurried them off the porch.

He spent the rest of the evening manning the front door for trick-or-treaters, which turned out to be few. The ones that did show up were very small children, obviously too young to appreciate or understand what happened last night and only knew that they wanted to dress up and get candy.

While waiting on costumed children, he took a call from Tyler. Between mouthfuls of powdered doughnuts, Tyler said Facebook, Twitter, and Instagram were flooded with traffic about the shooting and that cell phone videos of last night's events had gone viral. Good thing Mom had forbidden the use of any social media accounts until he graduated—they'd just offer more ways for people to intrude and annoy him. Summer called also and asked to stop by but he told her he didn't feel like having company.

Around nine o'clock he turned off the front porch light and took the half-full bag of candy to the pantry. A few mouthfuls of milk out of the carton and he headed down the hall. Again, he avoided looking at the family pictures, afraid of what photos of Abby might trigger.

He shuffled to his bathroom and took another large dose of cold medicine to help induce sleep. Walking out, he noticed light coming from underneath the closed door of his parents' room. A few steps in that direction brought the muffled sounds of crying. He leaned against the wall for a moment and listened to Mom grieve over Abby. Her words from earlier came back to him, and the thought of praying entered his mind but only for an instant.

Parker shook his head with a scowl and went to his room. He shut the door, flopped down onto his bed, and waited for the cold medicine to kick in. Though in total darkness, images and sounds of the shooting continued their haunting refrains. Tossing and turning, he begged the medication to hurry and knock him out.

CHAPTER 15

Plain and uninspiring, the small wood-planked house appeared dilapidated under the moonless night sky. Shrouded by tall, thick bushes on each side that nearly reached to the roof, the dwelling seemed to hide its rough appearance behind the dense, untrimmed foliage.

Marie concealed herself between two large evergreen shrubs that obscured most of the rusty, chain-link fence that separated the tiny backyard from the lot behind it. Though the clothesline in front of her twisted and danced in the cold wind like a billowing strand of spider web, Marie focused on the light spilling from the bedroom window.

Blinds wide open, Summer's entire bedroom was visible to anyone curious enough to sneak a peek—which was probably intentional. Summer did always like attention. It was how she landed Parker in the first place, parading around in front of him at the lake and showing off as much skin as she could.

Watching her now prance around in a T-shirt and panties while talking on the phone showed she hadn't changed in the least.

Marie cupped her hands over her mouth and blew into them, then returned them into the folds of her denim jacket as Summer grabbed a forest green book and crossed the tiny, cluttered room. She sat down on her bed with a box of Kleenex and slowly turned the pages of the book.

The way she was ignoring Parker's suffering, whose life was in shambles right now, was sickening. Instead of yakking on the phone with Tasha or whomever, she ought to be doing whatever she could to help her boyfriend. Sure, she'd called him once, and even though Parker said he didn't feel like having company, she ought to know how badly he was hurting and that he really did need her.

Parker deserved better. That was all there was to it.

With hunched shoulders, Marie stepped out from her hiding spot and moved a few steps closer to the house, her eyes fixed on the teenage girl.

Summer's conversation dragged on, interrupted now and then by a few sniffles or a soft laugh brought on by the apparent reminiscences about lifelong classmates now dead.

Marie inched closer to the window until she stood only a few feet away from the dusty pane of glass. A sleek, dark blue dress hung on the back of the bedroom door. Short and trim, it had shown off Summer's curves—and drawn attention—at the school's homecoming dance she'd attended with Parker two weeks ago.

She finally got off the phone and tossed the book aside. She wiped her nose and studied herself in a full-length mirror next to the bed. Puffy, bloodshot eyes and a pale face reflected back at her. With a brush of the hand, she tucked a rogue strand of blonde hair behind her ear and straightened up. A forced smile crept across her face.

Marie spat out a sharp breath, despite her clenched teeth. *Show-off.*

Though Summer's thoughts were foreign territory, she knew Parker's intimately. And Marie knew exactly what he thought of Summer's appearance. Studying the object of her charge's affection strutting in front of the looking glass, Marie toyed with the ends of her hair and then quietly surveyed her own figure.

The similarities were there: same curves in the same places, same soft, round face with cute dimples, same shoulder-length blonde hair. Yet, appearing as a carbon copy of Summer would never work, for a variety of reasons. So subtle differences had been added: green eyes, an inch of height, and a slight strawberry tinge to the hair. Just enough variation to be her own identity, but still close enough to ensure Parker would—

A presence quickly advanced on her and Marie sucked in a quick breath, her eyes wide with surprise. She spun around to confront the aggressor.

A cold, dry palm clamped over her mouth as a hard forearm thrust into her chest and shoved her up against the house with a thud.

Marie winced as the back of her head whiplashed into the wood siding.

"Sshh," the female's voice whispered.

The hushed voice confirmed the guardian's identity. Marie opened her eyes to a glaring Jerah, who silently raised a finger to her lips. If looks could kill, Marie would've dropped dead.

A shadow passed across the light from Summer's bedroom and stopped at the window. Both guardians held their breath and waited. A wind chime from the house next door clanged a choppy melody in the cold breeze.

Jerah's icy stare never wavered from Marie.

Summer finally backed away from the window and closed the blinds, allowing the guardians to slink off to the cover of the large evergreens at the backyard fence. Once safely out of view, Jerah grabbed Marie by the arm and jerked her close.

"Are you insane? She almost saw you."

"I was in the dark. She wouldn't have seen me," Marie insisted.

Jerah gritted her teeth loudly enough to indicate she probably could chew through metal.

"Just relax, Jerah. I was careful. Nothing happened. Everything's okay." Marie smiled, hoping her colleague would soften her posture.

"You're such an idiot. I can't believe they let you be a

guardian." Jerah spat out the words in a tone full of disgust and let go of Marie's arm. "We don't take risks like this. Ever."

Marie crossed her arms and dipped her head. "I'm just looking out for my charge. That's all. Isn't that what we're supposed to be doing? Finding and using every means to protect them?"

"Don't lecture me, *extrarium*. I've been protecting human souls from the enemy for thousands of years. You don't know the first thing about it. You spend all your time in human form, lurking around and following your charge as if...if..."

Marie tilted her head. "As if what? I'm just concerned about Parker."

Jerah's eyes narrowed. "There's a thin line between deep, abiding concern and obsession." She jabbed a finger at Marie. "And you're crossing it."

The warning was clear and unmistakable. And Jerah was a true believer who did not violate protocol. No doubt she'd report this incident to Uriel.

"I'm not trying to argue with you, but Parker's devastated right now. I mean, he's breaking, Jerah, I could lose him. Plus, Seth has his sights set on him, so I need all the help I can get. And you're one of the few who can."

Jerah gave a slight shrug. "Your charge is of no particular concern to me. If Seth takes him, he takes him. If not, good for Parker. But only one charge matters to me—*mine*."

Marie took a step back. Although she'd known Jerah for only three years, the heavy amount of time their charges spent with one another had allowed Marie to become familiar enough with her style and preferences to know Jerah was a hard case. Most true believers were.

But this level of indifference, bordering on callousness, was an all-time low.

Keeping her voice down, Marie said, "I'm only concerned with my charge as well. But there's—"

"You've got a strange way of showing it, Marie. Because

this isn't the first time you've spied on my charge." Jerah cocked her head and smirked. "Oh, yes, I've seen you appear and follow them, follow her. If I didn't know any better, I'd say you were—"

"No—no—no," Marie stammered, trying to prevent Jerah from making the accusation. "It isn't what you think. It really isn't. I promise." Marie's chest tightened with every word and heat raced to her cheeks. "It's just that those few people who are closest to Parker can make all the difference in the world right now, and I have to know where I need to try to influence him. That's all."

Jerah didn't flinch. An immovable figure of insensitivity to anything that wasn't directly related to her own mission.

Marie pressed her hands together. "Please, Jerah. Parker spends more time with Summer than anyone else. Help me just this once, and I'll never ever ask for your assistance again. Ever."

Jerah studied Marie for a moment then closed her eyes and took a deep breath.

"*Please*, Jerah." A gust of cold wind swayed part of the evergreen bush into the side of Marie's face. She flicked away the scratchy brush. And waited.

The icy guardian finally opened her eyes and stared in agonizing silence at Marie, who held her breath. Except for the edges of the evergreens that swayed and twisted with the chilly gusts of wind, nothing stirred between them.

Oddly, it was Jerah's status as a true believer that Marie banked on. Surely her zealous devotion to the cause would not permit her to let Seth to get an upper hand, despite her personal feelings.

The seconds continued to tick by without a word until Jerah finally said, "Markus must've owed you something fierce. That's the only thing that can explain it."

Although Jerah's tone didn't carry its usual bite, Marie sagged at the implication that her promotion into the guardian ranks had been based on anything less than merit.

She dropped her head and recalled the affair at the abandoned Italian monastery all those years ago. If not for that incident, she'd never have met Markus or even come to his attention. But what happened there was between the two of them and no one else. Marie raised her head and made one last appeal. "Please, Jerah. Please help me."

Her colleague remained as still as a statue, then glanced toward Summer's bedroom window. "All right," she said. "What do you want to know?"

A sigh of relief escaped Marie, and her muscles relaxed. *Thank you!*

"Okay. Does Summer really love Parker? I mean is she truly in love with him?"

Jerah paused as if she were debating again whether to actually help. She cast another quick look at the house, then said, "No."

"She doesn't?" Though Marie was genuinely surprised by the answer, she tried to suppress the smile that played at the corners of her mouth.

"No. She's likes him a lot, but she's not in love with him. She's in love with the idea of dating the quarterback, one that's really good and is going to get a college football scholarship and get out of Briar Ridge. Summer's determined not to end up like her mother. She knows she makes one false move and she'll turn out a single mom scraping to get by. She sees Parker as her ticket to getting something more."

"That's it? The last three years have all been about Summer using Parker?"

"Yes. But it's not just Parker." Jerah's voice softened as if her words might damage something fragile. "She's so desperate that she cheated on him with a college guy last summer when she was at cheerleading camp at Texas Tech. She thought maybe after a few days of making out with him that she'd have him on the hook and he'd want her to move in with him after she graduated. But she never heard from him once she got back to Briar Ridge. So Parker's her only shot now."

Jerah ran her fingers along an exposed piece of chain-link fence. "I'm embarrassed for what my charge has done. She doesn't listen…"

Marie pulled back part of the evergreen and looked at the house. The light in Summer's room turned off, and Marie shook her head. "Parker has no idea."

She'd always had her suspicions and doubts, but now Jerah's words confirmed them. Marie curled her fingers, and her nails dug into her palms, almost drawing blood.

Her colleague shook her head as if breaking from a trance. "Yeah, like I told you, Parker's of no concern to me," Jerah said, her words dripping with their customary glibness. "So, if you're done, this conversation is over."

Marie broke away from leering at Summer's window and nodded.

"Good. Now let's be clear on something." Jerah leaned in close. "You worry about your charge, I'll worry about mine. Stay on your side of the street, Marie. I mean it. Leave my charge alone and never come back here again."

Marie turned and leered at the house. "Glad to."

℮∕℈℮∕℈

Marie appeared behind the trunk of the large pecan tree closest to Parker's bedroom window and stepped around it without the slightest care for silence or camouflage. The backyard was large enough that the next door neighbors couldn't possibly see her, unless they were in the habit of scaling fences and spying on their neighbors at 3:00 a.m.

She walked up to the window, leaned her shoulder against it, and tilted her head against the cool pane of glass.

Parker slept on his bed less than three feet away, snoring under the influence of medicated sleep.

The thought of Markus or Uriel being upset with her appearing this close to her charge and violating some kind of privacy issue with him in his bedroom crossed her mind.

But only for a second.

No warnings or upset feelings mattered any longer. The risk of getting into trouble held no more sway. Parker was alone now. The one person he thought loved him was really a liar and a cheat. And would never be there for him, not in the way he needed. Not now. Not ever.

Time to do something about that. At first light, she'd go to work and plant the seed. And hope he'd listen and make the right decision.

With Seth still lurking around, the days and weeks ahead would likely get dangerous. Pressure and perils, taking many forms, would be thrown at him in order to steal his soul. And his safety was too precious to leave in the hands of people like Summer.

No, what Parker needed was someone who was utterly devoted to him. Someone whose every thought was spent on his well-being. Someone who would never lie to him, disappoint him, or ever leave him. Someone who would walk through fire to protect him.

Marie placed her hand against the window and caressed her fingers along the glass that overlooked Parker.

I'll always be here for you, Parker. No matter what.

She kissed her fingertips and pressed them up against the window, then withdrew into the shadows and disappeared.

CHAPTER 16

Sleep, when it came, didn't last long. Gunfire and Abby's piercing screams awoke him. His eyes popped open, and he sat up, trying to orient himself in his dark room. His chest heaved from fast, erratic breathing as sweat trickled down his temples. Parker swallowed, took a deep breath, and tried to steady himself, coming to the realization he'd been having a nightmare. A glance at the clock showed only a few minutes past one in the morning.

His body felt like a battered piece of driftwood. Whenever he was still with his eyes closed, it didn't take long before the sights and sounds of the shooting, especially those concerning Abby, came roaring back. The mental current of the images beat on him, tossed him about, and forced him in directions he didn't want to go. He tried to think of other things, but any attempt to block out the shooting proved tiring and useless.

Parker wrestled with the bed covers the rest of the night, dozing off for a few minutes here and there, but never falling into restful sleep. At 5:30, Mom opened the door and stuck her head inside. Fatigue prevented his eyes from focusing as well as they should have, and he reached for his bedside lamp. When the light turned on, she opened the door all the way and stepped into the room. Dressed in scrubs with coffee thermos in hand, she looked just as tired as he felt.

She opened her mouth to speak but cut herself off when she diverted her eyes to the bare corkboard, now devoid of any reminder of life before the incident.

She took a deep breath and exhaled. It was obvious she wanted to say something, something comforting and reassuring perhaps, but it was equally obvious she didn't have the strength to do it.

She walked over to the side of his bed, leaned over, and gently kissed the top of his head. "I'll be back in a few hours with your father. Remember, I need to you to stay around the house in case he needs anything."

Parker collapsed back onto his bed and stared into space, felt the onset of a major headache. Massaging his temples provided no relief, and though his eyelids were like sandbags, he dared not shut them. *Can't eat, can't sleep—I've got to get out of here.*

Unable to lie still any longer, he got up around 6:30 and wandered through the house in a mindless trance, trying to find anything that could be a distraction.

His phone rang with calls and texts from classmates letting him know he was the talk of the cable news world as well as every form of social media. There was something macabre about knowing he was all over the news that he couldn't resist, like being unable to turn from watching someone walk into oncoming traffic.

He turned on the television and surfed to the first news channel he found. Two of Parker's classmates appeared, giving a live interview describing the incident along with providing details about Parker.

"Yeah, he plays on the football team, dates Summer, you know, but he's not from here," the girl said when asked to describe Parker.

"No, he moved here from Houston a few years ago," the other girl piped in while smacking gum. "I mean, he's nice and cool and everything."

"Yeah, sad about his sister, though. I think she was like, retarded or something. But it's cool he went after Bobby.

Shows we don't mess around in small towns, you know?"

Not from here. Retarded sister. Heat rose through his neck and to the top of his head as his cheeks flushed. Eyes narrowed, jaw clenched, teeth gritted. His right hand, sore from punching the drywall in his room, balled into a fist. Only a bite to the lip kept him from screaming at the television. A change of the channel found more of the same on every news outlet. Apparently, nobody in Briar Ridge could resist their fifteen minutes of fame and were perfectly content to share their opinions about Parker with the world.

Outsider. Not one of us. Retarded. The words used to describe the Austin siblings repeated in every interview as if they'd all been reading from the same page. The words rattled inside him, stinging at first, but soon evolved into a smoldering fire of bitter contempt. *I hate this town!*

A commotion outside the house interrupted his thoughts. It was exactly eight o'clock on a Sunday morning, and what privacy remained vanished as he watched news crews set up in the front yard.

The first to arrive knocked on the front door and rang the doorbell, but as it became obvious no one would answer, they settled in as though preparing for a siege. The little band of reporters and cameramen soon expanded into a small army as more members of the national media arrived throughout the morning, overwhelming the front yard and lining both sides of the street for two blocks in either direction.

Irritated, Parker ignored their incessant knocking and doorbell ringing by planting himself on the couch in front of the television, but it didn't take long for the images from Friday night, now coupled with the insulting words from his classmates' interviews, to flood his mind. He closed his eyes tightly and pressed his hands to his head. His pulse quickened, his palms grew sweaty, and his hands shook. Anger stirred within him again, and the barrage by the media only intensified the rage.

He leaped up off the couch and roamed the house like a

wounded animal, desperate to strike back and protect himself.

And then an idea struck with the impact of lightning as he paced, bringing him to an abrupt stop and nearly toppling him over. He walked to the kitchen and sorted it out as he leaned on the breakfast table. His eyes stared at the wood grain of the tabletop, but his mind gleefully plodded over the details. The more he thought about it, the more it made sense, if anything could make sense again. But he knew what he had to do now, and the corners of his mouth curled into a grin.

He pulled out his cell phone and dialed her number. She answered on the second ring.

"Summer, I need to see you."

CHAPTER 17

On the drive home, Suzy sensed Kenneth wanted to be left alone. No surprise. He rarely talked in the car. To be honest, she really didn't have the energy to talk either. Discussing the funeral arrangements for Abby had sapped any need for small talk.

They decided that morning that Abby would be buried in Briar Ridge and not in Houston. Briar Ridge was their home now. They would have to relocate if Abby were interred in the city since the thought of being unable to visit her gravesite whenever she chose was unfathomable, but with the economy in its present state, moving seemed next to impossible.

They both felt comfortable with the decision, although Kenneth didn't say much. He was still devastated from the events of Friday night, even though he wasn't able to fully recall everything. The last things he remembered after Parker threw the touchdown pass were hearing gunfire, the overflow crowd stampeding in all directions, his attempting to move down the stands to get to Abby, and then darkness. The next thing he could recall was Suzy telling him Abby was dead.

From their intermittent conversations over the past two days, it became obvious that Kenneth held himself responsible for Abby's death. "I should've gotten to her, I'm her Daddy," he kept insisting. "It was my job to protect her."

My protective husband. Always looking out for everyone else. His sentiments were understandable. As the oldest child of an alcoholic, abusive father, Kenneth learned early on to look after his own. Brutal lessons no child should ever have to learn at that age.

She recalled the first time he'd opened up about it, when his father passed away just a few months before their wedding. Kenneth's father was often drunk and in a violent mood. The man hated the world and everyone in it. Kenneth would routinely redirect his father's anger and physical beatings toward him to shield his two younger siblings. When she'd asked how many times he'd sacrificed himself so his younger brother and sister wouldn't get hurt, he simply replied, "enough." His devotion and protective nature toward their own two children was one of the reasons she loved him so much.

The car turned off of Wabash and she placed her hand on his leg. "It's not your fault, sweetie."

"You weren't there. I was," he said staring out his window. "It's my fault."

"No, honey," she'd replied, her voice strained with fatigue and exhausting what little strength for conversation she had remaining. "It isn't. It's not your fault, it's not Parker's fault. It just…" Her energy depleted, she couldn't finish the sentence.

She made the turn onto Elliot and slowed. Vans and trucks, most with large antennas mounted on the roofs and pointing to the thick, immoveable gray skies, lined both sides of the street all the way to their house.

"Oh, my God. What's going on? Why are they at our house?" She navigated her car between the parked vehicles and the sea of reporters who jogged alongside them.

Kenneth perked up from his slumped-down position in the passenger seat. "Keep driving, pull into the driveway, park in the garage."

The gaggle of reporters, photographers, and cameramen followed them as they turned into the driveway and made

their way to the garage. Suzy pressed the garage door opener and waited, drumming her fingertips along the top of the
steering wheel while the garage door inched upward. The
reporters lined up on both sides of her Ford Focus, still covered in shoe polish from last Friday, and shouted questions
about Parker and Abby through the glass windows.

"Please go away, just leave us alone," Suzy repeated
several times as Kenneth glared at the reporters on his side
of the car.

The garage door finally opened and Suzy eased the car
inside and quickly pressed the button to close it behind
them. She walked Kenneth inside and escorted him to their
bedroom to make him comfortable before visiting with Parker, who apparently had barricaded himself in his room.

A knock on his door brought a terse response and she
peeked inside. He sat on his bed with the family's laptop
computer while his television showed a rerun of a sitcom
she didn't recognize. The room remained in disarray. Dirty
clothes sat in piles, and the pictures and mementos from the
corkboard still littered the floor. She stepped in, closed the
door behind her, and leaned back against it.

"How long have the reporters been here?"

"A little over an hour," he replied, his eyes glued to the
computer screen, his mind obviously engaged in something.

"Have they been bothering you?"

"Not really."

She paused, waiting for him to look at her. He stayed focused on the laptop and occasionally pecked at a few keys.
"What do they want?"

"Don't know, don't care."

She nodded and smiled to herself. The reporters would
never get what they wanted from him. "How are you holding up?"

He shrugged his shoulders. "Fine."

"I want to talk to you about Abby's funeral."

For the first time he broke free from the computer, but
quickly returned his gaze to the screen.

"Your father and I have decided to bury her here in Briar Ridge. The service will be on Tuesday around two o'clock up at the church." She waited for him to say something, but he only nodded his head.

"Family will be coming in tomorrow, too. So, be prepared to have some company." This elicited no response, which was no surprise. Both Kenneth's and her siblings lived out of state with their respective families, and Parker and Abby were rarely around their extended family.

"Well, I just thought I'd let you know." She turned, opened the door, and glanced over her shoulder. "Remember to get something to eat and listen for your father in case he needs anything." She paused, looked at him, and said, "I love you, Park."

She closed the door behind her and checked on Kenneth one last time before leaving the house again. Dodging reporters in the driveway and ignoring their questions as she backed out onto the street, she drove to Tealman's Funeral Home to make the final arrangements for Abby's service. Along the way she passed Summer Hayes, heading in the opposite direction. Good. Parker needed company.

She managed to get through the meeting with Tommy Tealman and Pastor Jim, who despite their apparent weariness and fatigue from helping plan so many funerals all at once, tried their best to be both patient and compassionate with her. Even though she and Kenneth had made decisions about the funeral service, it was hard to actually verbalize those answers about her precious Abby. Concentration was difficult, and her mind moved in slow motion, like trying to navigate through a thick, dark fog.

After an hour with the funeral director and her pastor, the final arrangements for Abby's service and interment were completed. She thanked them as well as she could, walked to her car, and sat in the driver's seat. She inserted her key into the ignition but didn't turn it. Alone in the quiet solitude of her car, she folded her arms across the steering wheel, laid her head on them, and burst into tears.

CHAPTER 18

Emoticons sucked. The smiling face blowing kisses at the end of Summer's text just smacked of blissful ignorance—or callous indifference. Either way, that mood was about to change.

Parker stuck his head into his parents' room. Dad lay propped up on the bed, the television casting a soft blue glow over the darkened room. Though the volume was turned down, he could detect faint pieces of a narrator's voice. Something about ship designs of the eighteenth century. *Yawn.* If that couldn't put Dad to sleep, nothing would.

"Hey, Dad. I'm gonna be in the backyard for a few minutes. Be right back, okay?"

His father stared unblinking at the television and gave a slight nod.

Parker withdrew and shut the door. He grabbed his letter jacket and stepped onto the screened-in back porch.

The skies were a dreary, melancholy gray. He buttoned his jacket against the chilly air as he walked briskly through the backyard, feet slicing through fallen leaves, through the gate in the still-damaged fence to the alley where Summer waited. Wooden fences and tall oak trees lined both sides of the narrow, unpaved road that separated the long row of ranch-style homes on Parker's street from the homes in the subdivision behind them. Used by the town's small waste management department to collect garbage, it also served as a quiet spot for some private time on dates. Hopefully, the seclusion would shield them from the prying eyes of the media.

Summer sat in her yellow Toyota Camry with the engine turned off, and she smiled as soon as he walked through the gate. He closed it behind him, looked in both directions of the alley, and crossed over to the passenger side when he was confident they were alone.

His stomach churned as he slid his fingers under the cold door latch and climbed in. A blast of warm air from the car's heater greeted him. With sweaty palms he unbuttoned his letter jacket so he wouldn't perspire. He settled in as best he could and looked at his girlfriend. The casual style of gray sweatpants and black Old Navy sweatshirt with her blonde hair pulled back in a ponytail made her look as cute as ever. For a brief instant he wanted to touch her, hold her, but resisted the urge.

Summer reached for him, placed her hand on his denim-covered leg. "You look really tired. You okay?"

His eyes fixed on her warm, smooth hand. "Haven't been able to sleep, been having some really bad dreams." Exhaustion weighed down his voice.

She cocked her head to the side. "So what's going on with you, Park?"

He shifted in his seat and cleared his throat. "Look, I've been doing some thinking lately, and uh…" The sentence remained unfinished, and he stared out the windshield, watching the cold wind blow through the trees lining the alley, leaves falling in gentle patches. Mouth dry, he took a deep breath, and decided to come out with it. "I want to break up."

Summer withdrew her hand. Her lips quivered and her eyes grew moist. "Why?" she asked hoarsely, her voice choked with emotion. "What have I done?"

"Nothing. Look, I don't want to make this any more painful than it already is, but it's just something I've got to do, okay?"

"No, it's not okay," she said. "People just don't break up with someone after three years together. There—there has to be a reason." She paused, clearly waiting for him to answer. When he didn't respond, she asked him, "Why are you doing this?"

"I just need to make some changes right now."

She didn't say anything, but kept her eyes locked onto Parker, her stare drilling holes into him. He could tell her mind was racing behind those watery eyes. She sniffed. "Is it me? Is it someone else? Is it Skylar? I swear if she has anything to do with this, I'm gonna puke."

He sighed, tapping his thumb against his leg. "No, it's not you, and I promise there isn't anyone else. But this is something that I've got to do."

A tear ran down her left cheek and she shook her head. "I—I don't understand. You have to tell me, I deserve that much."

Parker shrugged and shook his head.

"You're lying, Park. I know you're lying. You always think I can't tell when you're hiding something, but I can," she said, followed by another sniff and a few more tears. "You can't look me in the eye when you're hiding something."

That she knew him so well comforted him, but at the same time made what needed to be done more difficult.

Summer motioned toward the glove box. "Can you get me a Kleenex?"

He gave her a tissue and she quickly wiped her nose while waiting for him to respond.

"Tell me," she pleaded, her voice rising an octave.

When he refused to speak, she pressed on. "If this is something you think you have to do, please tell me what's behind it, maybe I can help you. We can work it out together."

"No." Going back was out of the question. "It's over."

Summer burst into tears. Parker rolled his eyes and looked out the window again. A basset hound crossed the alley in front of them. Its long, droopy ears grazed the top of the dirt and brown grass of the alley. Strange. No one on his block owned a basset. The long black and brown hound with its pudgy white underbelly stopped in the middle of the alley, turned and looked in the direction of Summer and Parker. It panted for a few seconds, yawned, and then waddled down the alley toward a thick tree.

The dog still held his attention when Summer began speaking. She pleaded for him to admit to the cause of the breakup, but his eyes were now fixed on the tree where the dog had stopped. Parker squinted and looked closely at the trunk. Focused eyes revealed someone lurking behind the tree, using the thick trunk for concealment as if they didn't want to be seen.

What in the world? Trying not to alarm Summer, Parker casually kept an eye on the mysterious figure as he tried listening to the conversation.

"Maybe you're feeling this way because of what you've been through. I'm hurting, too. The whole town is hurting. Maybe—"

"Screw this town." His head snapped in her direction, heat engulfing him like hot wind racing through a grass fire. "I don't care what anyone in this town thinks or feels. You got that?" He glared at her for a moment before he resumed his observation of the semi-concealed figure.

The dog sniffed at the person's feet.

"I'm just saying that maybe you feel like this because of all that's happened. I mean you're hurting, and if you give it some more time maybe you won't feel like this." She paused, obviously waiting for a response. "Is this because of Abby?"

He shot her a sideways glance, eyes shifting under half-open lids. "Don't talk about my sister."

"I'm sorry, Park. I'm so sorry for what you and your parents are going through. But you can't be breaking up with me over this. There has to be something that I've done. There's got to be a reason. What is it?"

Parker sighed and his shoulders drooped. He rubbed his eyes. "Nothing. You haven't done anything, all right? This is just something I have to do."

He turned his attention back down the alley. The basset hound raised a hind leg and urinated on the figure's pants. The stranger jerked away, revealing more of himself in the process. A camouflaged jacket, its hood pulled up and drawn tight, concealed most of his face.

Parker inched toward the door handle as the stranger looked up and froze, clearly discovered. The basset hound barked at the man, who abruptly turned and ran down the alley and out of view. The dog looked back at the two teenagers and trudged away.

Parker's mind swirled trying to figure out who the hooded man might be and why anyone would be loitering in a garbage alley, but Summer interrupted his thoughts.

"Look at me, Park. I can't accept that there's nothing going on. There's always a reason why people break up."

Silence.

When he didn't reply, she snapped. "Just tell me!"

Parker huffed, leaned against the cool glass of the passenger window and rubbed his eyes for a moment. Maybe full disclosure could speed the conversation along and provide an escape. "Fine." Exasperation strained his voice. "You want to know what's going on? Here it is."

He told her everything—the black Dodge Charger that had followed him, the note on his car, the conversation with Detective Boddicker, feelings of guilt over having caused the shooting that led to Abby's death, and the nightmares that haunted him every night.

He shared everything, including his plan for moving on and getting out of Briar Ridge.

Silence enveloped them as they both turned and stared through the windshield, watching the changing leaves dance and swirl in the cold November wind.

He wasn't sure how she would respond, but it didn't matter.

"You could've told me this sooner, you know? Look, the shooting wasn't your fault, and you breaking up with me because you want to graduate early is bullcrap."

She could provoke him all she wanted. It wasn't going to change anything. "Thanks, but my mind is made up. I'm sorry I'm hurting you. But I'm doing this. I'm getting out of here."

Summer's eyes narrowed, her head shaking in disbelief. "You coward," she said. "Just because things are really tough, you're bailing? I can't—I mean, you and I were supposed to be together. And after three years, you're just going to quit and run away? What the hell?"

Parker shifted in his seat, his body tensing. "I'm out. I'm leaving, all right? Why is that so hard for you to understand?"

"Whatever. You're having a really hard time and you don't even ask me to help. You don't even tell me what's going on. You just decide to break up with me, graduate early, and *leave*?"

"Look, Summer, I can't stay here anymore, all right?"

"But why? Why is this town so bad all of a sudden?"

Parker flinched and his face contorted. "Are you freaking kidding me? You know how people treat me here. I'm an outsider who's tolerated because I can score touchdowns. That's it. I hate this town, I hate everything about it. I hate the fact that we ever came here, I hate that I caused Abby's death, I hate that I have to walk past her room and her pictures every day. I'm reminded every second of every day about what happened, and there's no way I can ever escape it as long as I'm in Briar Ridge." His tone grew sharp, his voice rising.

"But Park—"

"And if that's not enough, I've got to listen to everyone remind me that *I'm not from here* or listen to them call Abby a retard. I hate this town! I hate it!" He slammed his fist into the dashboard, causing Summer to jump in her seat. Tightness formed in his chest, and a growing sense of desperation swelled within him, like he was drowning and desperately needed to breathe.

Summer frowned. "You hate this town and everything in it, huh? That includes me?"

Massaging his knuckles, he closed his eyes and inhaled deeply, waiting for the knot of hate inside to untangle. A slow exhale and the muscles began to unwind and relax. He looked at her. "No," he replied. "I don't hate you, Summer. I love you."

She rolled her soft brown eyes. "Yeah, but you're breaking up with me. I get it."

Parker shook his head. *Enough of this conversation.* "Look, this was exactly what I was afraid of. You're just not going to understand, all right? I'm sorry that I'm hurting you, but…" A search for the right words, anything that might soften the blow and help her understand, proved futile. And his patience had run out. "I just have to get out of this town." His gaze met hers. "Goodbye, Summer."

He opened the passenger door and stepped out into the cold, brisk air, glad to escape the awkward confines of her car. She yelled his name through the windshield while she burst into angry tears. Ignoring her, he passed through the backyard gate and swung it behind him. The metallic clank of the latch catching signaled the door had shut, but it wasn't the only thing he knew he'd just closed.

The crank of the ignition interrupted the silence, and the spin of tires on loose gravel sent small pellets of rock crashing into the fence.

When the sounds of her car faded into the distance, he opened the gate and re-entered the alley. He jogged down the rough gravel drive about twenty yards and looked behind the tree where the cloaked stranger had been hiding. The ground below was dark and damp from the dog, and at least half a dozen crushed cigarette butts littered the spot like large pieces of dirty confetti.

Squatting next to where the stranger had stood also revealed a half-empty bottle of Jim Beam whiskey. The fumes of strong alcohol burned the small hairs inside his nose. Still open, the remaining liquor slowly dripped onto the dry, brown leaves beneath it.

With tired eyes he examined the evidence. *You'd been waiting here for some time, hadn't you?*

CHAPTER 19

Marie kept her feelings about Parker's breakup with Summer pent up inside all day. She needed a release. The walk outside, alone in the misty fog, would do her some good. Somehow, doing cartwheels around the other guardians didn't seem quite appropriate. Those snobbish elitists would've recoiled in abject horror at such a display of emotional attachment and involvement, especially over something they'd consider so trivial.

But it wasn't. Not by a long shot.

Summer was a liar and a cheater, nothing more. The fact that she'd been unfaithful to Parker was proof positive she was all wrong for him. Parker deserved better. If only…

She stopped, closed her eyes, and took a deep breath. *C'mon. Get a hold of yourself. Get some perspective. It's not as if...*

Marie pressed her lips together in a futile attempt to suppress the smile that erupted across her face. Her eyelids lifted. She clasped her palms together as if she were about to pray, her fingers resting against her mouth and nose. A giddy laugh forced its way out and her shoulders bounced from the chuckle.

She passed through the parking lot of the Sleepy Cactus Motel, though her feet seemed not to touch the pavement. Nearly six miles outside town and on the other side of Wheeler Lake, the seclusion of the dilapidated roadside inn had kept it from being overrun by the influx of people who swarmed to Briar Ridge to cover the shooting. Only a few media vans and a couple of cars sat in the parking lot. The isolated motel with few guests made it the only spot for a sanctuary.

The cold, misty shroud that enveloped the motel would discourage folks from venturing outside. Plenty of time for a relaxing walk before looking for room two-thirty-four.

Marie strolled between two parked cars and around a large, red, diesel semi-trailer. Except for the occasional passing motorist, nothing moved. The motel's neon sign buzzed. She sauntered up to the covered porch that ran the length of the motel and wiped some of the precipitation from her face.

A motel room door opened, light spilling onto her. Marie jerked her head in surprise and squinted at the light. A figure emerged and stood in the doorway.

"Well now. What do we have here?" The man slurred his words, and he leaned against the doorframe. Two aluminum cans, remnants of a six-pack, dangled from plastic rings in one hand while he took a gulp from an open can in the other. He wiped his mouth with the back of his hand as his eyes roamed Marie's body.

Marie ignored the question. Better to avoid interaction, move on, and find sanctuary before something happened. She stepped away from the room.

"Hey, sweetheart. You don't have to run off." The man stumbled forward.

Marie couldn't call for help—any sounds of altercation would draw more attention. She turned and headed toward the parking lot. Surely the cold, wet weather would discourage a pursuit from the drunkard. Besides, the passing cars on the road could also serve as a deterrent.

Quick, heavy footsteps told her otherwise. The man gripped her by the arm and spun her around.

"Hey, darlin'. I'm talkin' to you."

Marie resisted but couldn't break free.

"Mmmm." The man's lips curled into a perverted smile, baring jagged yellow teeth. The foul odor of alcohol, cigarette smoke, and body sweat made her gag. "You're feisty. I like that."

The man's camouflaged hoodie froze Marie. She studied his wardrobe. Forest green with shades of brown and gray. She'd seen it before—but where?

The man pulled her close. "Yeah, that's better." Dirty fingers teased and twirled her hair. "C'mon, darlin'. I can show you a good time."

Marie swallowed. "I'm—I'm not that kind of girl." She wriggled in his grasp.

The man grabbed a fistful of Marie's hair near the scalp and pulled, snapping her head back. "Maybe you are and just don't know it yet."

The back of her head burned and tingled as though it were on fire. Pain forced her to wince. "Please, I don't want any trouble." Tears pooled at the edges of her eyes. "Just let me go."

"You heard her. Let her go." The woman's voice shot out from the misty night somewhere behind Marie. Only it didn't belong to a human. *Thank God, a guardian.*

The man stiffened and looked past Marie's shoulder. "Me and my girlfriend were just going back to our room." He grinned, his eyes twinkling with desire. "But you can join us if you'd like."

The guardian's tread against the pavement signaled her advance. "I know about the knife in your pocket and the restraints in your room. I'm not going to let you use them on her. Now *let—her—go.*"

The man blinked and his smile faded. His uncertainty opened the window for action. In one quick movement, the guardian sprang forward, snapped an aluminum can from the plastic ring still dangling from the man's hand and slammed it into his forehead. Foamy beer spewed from the punctured can upon impact.

The blow staggered the man. Marie slipped from his

hold. The guardian sent a kick to the man's groin, doubling him over and dropping him to the wet pavement. She looked back at Marie. "Sanctuary. Go."

Marie took off toward the motel porch and followed it around the back of the building until she reached two-thirty-four, the very last room. Blue luminescent paint, in the shape of a cross over the doorway, marked the safe haven. She banged on the paint-chipped door with her fist.

The door soon cracked open, a man's wrinkled face appearing from behind the lock's chain. "Identify."

"Marie. Sanctuary."

The man closed the door, and the sound of the lock sliding out of the latch signaled her access was granted. He opened the door again, just wide enough to let her pass. The door creaked shut behind her as soon as she stepped into the room, and the lock slid back into place.

Two guardians sat at a small table in the corner while two more guardians stretched out on the room's double beds. The door to the adjoining room stood open, candle-light flickered from within, and another guardian emerged.

A faint odor of burned flesh filtered through the air, and Marie surveyed her colleagues for the wounded party. The guardian on the farthest bed lay still, the skin of his right arm mangled and discolored from fire. The burn wounds extended up the side of his face.

Marie took a few steps in his direction. "Are you okay?"

The guardian winced and propped himself up on an elbow. "Looks worse than it is. I'll be fine soon."

"This is Marie," the gatekeeper announced behind her. He walked past her and stood in the middle of the room. Six pairs of eyes studied her.

Marie wiped her face with her hand and shifted her weight. "Um, hello."

One of the guardians at the table leaned back in his chair and crossed his arms over his chest. A quick nod was his only response.

"*Extrarium.*" The guardian propped up on the other bed

placed her hands behind her head and closed her eyes. The dismissive tone was all too familiar.

Marie placed both hands on her hips. "You got a problem?"

The guardian slowly opened her eyes, and her face contorted into a smirk. "Your methods are dangerous, and they don't belong here. That's my problem."

"Knock it off," the gatekeeper said. "She's a guardian, and she's here for the same reason we're here—to protect our charges." He sized Marie up. "I'm Crolius. Markus said you might be stopping by."

"Thanks, Crolius," Marie switched her attention back to the girl on the bed, "but I guess I won't be staying long."

"Suit yourself, but you're welcome to stay as long as you like. Just ignore Miss Congeniality over there and you'll be fine. We've got an altar set up in the adjoining room if you want to commune with Him." The guardian standing in the doorway to the next room pointed over his shoulder with his thumb.

"That's if Errol will let you use it," said one of the guardians at the table.

The man in the doorway turned on him. "Hey, I'm standing here, aren't I? You don't see me at the altar, do you?"

"'Bout time," came the reply.

"I'm sorry, Marie. It's not always like this," Crolius said. "Everyone's a little tense right now. All our charges have been affected by the shooting. Mine's lost a child and is thinking of committing suicide. Errol's is a recovering drug addict who's relapsed. Bart's charge is in the hospital and the prognosis isn't good. I mean, we're all struggling here."

Crolius massaged his forehead for a moment and took a deep breath. "And Seth's personal involvement has got us on edge. I mean, he's killed Yaris, and now..." He motioned toward their wounded colleague, who lay back down. "Seth did that to him last night. Which is another good reason to have a sanctuary. It's nice to have a safe respite where we can draw on each other for strength and support, plus strategize how to save our charges and combat the enemy."

The girl on the bed sat up. "I'm telling you, Uriel should just call in Michael and the Venantium. Let the demon hunters come in with angel swords and halos, create some breathing room for us, and give us a chance to influence our charges."

The Venantium—hunters of the fallen—the heavy artillery in combating demons. Marie had never seen them in action. *This could get interesting.*

Crolius glanced over his shoulder. "How do you know he hasn't done that already? The Venantium operate alone. Besides, that's none of our concern. Our only priority is to help our charges, regardless of circumstances. Period."

Marie nodded. "Well, I'd appreciate your prayers for my charge. He's in pretty bad shape, emotionally and spiritually, and I could use the help. Anyone want to pray with me?"

The girl on the bed deliberately turned away. One of the guardians at the table traced the grain contours of the tabletop with his finger. No one else moved, and an awkward silence prevailed.

Marie slouched and hung her head. *I'm sick and tired of being on my own. Just once I wish—*

"I'll do it." Crolius's firm voice struck a defiant tone. "I'll pray with you." He held out his hand. "When it's all said and done, we're on the same team, serving the same purpose." He surveyed the other guardians in the room, but his eyes lingered on the girl. "And some of you would do well to remember that."

Finally, a fellow guardian treating her as an equal. Marie exhaled and smiled, relief washing over her and melting her tension. "Thank you." She took hold of the outstretched hand and walked toward the door leading to the altar in the adjoining room.

Three loud knocks brought Marie to a halt. Crolius hustled to the door and cracked it open. "Identify."

"Elizabeth. Sanctuary." The voice shook.

No sooner had Crolius slid the chain out of the latch than Elizabeth barged through the unlocked door. She scanned the room, locked onto Marie, and stepped toward her with balled fists. "I oughta strike you down!"

Marie stepped back and recognized Elizabeth as the guardian who'd intervened with the drunkard in the parking lot. "What's wrong?"

"What's wrong?" Elizabeth's eyes flashed, seething with red hot anger. "Your stupid little stunt, that's what's wrong." Elizabeth closed the distance and Crolius stepped into the middle, arms spread wide, keeping the two separated.

"Wait a second. What are you talking about? What stupid stunt?" Crolius asked.

"Just because demons can't get in here doesn't mean you're safe." Elizabeth tried to advance toward Marie, but again Crolius blocked her.

"Stop it, Elizabeth. What are you talking about?"

"I'm talking about this outsider who thinks she can just appear around humans any time she wants. You should've seen her a few minutes ago, traipsing through the parking lot like she was on a stroll in Central Park. Only this time she drew someone's attention and it got ugly."

Crolius snapped his head in Marie's direction. "Is that true? You appeared to a human?"

"I didn't appear in front of anyone. I was just out there by myself, okay? I was alone, and then this drunk guy showed up out of nowhere and grabbed me."

"How'd you get away?" Errol asked.

"Me," Elizabeth growled. "I smacked the guy in the head with a beer can and then kicked him in his balls."

"Sweet move," commented a guardian at the table.

"It was, and I'm thankful for it," Marie said, nodding. "It all worked out, so I don't understand why you're so upset with me."

Elizabeth pursed her lips and her eyes narrowed, her chin quivering. "Because that man is my charge."

The air sucked out of the room and time screeched to a halt. Moments of insufferable silence passed before Marie could speak.

"That man was your charge?"

Elizabeth nodded. "Yes. Darryl's my charge and I beat him." Elizabeth's hands trembled. She wobbled to the edge of the closest bed, sat down, and placed her head in her hands. "I physically assaulted my own charge."

Crolius spoke up, his words slow and measured, no doubt speaking what everyone else in the room was thinking. "You directly intervened and changed the course of your charge?"

Elizabeth crossed her arms over her stomach, and the color drained from her face. "What was I supposed to do? He was attacking a guardian. I—I just couldn't—" She lifted her head and looked directly at Marie, eyes ablaze. "Why? Why did you have to appear like that?"

Any answer was bound to be wrong, as emotional as Elizabeth was at the moment. Better to remain silent and let her get control of herself.

The girl on the bed sat up. "I told you she doesn't belong here. Her carelessness is a liability. She puts us all at risk." Smug contempt dripped from every word. "Markus needs to fix his mistake before anything else happens."

"That's enough, Cylene," Crolius said, glaring at her. "One more word out of you, and I'll banish you from this sanctuary."

"You didn't have to do that, Elizabeth. I could've fought him off." Marie's own attempt at reassurance didn't sound convincing, though maybe her colleague would at least appreciate the gesture.

Elizabeth shook her head. "You have no idea what he would've done to you if he'd gotten you into his room."

Marie took a step back and leaned against the wood-paneled wall. "You mean he would've—killed me?"

Elizabeth paused as if reluctant to confirm the worst, but soon nodded. "Yes," she whispered. "Darryl would've raped and killed you." She rubbed her palms on her jeans. "Your spirit wouldn't have been allowed to take human form again. Ever."

The revelation of Darryl's true intention sent the room spinning like a carnival ride. Marie bent over and caught herself, placing her hands on her knees. *Breathe—just breathe.*

Being killed by a demon from angel fire or an angelic sword was permanent. But for a guardian to die at the hands of a human was almost as bad. Once a body containing a spirit died, that spirit could not return and take human form again. Ever. No more appearing around Parker, no more being close to him, no chance of ever—

That was why Markus and the others made such a big deal about appearing. The risk was too great.

Marie finally straightened up and placed a hand over her mouth. "I'm sorry, Elizabeth. Truly I am."

Elizabeth sniffed and wiped her nose. "Whatever."

Crolius kneeled in front of Elizabeth. He slid both arms around her and she leaned into him, resting her head on his shoulder. She closed her eyes, and Crolius whispered to her.

Everyone watched in quiet reverence as one guardian drew strength from another. Crolius continued whispering into Elizabeth's ear.

The two guardians finally ended their embrace. They stood and walked toward the adjoining room but stopped before the doorway. Elizabeth turned and faced Marie.

Crolius placed a hand on Elizabeth's shoulder, spoke something to her, and nodded. He stepped into the next room.

Elizabeth lingered, still studying Marie, obviously working something over in her mind. But what?

At last she spoke. "I'm sorry I snapped at you." Her eyes drifted to the floor.

Marie slid her hands into her jeans pockets. "Forget it."

Elizabeth nodded and took a step toward the adjoining room, but paused. "One other thing. Darryl's last name is

McGonagill." She looked up and locked eyes with Marie. "Your charge, Parker, is in grave danger."

CHAPTER 20

Uriel placed his hands behind his back, swept his silver wings into a tucked position, and surveyed the grove. Long lines of trees stretched into the indefinite distance, offering deep pockets of cool shade. Why he always chose to stroll here when conferring with Markus remained a mystery—even to Markus.

Perhaps the quiet solitude of the grove appealed to Uriel's nature—he was a guardian of very few words after all. In fact, turtles spoke more frequently than Uriel. But that was just on the surface. Markus knew that underneath the placid exterior lay a brooding, strategizing spirit. A spirit roillng with determination, or ruthlessness depending on one's point of view, to protect every charge on Creation.

"So, my friend, what is it that you wish to discuss?" Markus asked.

Uriel embarked on a slow, methodical walk under the shadows of the overhanging foliage. "Your recruit."

Markus had heard the grumblings from the rank and file, but the fact that Uriel paid heed to them was a bit surprising. "What about her?"

"Is she up to it?"

Markus shrugged. "I wouldn't have recruited her if I didn't think she could do it. Besides, Gabriel speaks so highly of her."

Uriel stopped next to an apple tree and glanced upward

at the spheres of red fruit. The smallest trace of a smirk appeared on his smooth face. "Gabriel likes everyone."

"Sure. But I believe in Marie. She's on her eleventh charge now, and she's done well so far, despite the cold treatment from her colleagues."

A small branch recoiled from the pluck of an apple. Uriel rubbed the fruit on the sleeve of his robe. "She employs unusual methods."

Markus sighed. "Granted. Her approach of frequently appearing human is a bit unorthodox."

Uriel's gaze slid out of the corner of his eyes and fixated on Markus. "It's dangerous."

"Yes, but you and I have done it before. Lots of us have. It's not as if—"

"The rest of us have never done it with such regularity. Or with such a cavalier attitude." Uriel studied the apple for a moment and then sank his teeth into it.

"Perhaps she spends so much time being human because so many other guardians—her own kind—shun her, give her such a hard time." Markus's wings ruffled in irritation, and he leveled his gaze at Uriel. *You're not the only one with a point here.*

Uriel's jaws bulged as he chewed, his eyes never leaving Markus. He ate in silence until he swallowed, then wiped his mouth with the cuff of his sleeve. "Do I detect defensiveness in your tone?"

"What's my tone got to do with anything, Uriel? That you and the other guardians have been less than kind to her is a fact. They even have a name for her. Haven't you heard?"

Uriel turned and beckoned Markus to continue walking with him. "Yes. It's unfortunate. Not surprising, but unfortunate."

"Unfortunate?" Markus spat out the word with contempt. "It's disgusting. It's wrong. We don't do that to one of our own."

"Then speak to her. Get her to see the risks of appearing

human so often. It would help if she toed the line better."

Markus offered a slight chuckle. "I have. She's pretty headstrong." A blue jay chirped overhead, but Uriel seemed not to notice—or care. "That's one of the reasons I like her. She's determined, bold, unafraid to take risks."

Uriel took another bite of the apple. He chewed for a moment and then swallowed. Holding the half-eaten fruit aloft in front of Markus, he said, "Taking risks when one should heed what he's been told—we've seen that story before. And it didn't end well, did it?"

With so much at stake, the point was well taken. The current operation would be tough on any guardian—it had already resulted in the death of Yaris—but it might be too much for Marie. Even if she did proceed in the manner they anticipated, she may not be the same when it was over.

"If things progress the way we think, and if we move forward like we've planned, it will take a toll on her. A heavy one."

"The end game is much bigger than her, Markus."

"I just don't want to see her hurt and confused. Even if she makes it through this, she's not going to understand."

Uriel tilted his head slightly, eyes narrowing to probe for hesitancy, maybe even regret. "Do you want to call it off?" he asked quietly.

Whether Uriel would really cancel the operation wasn't clear. Without her knowing it, five hundred years of preparation had been invested in Marie just for this one assignment. And if another opportunity did present itself, when would that be? Another millennium or two? With Lucifer's ranks growing with each passing century, the time to strike was now, despite having to thrust Marie blindly into harm's way.

"No."

Uriel tossed the apple aside. "Then do what needs to be done." He clasped his hands behind his back and continued his walk alone.

CHAPTER 21

They buried Abby on a sunless Tuesday afternoon. Her funeral, one of nine scheduled for that day, provided another opportunity for a three-ring media circus to appear.

Marie's gaze fell on the reporters huddled in large packs around the front steps leading into the sanctuary from Wabash Avenue. Hovering and circling like buzzards to prey upon a hurt and wounded family should be a crime. Why couldn't they show a little respect?

Inside the sanctuary, the most beautiful arrays of lilies and roses flooded the large room in a sea of bright, sweet-smelling petals. So many flowers had been received that the vases and pedestals filled the choir loft as well. A grieving nation had been following the news of Parker and Abby, and many felt moved to send their condolences.

Marie's chest swelled briefly. It was comforting to see so many people, total strangers, moved to acts of kindness and compassion in spite of the horror Seth had brought about.

Not an empty seat could be found in the sanctuary. Many who attended were Abby's teachers, fellow students, and their families. Friends and coworkers of Kenneth and Suzy were there, as were the families of some of Parker's teammates, though many were nothing more than curiosity seekers.

Parker's family made the service more a celebration of

Abby's life than a grieving and gnashing of teeth kind of moment. They sang several hymns throughout the service, including "It Is Well With My Soul," "Amazing Grace," and "Be Still, My Soul."

Marie always liked "It Is Well" and truly loved the story behind the song. But disappointment darkened her mood when Parker refused to sing any of the hymns, choosing instead to sit with his arms crossed and staring at the floor.

A few people gave remarks about Abby, including her second-grade teacher, Mrs. Paris, who shared a story about Abby's great sense of empathy and caring. Years ago at Halloween, the kids in Abby's class who dressed up got to go trick-or-treating from classroom to classroom. Not all of the kids had costumes, so a few of her classmates had to remain behind in their room while their friends collected candy. Even though it had been difficult for Abby to get around in her walker, she'd insisted on going to every class-room. When she returned, she donated all of her candy to the kids who had remained behind.

"Such was Abby's caring nature," Mrs. Paris said, her voice choking with emotion. "Having known the feeling all too well, Abby never wanted anyone else to feel left out."

Pastor Jim spoke briefly, poor guy. Nothing in this world could've prepared a small-town pastor for a spiritual crisis of this magnitude, and the dark, heavy bags under his eyes served as testaments to his exhaustion. He had five funerals to conduct in a forty-eight-hour period, not to mention all of the grief counseling and spiritual support he was providing to the other grieving families and members of his congrega-tion. Probably the only thing keeping him going was the coffee from Gibson's Pharmacy.

Marie was pleasantly surprised when, after reading some scripture, the pastor likened the passing of loved ones to watching a passenger ship set sail on a long voyage.

"On the dock are many family members and friends, watching the ship carry their loved ones out to sea, the ship getting smaller and smaller as it nears the horizon." His eyes squinted as if trying to find a distant object. "Eventually it vanishes, whereupon everyone at the dock says with a quiet sadness, 'She's gone, she's gone.'"

He bowed his head for a moment, then looked up with misty eyes. Pursed lips broke into a smile, dimples appearing on either side. "But on the other side of the vast ocean, completely out of sight, is another dock filled with even more people, eagerly casting their eyes to the distant horizon searching with anticipation for the passenger ship. When it first appears as a tiny dot, they immediately shout for joy. As the ship draws closer and closer to its new port with its precious cargo, the crowd excitedly proclaims, 'She's home! She's home!'"

Marie smiled. *Finally, a pastor who gets it.* He didn't drone on about 'it was all God's will' or that 'the Lord giveth and taketh away.' *No, this one got it pretty close to the mark.*

Parker, on the other hand, was a different matter. Not only did he not sing any of the hymns, but he'd also refused to participate in any of the prayers, which troubled her. He sat with his arms crossed, staring at the floor throughout most of the service, his face utterly devoid of expression. The detachment could've been attributed to exhaustion. The recurring nightmares were getting worse, and the lack of sleep was evident from the dark circles under his eyes.

Yet she knew better. Grief and hostility seethed under his aloof exterior, and it was only a matter of time before something gave way and the emotions poured out.

The thunderous crack in his veneer came minutes later when they played a highlight video of Abby taken from home videos set to some of Abby's favorite songs from Taylor Swift.

The footage of his sister smiling and laughing had been too much for him and he gave way to heavy, uncontrollable sobbing.

The dam had finally broken. Marie pressed both hands against her chest and bit her trembling lip to suppress the scream that yearned to be released. Her eyes watered quickly.

"Oh, Parker," she whispered, doing her best to keep her own composure. For the pain of seeing someone you deeply care about hurt could only be equaled by the pain of being unable to comfort them.

More than anything she wanted to appear in the pew next to him, wrap her arms around his broad shoulders, and draw him in to cry on her shoulder. She'd whisper into his ear that he wasn't alone and that everything would be okay.

And she'd hold him, feel his heart beating in his chest against her, and his warm breath on her skin. Not just be there for him—she'd always done that—but be there *with* him.

Still, no matter how badly she wanted to do it, she knew she couldn't. And it was killing her.

Marie dropped to her knees and held her head in her hands. Warm tears fell from her eyes as she continued watching Parker from her ethereal home.

He filed past Abby's open casket to view his sister for the last time, lingering for quite some time while he said his goodbye to her. He eventually made his way to the rear of the church with his family, where the hearse and their families' cars were parked so as to avoid the throng of reporters outside the front doors. He rode in silence with his family to Bluebonnet Hills Cemetery, the only cemetery in Briar Ridge, where Abby would be interred.

A quiet place on the western edge of town, it was an open field of a few acres, dotted here and there with an occasional live oak or pecan tree, with a few rolling hills in the distance. Its peacefulness and serenity shattered by the throng of reporters that soon arrived.

Vultures. Thankfully, a cordon of police officers guarded the entry into the cemetery so only attendees of the graveside services could enter.

Marie watched Parker walk with his parents toward the green tent pitched on the far side of the cemetery, close to the barbed-wire fence that separated it from the neighboring pasture. They meandered past tombstones of various heights and designs, some still pristine while others were moss-covered and beginning to crumble. Several dozen mounds of fresh dirt at various plots around the cemetery served as a stark reminder of the staggering toll the tragedy had taken. A work crew stood near one of them, idly leaning or sitting on their equipment while waiting for the conclusion of Abby's graveside service.

The wide open space of the cemetery allowed her to appear. Dressed in the obligatory black dress with elegant black gloves and sunglasses, she moved incognito through the crowd to an isolated spot, holding a small bouquet of tulips. A large tombstone of pink Texas granite afforded the opportunity to observe from a quiet distance. She stood alone, watching Parker and the other attendees find their seats under the green canopy when an attractive, dark-haired young man joined her. His crisp black suit fit tightly against his trim body.

"Hello, Markus."

He nodded in reply. "Nice shoes."

A slight grin. "Thanks."

"You seem to be taking a lot of risks lately with all of this appearing, don't you think?"

"Whatever you heard about the motel, it wasn't that bad. Besides, just because everyone else does it differently doesn't mean I'm wrong."

"Everyone else does it differently for a reason." The displeasure in his tone was obvious.

Really? He wanted to argue about this during Abby's graveside service? She bit her lip. "Do you want me to do my job or not?"

"Yes, but in a manner that doesn't create the potential for more harm."

Whatever.

They stood in silence, as still as the tombstones around them, pretending to pay respects to the grave in front of them. She bowed her head. Strange, the grass around this grave seemed to have been burned recently.

Moments of awkwardness passed until Markus broke the quiet tension. "I'm concerned with how things are progressing."

A reluctant sigh escaped from her. "I know. I'm—I'm having trouble getting through to him." Hands fidgeted with flower stems as the heavy stare from Markus weighed on her. "But I'm working on it. I'm working on it." The sound of her voice belied her confidence.

She returned to observing her charge. Her brows furrowed when Parker ominously refused to bow his head and pray just as he had done during the funeral service. An eerie defiance emanated from him.

"He's slipping away." Markus evidently noticed it as well.

The service ended and the attendees shuffled away from the tent and toward their parked cars on the opposite side of the cemetery.

"He's in danger now."

"I know," she replied, her voice heavy with sadness. "I've been speaking to him nonstop, but he's shutting me out. He's not listening. I'm trying everything I can to reach him before anything happens."

"Are you sure you know what you're doing?"

The implication was inescapable. She turned and looked at him. "Yes," she said, mustering as much force as she could. "I may not have been a guardian as long as you and everyone else, but I know exactly—"

The alarm inside her went off. A glance over her shoulder revealed Seth casually strolling between the headstones with two of his cohorts. His long, black trench coat, buttoned down and tied smartly at the waist, billowed in the cold wind.

Markus scanned their surroundings. "Keep cool. There're too many people around."

Her right hand twitched. The thought of striking the

three of them was appealing. If it was quick enough, maybe nobody would notice.

Seth approached and stopped in front of them.

"I thought I told you to leave him alone, Seth," Marie said.

Yellow eyes flared as Seth's pale lips snarled. "Shut up. Like your words carry any weight with me." His words dripped with bitter contempt. "I have as much right to him as you do." Seth's two sick-looking colleagues smirked at Marie and Markus with his retort.

Marie set her jaw and cocked her head upward. "Try all you want, you'll never have him." It struck a confident tone, but could it hide the growing fear and self-doubt?

Seth sneered. "How pathetic you are. Look around you. Half the people here are breaking and losing their faith, if not openly questioning it. Do you honestly believe he's any different, especially after what he's just experienced with his sister?" Seth glared at her, as if daring her to respond. "Of course not. Already he's slipping through your fingers. He's through the looking glass. He's pulling back the curtain and finally seeing the truth. And you know what? He'll be freer because of it."

"Liar," Marie replied.

Seth's eyebrows raised in mock surprise. "Really? I'm the liar? 'Never will I leave you, never will I forsake you.'" Seth shrugged. "Where was He the other night?"

Marie rolled her eyes and shook her head.

"'No, I will not leave you or abandon you as orphans in a storm.' These people look pretty abandoned to me."

The heat rose to Marie's cheeks. How much longer could she endure his taunts?

"'And we know that in all things God works for the good of those who love Him.' So where's the good in all of this? I guess He doesn't love the people of Briar Ridge." He paused, intensifying his gaze as he stepped closer. "'For I know the plans I have for you, says the Lord, plans to prosper you and not to *harm you*.'"

The recitation of a verse Parker knew so intimately shook Marie. In fact, he'd been thinking of this very verse the past several days, and it hadn't been pleasant. Parker's every thought was known to her, and they were taking him down a path that had but one outcome.

"No," she whispered as she turned and watched Parker make his way across the cemetery. She called to him, his name escaping her lips in a hushed tone. Could he still hear? Would he even listen? Seconds ticked by, and the lack of a response crushed her heart.

"He's burying more than his sister today," Seth whispered, an unmistakable trace of glee in his voice. "You're losing him."

The thought burned inside her. Her eyes watered. She clenched her jaws, and her hands trembled. She wanted to strike Seth now more than anything, but couldn't, not with so many people around. Seth had to know there wouldn't be a fight.

The church. The hospital. The cemetery. He seemed to only choose public places for confrontation, probably knowing full well he could antagonize without consequences.

This revelation incensed her even more and her self-control finally broke. She spun around and slapped Seth across his pale, ghostly face as hard as she could. The sting of the impact forced him to recoil and stagger backward. Markus's firm hand rested on her shoulder, a not-so-subtle hint at restraint.

Seth steadied himself and faced her. Callous, yellow eyes bore into her for a moment and then, quick as a rattlesnake, a cold, icy hand shot up against her throat, gripping it in a steel-like vise.

Her windpipe nearly crushed, she dropped the flowers and frantically grabbed at his wrist in order to break his hold.

Seth pulled her toward him. His dank, foul breath watered her eyes. "I will have your charge if it's the last thing on Creation I ever do." His voice was low and quiet but filled with undeniable hatred that turned Marie's blood to ice.

Markus stepped forward. "That's enough, Seth. Release her. *Now*."

Seth calmly looked at Markus while Marie struggled for air. "As you wish." He released his stranglehold on Marie, who dropped to her knees, taking in oxygen with deep, desperate gasps. Seth towered overhead, smugness plastered across his gaunt face. "What a huge price you're about to pay for a little flare of temper." He turned, but stopped, his face hardening with contempt. "Now get up before you ruin that beautiful Oscar de la Renta." He slithered away, his associates trailing in his wake.

Markus squatted next to Marie and placed his arm around her. Wincing, she coughed and massaged her aching throat. As Seth disappeared into the crowd of black-clad mourners, she apologized to Markus.

He frowned. "You knew better than to do that, although he definitely had it coming."

She took hold of his extended hand and rose to her feet. One glance at Markus indicated something else was coming.

He lowered the boom. "We need to talk."

CHAPTER 22

Parker peeked from behind the living room window curtains and watched Pastor Jim sidestep through the throng of reporters. Dad let him in amidst shouted questions and flashes of photography.

"Thanks for coming, Pastor Jim," Dad said, gripping the minister by the hand.

"No problem, Ken. I'm glad to help in any way I can." The preacher's eyes shifted to Parker, who shook his head and looked away.

Dad cleared his throat. "Park, what did I tell you about this?"

Parker pursed his lips and glanced at Pastor Jim. A quick nod was all he was willing to give.

Dad extended his arm toward the kitchen. "Pastor, the kitchen is right through there. I think Suzy's got some coffee if you'd like."

"Sounds good. I could use some actually."

Coffee, snacks, money—not even the scowl from Dad could offer enough motivation for Parker to take part in this conversation. Talking about it only brought everything back up again. Besides, there was nothing he had to say anyway.

"Parker." The terse command from Dad broke him free of his spot. Heavy feet carried him out of the living room and into the kitchen where everyone sat around the break-fast table, sipping coffee. Though an empty chair sat opposite Dad, the space behind the counter seemed far more appealing.

"Park, will you have a seat?" Mom asked. "Pastor Jim is going to help us write a statement. Maybe that way the media will leave us alone—hopefully."

Parker didn't move.

Mom sipped from her cup and placed it back on the wooden table. "We want to know if there is something you want to say specifically. Anything you really want to convey?" She looked at Dad and Pastor Jim, then turned back to Parker. "Park, will you please help us?"

Again, Parker refused to acknowledge the request.

"Sit down," Dad commanded, obviously irritated at the lack of responsiveness.

Parker looked out the bay window at the backyard and watched fallen leaves dance in the wind. He shrugged his shoulders. "I told y'all, I don't care what y'all tell them." He turned to leave.

His mother extended her hand in his direction to beckon him to reconsider. "Park, please."

Dad pushed back from the table. "Parker, get back here." He placed his hands on the tabletop and appeared ready to stand and forcefully drag Parker to the table when Pastor Jim interrupted.

"It's okay, Ken. Let 'im go. It'll be all right."

Parker disappeared down the hall and returned to his room, leaving his parents and Pastor Jim to craft the message to the media. About thirty minutes later, someone knocked on his bedroom door.

"What?"

The door cracked open and Pastor Jim's face appeared. "Hi, Parker. Can I come in for a second?"

Parker sat on his bed with the laptop, typing on the keyboard. He glanced at the minister and shrugged his shoulders. *Whatever.* The typing resumed without a word.

Pastor Jim stepped inside and closed the door behind him. "I don't want to bother you or intrude in any way. I—I just want to check on you, see how you're holding up."

Parker ignored him and continued working on the laptop.

The preacher paused for a moment, then continued. "I didn't see you in church this morning with your parents."

Parker remained fixated on the computer screen.

"Park," Pastor Jim began as he reached up and ran his hand through his thinning hair, "I know you're hurting, and I kind of know how you feel." He stepped toward the bed and slid his hands into his pockets. "You probably don't know this, but my older brother died in a car wreck when I was twelve."

The typing continued unabated.

"Samuel was his name. A really good guitar player, too. He was seventeen at the time." Pastor Jim paused, reached up, and scratched at the stubble on his chin. "You see, I was a baseball player. And one day, our coach cancelled practice. Well, instead of doing the responsible thing and calling my parents to let them know, I rode my bike to a friend's house. My brother always picked me up after practice, and that particular day he was running late."

Parker's fingers paused and hovered over the keyboard.

Pastor Jim took a deep breath and continued with his story. "And not wanting his little brother to be left at the ballpark by himself, he drove pretty fast to come get me. He made a sharp turn at a high rate of speed, lost control, and flipped his car several times before crashing into a big oak tree. He died instantly."

Parker turned his head and tugged at his T-shirt. The room suddenly felt stuffy.

"Not a day goes by that I don't think of what might've happened had I just stopped for twenty seconds and picked up the phone to call home. And I'm not going to lie to you and tell you that you'll get over this, because you won't."

Pastor Jim bowed his head for a moment, then continued, his voice growing softer. "But over time, you'll see it gets easier to live with. That void is still there, mind you, but you learn to cope and move on."

Parker leaned back on his hands and blew out a sharp breath between his lips.

"I just remember having that awful sense of guilt, that it was my fault Samuel died and feeling so angry because of it." Pastor Jim glanced at the barren corkboard, his eyes roaming the empty spaces. "Looking back, it's amazing that I'm where I am today. And I believe that's due to the love, grace, mercy, and compassion that others showed me." He looked back at Parker. "I guess what I'm trying to say is that people were there for me—whether I thought I needed them or not. And I want you to know that there are people here for you now, like me."

He took another step toward the bed. "Is there anything I can do for you?" he asked quietly. "Anything at all—even if it's just to listen."

Parker slowly nodded.

"What can I do?"

Parker turned his head and faced Pastor Jim. "Get out."

The preacher sighed and dropped his head. As he opened the door, the minister looked over his shoulder. "Park, please know I'm praying for you. If you need anything, anything at all, you can call me twenty-four-seven. I'm here for you." The door shut behind him.

Parker resumed his work on the computer, but the TV remote sitting next to him proved too distracting. He scooped it up and pressed the power button.

CNN carried the live broadcast of Pastor Jim standing on Parker's front porch, dozens of microphones jammed in his face.

The preached unfolded a piece of paper. "I'd like to read a prepared statement from Mr. and Mrs. Austin." He cleared his throat. "'We cannot begin to find the words to express our sincere and heartfelt gratitude for the kind and affectionate support everyone has shown for the recent loss of our precious Abby. We grieve with the other families whose loved ones have also been called home too soon. Our son Parker is exceedingly thankful to have been able to do something that might've helped prevent more tragic deaths, and we simply request that our privacy be respected as we continue to grieve for Abby and all the others who've been lost. We pray for the healing of those who are still recovering from their wounds, and we pray for the families of all those who've been affected by this tragedy. We look forward to the day when the sun will shine again in Briar Ridge, and the sound of its children's laughter ring out with joy and love. Thank you."

Pastor Jim looked out upon the sea of cameras. "I want to stress that the Austin family will not grant any interviews, and any communication the family wishes to make in the future will be through prepared statements."

The reporters milled around for another hour, but soon lifted their siege, and, by late afternoon, they vanished altogether.

Around five o'clock, Mom stopped by his room and suggested he get out of the house.

"What for?"

"Park, with the exception of the funeral, you haven't stepped one foot outside this house. You've been cooped up in here for over a week now. I just think it would be good to get out the house for a bit now that the reporters are gone."

"There's nowhere I want to go," he said and dismissed the suggestion with a wave of his hand.

"Okay, then just go for a drive. You can't keep sitting here in your room like this."

His mouth curled into a smirk. "School starts back up tomorrow. I'll get out of the house then."

"That's not what I meant. You need to get up, get moving again, not be afraid to re-engage with the world."

Parker sat up. "Seriously? You think I'm afraid?"

"Honey, we just don't want you isolated like this. It's not healthy."

Gritting his teeth, Parker stood. "Fine, I'll go for a drive if that will make y'all happy."

Mom smiled. "Yes, and what would make me even happier is if you could stop by Dairy Queen and pick up dinner on your way back."

Parker threw on his letter jacket, grabbed his car keys, and walked through the garage to his car. The seemingly permanent gray skies continued filtering out the daylight, and strong gusts of wind blew into his face. Would the sun ever come out again?

He got in his car and turned left out of his driveway onto Elliott Street. A few houses down, he passed a red semi-trailer parked on the side of the street, which nearly took up half of the roadway. Its big diesel engine roared to life, and the rearview mirror revealed the truck lurching forward into the street.

"Now what," Parker muttered as the semi-trailer followed him through several turns. He made his way to Wabash and headed east to the Highway 19 intersection. A turn south at the crossroads toward Eastmoor might confirm his suspicions and tense nervous eyes checked the rearview mirror to see if the truck made the turn as well.

A few seconds later, the semi-trailer appeared and turned south onto Highway 19. Parker accelerated. Would the truck speed up to catch him if it fell behind? His eyes remained riveted to the rearview mirror as if in a trance. Parker's heart leaped into his throat as the truck sped up and rapidly closed the distance.

As he neared the Dairy Queen, a tap of the brake pedal brought the truck to within a few car lengths. Without using a turn signal, Parker turned sharply into the Dairy Queen parking lot. The tires screeched on the pavement as he pulled into the drive-thru lane and slammed on the brakes.

The big rig tapped its brakes but the vehicle continued southward toward the edge of town. A sigh of relief escaped Parker's lips.

He edged his car forward and placed his order for the hamburgers. Had the truck driver been following him or not? Maybe he was just making his way out of town to deliver something. Then again, nobody who drove a big, red diesel truck lived on Elliott Street, so why was he there at all? *C'mon, dude, stop being paranoid and get a hold of yourself.*

A tumbleweed drifted across the empty highway. The Dairy Queen sat on the periphery of Briar Ridge, and traffic was light on this stretch of road. A lone, dark-colored car appeared, heading south.

It meant nothing at first, but as it neared something about the look of the car captured his full attention. He sat up straight and leaned forward into the steering wheel, eyes straining.

Dark, sporty, tinted windows. It drew closer, and Parker's mouth fell open in disbelief.

"No way," he whispered. A black Dodge Charger sped past Dairy Queen. Sandwiched between two cars in the drive-thru lane, Parker couldn't get out. He rolled down his window, stuck his head outside, and yelled at the driver behind him. "Back up, back up, back up!"

The driver frowned and refused to budge. Only when Parker opened his door and stepped out of his car with a menacing scowl did he back up a few feet. Parker returned to his vehicle, revved the engine, and bolted out of the drive-thru lane.

He peeled out of the parking lot, smoke billowing from burned rubber, and turned south onto Highway 19 in pursuit of the Charger. He pressed the accelerator to the floor and spied his phone in the dashboard cup holder. He could dial nine-one-one and tell the dispatcher to let Boddicker know he'd found the mysterious vehicle. But what if he was wrong? What if this wasn't the same Dodge Charger that had tailed him the entire day of the shooting? Getting it wrong and chasing an innocent person across Joe Wheeler County would make more headlines. That was the last thing he needed at the moment. No, better to make sure and *then* call the police.

He continued to speed, never taking his eyes off the Charger. As he neared, he switched into the opposite lane and pulled up beside the car. A sudden chill swept through him, and he shivered.

Between glances at the road ahead, he looked at the Charger to identify the driver, but still couldn't make out the person through the tinted windows. At least the driver was alone.

Parker honked his horn and pointed. "Pull over!"

The Charger kept going without the slightest indication it would comply.

Undeterred, Parker edged closer so only a few inches separated the two vehicles. *Time to find out who you are.*

More honks and commands to pull over, but the driver refused to yield. His palms sweaty on the steering wheel, Parker checked the road in front of him and in his rearview mirror for any traffic. Once assured his maneuver wouldn't pose a threat to anyone else, he took a deep breath and swerved slightly to the right. The dull clang of metal banging into metal confirmed he'd hit his mark.

The other driver swerved to the shoulder of the highway upon impact, overcorrected, and veered toward Parker, who jerked his car to the left.

The sudden maneuver caused Parker's Firebird to fishtail. His stomach did a somersault and his heart nearly exploded in his chest from almost running off the road. Parker slowed and regained control of his car. The Charger sped onward, showing no signs of stopping.

Parker gripped the steering wheel, his knuckles turning white, and slammed the accelerator to the floor. His car shot forward and soon pulled even with the Charger.

Mouth dry, heart racing, Parker spun the steering wheel hard to the right. The old Firebird rammed into the now-dented Charger, forcing it off the shoulder entirely. The scene unfolded in his rearview mirror like a movie. The black car left the road, dipped into a small ditch where it hit the embankment, and went airborne.

Tires spinning in the air, the car sailed for twenty yards, clipped a barbed-wire fence, and then crashed down onto the brush of a dry cow pasture. Parker slammed on his brakes. The high-pitched screech of the wheels pierced his eardrums as the car spun around.

He looked up in time to see the Charger in mid-roll, flipping over its left side and coming to rest right-side-up amid a cloud of dust and debris. Parker sped back to where the car left the roadway and parked on the shoulder. Despite the warm air coming from the car's heater, a chill raced through his body. He crossed his arms and leaned into the steering wheel.

Who's in that car?

Sitting on the side of the empty highway, Parker watched for any movement from the wrecked car as occasional gusts of strong wind gently rocked his idling Firebird. Except for a stream of white smoke billowing from the damaged hood, nothing stirred around the Charger.

Parker glanced up and down the highway, saw no one approaching, and quickly exited. He crossed the ditch and climbed the slight embankment, stepping over the mangled barbed wire as he entered the pasture. Prickly bull nettles and dry, thorny scrub brush grazed his jeans.

With his heart thumping like a jackhammer, Parker walked to the driver-side door and wiped cold sweat from his forehead. The driver remained motionless in the front seat. Another quick look to see if any passersby had noticed them—but there was nobody on the road in either direction. He breathed deeply to steady his nerves before he pulled opened the scratched and dented door.

The driver lay slumped forward over the steering wheel. Blood oozed from a gash over his left eye. He moaned. Parker reached in and pulled him backward into the seat. He studied the young man's blood-soaked face. Rounded chin, soft cheeks. He looked somewhat familiar, in his mid-twenties maybe, but he couldn't quite place him.

"Hey, can you hear me?" Parker waited for a response, but didn't get any. He asked again, but the man remained motionless, eyes still closed. He jostled the driver's shoulder, and the man's eyes fluttered a few times. "I know you can hear me."

Parker scanned the young man for any signs of serious injuries but found none. Other than the bleeding wound over his left eye, the man seemed uninjured. Parker surveyed the interior of the car. Several Ziploc bags of what looked like oregano—but obviously wasn't—lay in the backseat. Strewn about the floorboards were syringes and small baggies of a white substance.

A prescription bottle rested in the passenger seat. He reached across the man, picked it up, and read the label of the half-filled bottle.

"Darvocet," Parker read out loud. Darvocet? Mom had said nurses sometimes got hooked on prescription drugs while working in hospitals. Darvocet was one of their favorites.

He looked at the driver. "No wonder you're not feeling anything."

Parker squatted next to the driver and gently slapped the man with the back of his hand, causing him to recoil and open his eyes.

"Who are you?" Parked asked forcefully. The man looked at him, turned his head away as his shoulders slumped.

"I'm sorry," the driver mumbled.

Parker reached in and pulled the man toward him, grabbed his chin, and turned his head so they were face to face.

The man opened his eyes and sheepishly dropped his head. "I'm sorry," he repeated, as if the simple act of speaking required great effort.

Something about the man's face reminded Parker of someone, a person whom he'd seen before on several occasions. Brown eyes and hair, high forehead and freckles, slow speech and movement—he'd seen it all before. He looked down at the pill bottle in his hand, thought of the drugs in the car, and looked at the familiar face again.

"Gibson," Parker whispered to himself. The man's eyes looked at him, confirming Parker's suspicion. "You're one of the Gibson kids, aren't you? You're the one who had the drug problem and couldn't get into pharmacy school." Parker concentrated, tried hard to recall the name. After a moment, it came to him. "Gary Don, Jr., you're Gary Don, Jr."

"I—I didn't—know," Gary Don said, sputtering out the words, "that they were going to do that." Blood ran into his mouth and he tried to spit it out, but it only drooled down his chin. He shook his head. "I swear, Parker, I didn't know."

Parker unbuckled Gary Don's seatbelt, grabbed him by his shirt collar, and yanked him out of the car. Standing on wobbly legs and teetering against the side of the car, Gary Don whimpered liked a shamed puppy. Parker watched him with balled fists, felt the heat rising within.

"Were McGonagill and that other guy in the car with you the day of the shooting?"

Gary Don blinked slowly and nodded. His lips quivered.

"Why were you following me?"

Tears streamed down Gary Don's bloody face. "Bobby said he wanted to pull a prank on you. Said I could have the car if I went along." Gary Don slowly lifted his hands. "Park, I'm sorry, I swear I didn't know they were going to shoot anyone. They just wanted some drugs and promised to give me the car if I pointed you out and drove them around."

Parker remained silent, though every muscle twitched and bucked under rising tension.

Gary Don continued to plead his case. "We just drove around, getting high, that's all. They cut me loose that afternoon and let me have the car, just like they said." He paused as if waiting for Parker to respond. "I didn't know they were going to kill anyone," he insisted. "You gotta believe me."

Parker swung as hard as he could, his fist slamming into Gary Don's jaw like a sledgehammer. Gary Don's body twisted and crumpled to the ground. Hands shaking, eyes watering, Parker towered over him, rage coursing through his body. Alone in the empty field, the thought of kicking Gary Don to death and leaving his body to the buzzards consumed him.

Gary Don squirmed and propped himself up on his elbows. "I deserve to die," he said with difficulty, apparently due to a broken jaw. The tears continued to flow and he cried even harder, his torso shaking with each heavy sob.

This pathetic specimen had played a role in Abby's death. The thought of beating Gary Don into a coma, or worse, made perfect sense.

Kill him. He's a drugged-out loser. A zero. Nothing more. Kill him. He's responsible for Abby's death. If not for him, none of this would've happened. He might as well have pulled the trigger himself. Just kill him. It's justice. No one would argue. Nobody would mind. Just kill him!

Every muscle, taut and tense with fury, ached to be unleashed.

Still, an inner voice urged restraint, pulling him in the opposite direction. Soft, quiet, but powerful. The voice triggered images of Abby, flashing like lightning in his mind, and sent him staggering away from the car. He looked up at the gray skies for a moment, shut his eyes, and pressed his hands to his face. An intense, blood-curdling scream erupted from his lungs as he teetered on the brink of losing control. He turned and tried to resolve what to do. This piece of scum had played a major role in the shooting—the shooting that took Abby's life. There had to be a reckoning. Somehow. Someway.

He looked westward, toward the far horizon where the bleak, gray sky came down to touch small, distant hilltops covered in scrub brush. The frosty wind teased his hair and prickled the tops of his ears, turning them cold. Abby used to say the wind was God tickling you.

Parker closed his eyes and tried to swallow past the lump that quickly formed in his throat at the memory of Abby.

Gary Don, still heaving with tears, begged for for-giveness. "It's my fault—it's my fault. If only I'd said no, it wouldn't have happened." He paused, gasping for breath between heavy sobs. "I'm sorry about—your sister. Please—forgive me."

At the mention of Abby, Parker spun around, reached down, and forcefully dragged Gary Don to his feet. He grabbed him roughly by the arm and jerked him through the field toward the highway. "I'm taking you to the police."

Gary Don's head jerked. "You're not—you're not gonna kill me?" Tears ran down from his wide-open eyes, mixing with blood and a runny nose.

"No." Parker gritted his teeth. "She wouldn't want me to."

CHAPTER 23

Classes at Briar Ridge High School resumed on Monday, a full ten days after the shooting.

That first day back stood as the biggest hurdle to moving on without Abby. No music blared from her room. The box of pop tarts remained in the pantry. No Sycamore Elementary as the passenger seat sat empty. The drive was too quiet now. Taylor Swift didn't seem so annoying anymore.

As Parker pulled into the parking lot, media personnel swarmed like locusts in front of the school, interviewing students. Most of them conducted their interviews near the Bobcat statue, which now had been inscribed in various ink colors with the names of the dead. A sea of flowers, teddy bears, and other trinkets surrounded the makeshift memorial. The area had also served as the location for a recent candlelight vigil.

Enter the fray in front of the school? No way. Not after that episode on the highway. Better to go around and slip inside from the back.

The hallways seemed odd. Not only was he out of his regular routine, but the news of his apprehension of Gary Don, Jr. had rocketed through the student body. Everyone stared and whispered in hushed tones as he passed.

He made it to his locker and picked at the flowers and other decorations Summer had fastened to it. Avoiding his ex-girlfriend proved difficult due to the stupid narrow hall-ways, and he froze as she squeezed passed him. Summer dropped her head, but not before he caught a glimpse of her bloodshot, puffy eyes.

Awkward. Were they tears of anger or sadness?

Hopefully schoolwork would distract from the rampant gossiping and the drama of dealing with an ex-girlfriend. He entered his government classroom and took his seat by the window. Several chairs sat empty, some of which would not be occupied again for the remainder of the year. He slumped in his chair, stared out the window at the cold, gray morning, and tried—without success—to block out the glib chatter of his classmates.

"So how many are dead?"

"Thirty-eight," came the reply. "Now that Jason Hol-loway died in the hospital in Abilene last night. Another one hundred and seven wounded."

"Yeah, I heard that makes this the deadliest shooting in the world."

"In America, genius."

"No, I think they said the world."

"No wonder you're making a D in this class."

An announcement from another student interrupted the conversation. "Hey, I just got a text from my brother that people are smashing the windows at Gibson's. They're like ransacking the place or something."

The news of the violent protest at one of Briar Ridge's most established institutions set the classroom abuzz. *Wonder where the old timers will get their coffee now?*

"Good job, Barney Fifes. Way to keep the details of the investigation under wraps," a student proclaimed while clapping his hands in mock approval.

"Wow, the Gibsons are going to have to move out. I mean if Gary Don, Jr. was supposed to have been the third shooter."

"No way. Gary Don's harmless. My sister went to school with him, said he'd faint if he sneezed too hard."

"Doesn't matter. He got Bobby and that other guy all juiced up so they could go on a rampage. He might as well have been a third shooter."

"Yeah, they'll have to go into hiding, just like the McGonagills."

At the mention of the McGonagill name, Parker's muscles tensed up.

"I heard they're staying with family in Wichita Falls...or Midland...or was it Brazil?"

"Really? You heard they're either in Wichita Falls, Midland, or...Brazil? How did you even make it to the twelfth grade?"

The student in front of Parker spun around in his chair. "I heard they're at the hospital in Fort Worth to pull the plug on Bobby because he's brain dead."

"Anybody would be brain dead if they got bashed in the head a hundred times with a football helmet."

All eyes turned to Parker, who nearly collapsed under the weight of their stares.

Little schoolwork was accomplished. Parker's teacher seemed too out-of-sorts to keep the class focused, so the entire class period devolved into nothing more than a gossip fest. Without a word to anyone, Parker bolted from his seat when the bell rang and headed for his locker.

For the remainder of the day, every class held similar conversations. He tried every way to ignore them—reading textbooks, singing songs in his head, leaving the room multiple times to go to the restroom. At one point during drama class, he tried to go to sleep, although the stiff wooden chair made it difficult. He eventually dozed off but woke as he almost jumped out of his chair to the sounds of gunfire and screams in his sleep.

Skylar, sitting nearby, looked in his direction often, but didn't speak to him.

Monday also marked the first day of football practice since the shooting. Last week's game against Island Park had been canceled, and the monumental task now was simp-

ly getting back into the routine of practice despite the obvious absence of teammates who had been killed or wounded.
The official tally of casualties to the varsity football team
stood at nine. Two dead and seven wounded, including
Coach Sinc, who had been released from the hospital in
Gatling only yesterday but was already back at work. He'd
been shot twice, once in the thigh and once in the hip. The
latter had been the more serious of the two wounds, and resulted in giving him a limp that required the temporary use
of a cane.

Yet as the week wore on, everyone fell back into the routine of game preparation. They even seemed to enjoy the
distraction the time on the practice field provided. But Parker moved and thought in slow motion, usually lagging behind his teammates between drills. With each passing day,
his detachment from the team deepened.

When Friday arrived, Parker knew he wasn't ready. He
awoke that morning after another night of abbreviated, intermittent sleep interspersed with more nightmares. This
time he'd awoken at three in the morning with both of his
parents at his bedside trying to calm him down from the
screams in his sleep. He lay awake the remainder of the
night, apprehensive about repeating the same nightmares.

He rose at a quarter to seven with his usual bout of
game-day nausea, but the queasiness faded altogether when
he left the house. A strange aloofness enveloped him as the
school day began, completely out of his regular game-day
routine without Summer. He drifted through each of his
morning classes, ate lunch at McDonald's instead of Sonic,
where Summer usually ate, and then cruised through drama
and business applications without a word to anyone. Oddly,
Skylar thrust a note into his hand while exiting the auditorium.

He skipped the pep rally and drove home, where he spent
the remainder of the afternoon zoning out in front of the
television.

With no desire whatsoever to drive to the church and

pray, he stayed at his house until five o'clock and then drove to the field house to prepare for the game.

"Hey man, where you been?" Tyler asked when Parker walked into the locker room and headed straight for his stall.

"Went home to relax."

Tyler walked over to him, already dressed for the game and snacking on a bag of pretzels.

"You went home? Why?"

"Just needed to get away, that's all."

Tyler chewed a mouthful of pretzels. "This doesn't have anything to do with Summer, does it?"

Parker rubbed his eyes. "I'm fine." He went through his normal pre-game ritual, except he wore the standard issued Under Armor shirt instead of the one emblazoned with scripture. He also skipped his preferred pre-game Christian rock music.

While getting his ankles taped, the image of Abby scooping ice cubes into small coolers gnawed at him. Their last conversation together had been right here, and a lump formed in his throat. *I don't know if I can do this.* He swallowed and slid off the table to join his teammates on their way to the field for pre-game warm ups.

Emerging from the field house doors, he paused at the foot of the gravel drive leading to the stadium, his mind flooded with painful memories. Teammates jogged by like a current rippling past a protruding rock. His hands shook, and he took a deep breath to steady himself, finally moving forward in clumsy, uncoordinated steps while ignoring the cheering fans lining the gravel drive.

Already filled to capacity, the stadium erupted as the team appeared on the field. Fans stood and chanted "We are Briar Ridge!" as a long row of reporters and television cameras filmed them from outside the fence bordering the north end zone.

Pre-game warmups were handled in a robotic fashion. He tried to focus, but everything seemed fuzzy and detached. The stadium, always a place he embraced, felt different now. Surrounded by thousands, the arena prompted nothing but a sense of isolation.

The fans stood and cheered incessantly, giving the impression that the crowd thought it could help heal the town's wounds by cheering themselves hoarse. The louder and more boisterous their cheers, the more they could make everything right again. But it only made it clear how desperate they felt.

After warming up, Parker stood near mid-field with Hayden Hyghtower. The skies had darkened and the stadium lights flooded the field in an eerie, incandescent light. Cool and crisp, the evening air contained a slight breeze as the American and Texas flags gently waved from their flagpoles at half-staff.

"A lot of 'em," Hayden said as he nodded in the direction of the television cameras.

Parker surveyed the throng of cameras and news vans parked on the street behind them. At least twenty of them. They all seemed eager to document Briar Ridge's return to the scene of the massacre.

Coach Sinc, grimacing, limped over to the two quarterbacks. "Are y'all loose?"

Both quarterbacks answered in the affirmative.

"Good." Coach Sinc looked at Parker. "Park, how you feeling?"

Parker shrugged his shoulders. "Fine," he replied. The sooner the game started, the sooner it would be over and he could get out of this place.

Coach Sinc looked at him intently, forcing Parker to break eye contact and look down at his cleats.

Coach Sinc limped forward, leaned on his cane, and placed a hand on Parker's shoulder. "Look at me, Park," he said gently. "You can do this. I believe in you, okay? But I need you to remove the clutter and focus. Got it?"

Parker nodded. Pre-game jitters usually struck at this time, but tonight brought nothing but complete and total ambivalence. He cast his eyes around the crowded, emotionally charged stadium. A strong, overwhelming desire to leave consumed him. Anywhere was welcome, anywhere but Bobcat Stadium.

Coach Sinc hobbled away and conversed with an assistant coach. Hayden stared at Parker with an uneasy look on his face, as though he knew something bad was about to unfold and he could do nothing to stop it.

"What's your problem?" Parker asked.

"Nothing, Park. Just—look, you're okay, right? I mean—"

"Shut up and quit worrying. If you have to play, you'll be fine."

Hayden's face paled like he'd just received a death sentence, but Parker didn't care.

They followed the rest of their teammates to the field house, past a hundred screaming, cheering fans lining the gravel drive to the field house doors. Parker ignored all of them—even the hands of the little kids stuck out to give him "five."

Inside, Coach Sinc talked about the desperate need to get back up when knocked down, but Parker heard none of it.

When he got back to the sidelines, the small table where tiny cups of Gatorade sat jumped out at him. The bench area, though full of people, now seemed empty.

His eyes roamed the ground until he found the area where she'd died. Seeing the spot again triggered a wave of cold nausea. His palms grew sweaty. The memory of Abby's screams came back and blended with the noise of the crowd. Parker shuffled over to the spot as he remembered Abby's final moments and examined the grass with his cleats. No blood. At least those stains could be washed away.

He forced himself to turn around and waited through some additional pre-game rituals. One of the students came across the stadium's intercom and led everyone in a moment of silence, followed by a presentation of a large wreath and flowers at mid-field by the president of the Boonsboro High School student council to his Briar Ridge counterpart.

The coin toss out of the way, he waited for the kickoff. He spotted Summer. She met his gaze but soon turned away.

The crowd cheered when Royce Brown returned the kickoff to the thirty-yard line. Parker put on his helmet and walked out onto the field with his teammates.

Coach Sinc called out to him. "Park, you can do this!" he shouted while leaning on his cane. An assistant coach stood next to him to give the signals since it proved too awkward for him. Coach Sinc instructed the assistant to signal the first play of the game: "Brown, Moose."

Parker awaited the snap. He got the ball and handed it to Royce Brown who ran for a gain of five yards.

The next set of signals came in: "Black, Aussie." Simple play. So routine he could've made it in his sleep. He took the snap, looked to his left, and threw a bad pass well behind Tyler's outstretched arms.

On third down Parker fumbled the snap and dropped to the ground to recover it before a Boonsboro defender got it first, which resulted in a loss of four yards. He jogged off the field, trailing his frustrated teammates. Coach Sinc greeted him by grabbing his arm and tapping the side of Parker's helmet. "I need you to stay in the game, got it?"

He'd expected a comment from Coach Sinc, but it didn't matter. Nothing anyone said mattered anymore. He was just a tiny blip floating on a sea of indifference.

Parker gave an obligatory nod and walked to the bench to sit down. A student trainer handed him a cup of red-colored Gatorade. He unbuttoned his chinstrap, slid off his helmet, and gulped down the cold beverage. Tyler came over, but he waved him off. The far end of the bench area, furthest away from everyone, beckoned.

The defense struggled to stop Boonsboro. The Bears moved the ball down the field and looked poised to score.

He glanced at the cheerleaders. Summer watched him, but she looked away and rejoined the rest of the squad in a rowdy cheer.

He looked around the giant aluminum stadium at its sea of forest green. For a place he'd always seemed to connect with and thrive in, it now seemed forever tainted and scarred.

Hearing the fans on the other side of the stadium erupt in a chorus of cheers, he looked up to see Boonsboro had scored a touchdown. Rising, he put his helmet back on and buckled his chinstrap. The walk to rejoin the team was a slow procession of reluctance.

Zach Douglas returned the kickoff to the thirty-four yard line. Lethargy weighed Parker down as he trudged out onto the field again and turned to get the signals from the sideline. He took the snap and handed the ball to Royce Brown who gained seven yards. On the next play, Parker mishandled the handoff and scrambled to recover it, resulting in a five-yard loss.

He slowly got to his feet and became preoccupied with brushing some dried grass off his uniform.

On third and eight, the Briar Ridge fans rose to their feet, cheering and yelling with desperation, as if they could will their team to a victory and help begin the healing process for the town.

The signals from Coach Sinc didn't compute. Everything seemed to lose focus, the roar of the crowd filtered out as subtle, incoherent background noise. Royce Brown tugged on Parker's sleeve.

"Hey, man, did you get the play?"

"Huh? Uh, yeah," Parker replied, trying desperately to recall the signals. He couldn't remember. "What was it?"

Royce stepped closer. "Green, Magic."

Parker nodded and awaited the snap. His mind drifted into a trance again. The ball came at him while Parker's hands were at his sides. He snapped to attention as he became aware of everyone moving, a brown object flying toward him. He shot his hands up and caught the ball, bobbling it a few times before securing it firmly. He stepped backwards, looked to his left, then to his right, and threw the ball.

A poorly thrown pass, the ball sailed high and behind Tyler. It landed in the arms of a Boonsboro player who raced toward the Briar Ridge end zone.

The crowd erupted as the players reacted to the turnover. Parker, with the best angle to pursue and tackle the Boonsboro player with the ball, stood and watched as the Boonsboro defender raced untouched to the south end zone.

Parker didn't wait for him to score. He exited the field, unbuckling his chinstrap with a sharp tug. The rest of his teammates jogged back to the sideline, but Parker angled for the main gate of the stadium off to the side of the south end zone.

He ignored shouts from teammates and coaches as he approached the gate, passing several puzzled fans and spectators, one of whom stared at him intently. Faded blue jeans fit tightly around her shapely legs, and a black scarf topped off a forest green sweater. Her hands were clasped together, as if praying. Strawberry-blonde hair, billowing like golden streamers in the evening wind, caught his attention. He had seen her face once before, at the hospital the night of the shooting. Was this a coincidence? The thought almost stopped him in his tracks. For a moment he reconsidered his decision to quit, but he continued his trek out of the stadium.

Only a hundred feet to go. Halfway down the gravel drive his parents called to him. He stopped and turned to see them hurrying after him.

"Parker, what's the matter with you?" Dad shouted, visibly irritated. Mom grabbed him by the arm and said something, but he only shook his head in response.

Now what?

"What's going on? Where do you think you're going?"

"I'm done," Parker answered matter-of-factly.

Mom opened her mouth to speak, but Dad cut her off.

"What do you mean you're done? You can't quit like this, son. You need to get back out there and finish the game. Then we can talk about what's going on, understand?"

Dad wore his usual Briar Ridge baseball cap, but even the semi-darkness away from the stadium lights couldn't hide that Mom sported a button with Abby's picture on it. It held his attention until she stepped forward and placed her hands on his shoulder pads.

"Sweetie, talk to us."

He looked past them, toward the stadium's entrance, and tried to locate the girl he'd seen. A search of the fans passing back and forth between the bleachers and the concession stand yielded no results. He took a deep breath, inhaled the aroma of hot dogs, nachos, and chili for the last time.

"I'm just done," he said with a shrug of his shoulders. He looked at both of them. "I don't want to play anymore."

Dad stammered, "Quitting's a poor example, Park. It's unacceptable."

"I don't care."

With an increase in volume and intensity, Dad said, "You're letting down both the team and the town."

The town? Parker bit his lip to keep from yelling back.

Mom watched him intently, probing his eyes, studying every facial expression and reaction, apparently looking for some clue that might help her discern what was going on with him.

"Dad, you're just not going to understand, okay? You can be angry and disappointed with me all you want, but it's not changing anything. I don't want to play anymore."

Mom nodded. She reached up and hugged him for a moment, then let go. Parker turned, eager to leave, to leave it all behind for good. Dad called out, but Mom cut him off. "Let him go, honey, he's hurting. Just let him go."

The rusty metal doors of the field house creaked open, his cleats clacked down the concrete hallway to the locker room. He walked straight to his locker and got undressed, throwing off his shoulder pads and the rest of his uniform.

He put on his clothes, grabbed his letter jacket, and stuffed his personal effects into his pockets.

Parker slid the nameplate at the top of his locker out of its holder and surveyed the locker room. He took in the smells of body odor, sweaty clothes, mildewed towels, and unhealthy levels of deodorant and cologne for the final time. After one last, lengthy look, he tossed his nameplate into the large trashcan next to the door and walked out. The metal door clanged shut behind him.

He emerged through the chipped-paint doors that opened onto the practice field and trekked across the dry, crunchy grass. The wind picked up and the temperature was dropping. He stuffed his hands into the front pockets of his jeans to keep them warm and felt a folded piece of paper. Skylar's note. He pulled it out and unfolded it. It simply read, "Call me!" with an exclamation point, except a heart took the place of the period at the bottom of the punctuation. *Really?*

He didn't feel like talking to anyone but for some reason he kept telling himself to call her. Why not? No harm could be found in simply finding out what she wanted. He took out his phone and looked her up in the senior class directory.

She picked up after the third ring. "Hello?"

"Sky, hey, it's Parker. Um, you asked me to call you. So what do you want?" The background noise coming through the phone clearly indicated she was still at the game.

"Nothing, you just seem a little off this week, so I thought I'd check on you. Did you just quit in the middle of the game? Everyone's talking about it. You okay?"

"I've been better," he replied as he got closer to his car and fished in his pocket for the keys.

"Sorry to hear about you and Summer."

Parker laughed out loud. "Yeah, I bet you are."

"No, I'm serious. I'm sure it's been tough on you…" She kept talking but Parker tuned her out as he abruptly stopped.

"You gotta be kidding me," he said as he cut her off in mid-sentence.

"What's the matter?"

"I've got a flat. Look, I better go. I need to call my dad since I don't have a jack or a spare."

"What do you mean you don't have a jack or a spare?" Skylar giggled. "You live in the country, for crying out loud."

"Hey, it's not like I go off-roading or anything, so give me a break." He stepped closer and examined the deflated tire.

"Well, I can help you out, Mr. Quarterback. My daddy taught me that a girl should never be without a spare tire and tools. Where are you?"

"Sky, you don't have to do that. I can handle this, okay?"

"Whatever. I'm already walking to my car. Where are you parked?"

Parker sighed. Calling Dad would probably be awkward in light of their recent conversation. "Next to the practice field."

"Great. Be there in a second."

He ended the call and leaned against his car. The speakers and the roar of the crowd in the distance sliced through the night air. He listened to ascertain if they were winning or losing, but his mind wandered to the strange girl he'd seen when he'd left the stadium. Who was she? And why all the staring?

His thoughts were interrupted when headlights rounded the corner, brakes squeaking. Skylar pulled up in her Kia Sportage, parked in the middle of the street next to his car, and got out.

"All right, big boy, Miss Skylar is here to take care of your little flat tire." She headed to the rear of her vehicle and pulled out the jack. She lifted the flooring of the cargo space to retrieve the temporary spare.

"Thanks." Parker walked up next to her and hauled out the tire and carried it to the front of his car. She followed behind him with the jack and then sat down in the grass while he positioned and adjusted the jack under his car. Fortunately, he'd parked close to a street lamp that gave him enough light to see.

"Um, you probably don't want to sit there," he said when he noticed where she sat. "Ants in the grass." She jumped up and swiped at the back of her jeans.

"Are there any on me?" She edged up close to Parker and bent over, resting her hands on her knees and looking back at him over her shoulder. The attractive features of her swimmer's body in her tight denim provided quite a sight.

Parker cleared his throat. "No. Um, you're fine," he answered quickly.

She smiled and straightened up, backed up a few paces, and let him work on changing the tire. "Do I really make you that nervous?"

Why can't you just stand there and be quiet? He cranked the jack, and the front of the car slowly rose off the pavement. "No, it's just that all my time with Summer, I've tried to avoid any compromising situations. She's kinda territorial, you know, over-protective."

"Is that why you broke up with her?"

"I really don't want to talk about that, okay?" He studied the car, satisfied he'd elevated it enough to accommodate the temporary tire. Skylar rambled about the cancellation of the school's musical, which he tuned out as he worked.

"Aw, a puppy. Where'd you come from?" Skylar squatted as a basset hound waddled up next to her, its droopy ears flopping with every step. She scratched the top of the dog's ears, and it whined in satisfaction.

Strange. Briar Ridge was suddenly a Mecca for bassets. And, did all bassets look alike? Same black-and-brown coat. White-tipped tail. This one sure looked familiar.

The dog yawned and waddled up the street with slow, measured steps.

Parker reached for the flat tire and placed his hands on either side to pull it off after he'd removed the nuts holding it in place. His right hand touched something odd, out of place. He leaned forward, his eyes focused.

His jaw dropped at the sight of a steak knife protruding from the tire. The gray, almost silver-looking handle with a gold circle in the middle of it froze Parker. The blade had been inserted into the tire almost to the hilt, leaving a gash in the rubber nearly an inch wide where the air had escaped. He jerked his head up and scanned the area. Nothing but the parked cars of his teammates and a big semi-trailer truck at the end of the block stood on the street.

"What's wrong?"

"Nothing," he replied as calmly as he could, not wanting to alarm her. Somewhere off in the dark, a dog barked.

He pulled out the steak knife and shoved it into the pocket of his letter jacket. He changed the tire and thanked Skylar for the assistance, promising to return the temporary tire as soon as he got it replaced. He walked back to her car and put the tire jack where it belonged and then wiped his hands on his jeans. When he came back to his car, Skylar sat on the front hood, her legs dangling off the side.

"Um, what are you doing?" he asked.

"Just checking out your handiwork," she replied with a smile. She wiggled and bounced on the hood a few times. "You do good work, Mr. Austin. Not bad at all."

"So relieved that you approve." Parker stepped closer to her and Skylar scooted up to the edge of the car and sat up straight. He stood a few feet in front of her, their eyes meeting, but refused to move any closer. She looked at him intently. He held her gaze, but the glint in her eyes made him nervous, like she was famished and he was the meal.

No wonder it'd been difficult choosing between the two. Taller than Summer, Skylar had an athletic, toned body from constantly swimming at the lake. Her dark hair, bright blue eyes, and high cheekbones added to her attractiveness.

He recalled the few times that he and Skylar had spent together when he'd first moved to Briar Ridge, back when everything was new and different. He remained lost in those thoughts when he suddenly realized she was calling him and motioning to him with her index finger.

The steak knife, the football game, his parents, Summer, school, even the shooting, faded from memory for the moment. His body moved toward her. She grabbed him by his letter jacket and pulled him close.

The dog continued barking, followed by the start of the big semi-trailer's diesel engine at the end of the street. He turned his head in the sound's direction, but a smooth, silky hand guided him back to Skylar. His mouth opened to speak, but she held a finger to his lips to shush him as she wrapped her legs around his waist. Skylar leaned toward him, and her moist lips parted.

The abrupt sound of someone clearing her throat stopped them. Parker and Skylar turned in the direction of the noise to see a figure strolling down the sidewalk on the opposite side of the street. The silhouette of long, cascading hair clearly showed the person was female.

Skylar scowled as if to say, "Beat it."

The girl slid her hands into her pants pockets and lingered for a moment, then continued her slow trek. The beam of the street lamp revealed strawberry-blonde hair and a green sweater.

"Now—" Skylar flashed a devilish grin. "—where were we?" She moved toward him again.

"Um, wait a second." He pulled back. "This…" He paused, as an uneasy feeling gnawed at him and he searched for the right words. "…this doesn't feel right."

Her shoulders slouched and her body went slack. "What do you mean? What's wrong?"

He scratched the back of his head. "Look, I'm sorry, okay? But, I just can't do this right now." The words tumbled out slowly, as if his mind struggled to comprehend that he was really rejecting her.

No response came from Skylar. Her jawline hardened, no doubt from disappointment. She studied his face, maybe hoping he'd reconsider.

He shook his head. "I'm sorry. I can't."

She bit her lip, slid off the car's hood without bothering

to ask him to step aside, and brushed past him. She shuffled to her car without another word and drove off.

CHAPTER 24

Suzy watched in silence as Parker walked away and went inside the field house. Since he wasn't playing, there was no point in staying for the game. So she decided to go home with Kenneth. She knew it was a mistake as soon as she closed her passenger door.

"He quit. Unbelievable!" Kenneth muttered in disgust as he slammed his door shut. "What in the world was he thinking?"

She let it pass. Maybe he just needed to vent a little.

The car sped out of the parking lot, gravel kicking at parked vehicles as they exited. "Never thought I'd see my boy quit like that."

The brakes squeaked as they made a sharp turn onto Wabash.

"Honey, please slow down."

He shot her a sideways glance and shook his head. "I don't know why you're not upset about this. Doesn't his quitting bother you at all?"

She sighed. *Should've stayed at the game.* "Yes, but I think there are bigger issues here than Park playing football."

"Bull. Quitting is going to cause him even bigger problems down the road. He's just going have to admit he made a mistake and ask to rejoin the team. That's all there is to it."

She leaned back in her seat and folded her hands in her lap. "That's not all there is to it, I'm afraid."

They got home before Parker and decided to wait for him at the breakfast table in the kitchen.

"He's got to play," her husband said, sucking on a piece of butterscotch from their stash of leftover Halloween candy. "He just has to."

Suzy brought over a steaming cup of hot chocolate and set it on the table in front of him. She sipped her coffee and pulled out the chair across from him. "Why?"

He rolled the candy in his mouth and slid it to one side. "Because playing football is the best thing for him right now, honey. He needs to be around his teammates. They can support him."

"He needs to be around his parents."

"I'm not saying he doesn't, but being around friends every day can help him in ways we can't."

Suzy blew across the top of her coffee mug. "He's been around them all this week, and it doesn't seem to have helped." She took a sip. "Pass me some chocolate."

Kenneth shoved a piece of candy toward her.

Almond Joy? Yuck. "You know I don't like coconut." She tossed aside the candy bar. "Give me that one," she said, nodding at a different piece.

Another bar slid across the tabletop.

"Is this a joke? I don't eat dark chocolate. What's the matter with you?"

He snickered.

"What are you, eight years old? Forget it, I'll get my own." She reached across the table and rummaged through the candy pile in front of him. Reese's Peanut Butter Cups. *That's more like it.* She unfolded the wrapper and sank her teeth into the candy. Was there any better combination than chocolate and peanut butter?

She finished the first cup in two bites and licked the smudged chocolate off her fingertips. "Sweetheart, I understand he needs his friends, but from what I've seen this past week, they haven't helped. I mean, Park seems to be getting worse. The way he went after that Gibson boy—we're lucky that car was stolen and that kid was involved with the shooting. Otherwise—"

"Please. You saw the look on Boddicker's face. He was glad Park did what he did and turned him in. Otherwise, the police would still be looking for a big piece of the puzzle." He brought the cup of hot chocolate to his mouth but stopped. He frowned. "No marshmallows?"

Suzy glanced at the refrigerator adorned with Abby's artwork and report cards. "No, I haven't been to the store yet." Shopping for only three wasn't something she was looking forward to. She forced herself to turn away from the refrigerator and ignored the knot in her stomach.

Kenneth took a big gulp from his mug and set it back down. "Look, all I'm saying is that he needs structure right now, and football can give him that."

"Honey, who cares about football? He's a senior. Football season is almost over anyway. It's not like he'll just keep on playing forever and will always have that *structure* around him."

"But he needs everything that can possibly help him right now."

"Yes, he needs all the help he can get, but we're the ones who need to help him the most—not football. In fact, playing right now may not be such a good idea."

"I'm all for helping him, honey, so let's get him to talk to us."

Suzy took out the second peanut butter cup and unwrapped it. "Okay, but we can't force it on him. Let's—"

"Wrong. The best way to help him is to handle this like an intervention. Confront him, make him talk to us."

"Confronting him may turn him farther away."

"No. That's how you deal with this stuff. I've seen it before. You can't ignore it or hope things just get better on their own. You have to take a stand and deal with it."

They waited for over an hour. Eventually, a haggard-looking Parker walked through the garage door. When he entered the kitchen and saw them sitting at the table, he stopped dead in his tracks.

Suzy cleared her throat and spoke first. "Park, your father and I would like to talk with you about how you're doing. We're concerned about you. Can you sit down, please?"

He sighed. "Look, I'm really not up to this right now. I just want to take a shower and go to bed, okay? Can we do this later?"

"Park, we're worried about you. We haven't talked much since the shooting. I mean, we really haven't talked as a family about what's happened." She took another sip of coffee. "You didn't go to church with us the last two Sundays, you broke up with Summer, you've grown distant, and now you've quit football."

"Not tonight, okay?"

Kenneth looked directly at Parker. "Son, what's going on with you? Why did you quit on your team in the middle of the game?" The edge in his voice was sharp enough to cut metal.

Suzy winced and bit her lip. Thoughts of smacking Kenneth appealed to her, but self-control won out. She glared in his direction and then turned back to Parker.

"Park, we're worried. Our family has been through a lot lately, and we just need to check in with you. Can you please talk to us? What can we help you with?"

Parker shrugged. "Nothing. Let's do this later. I really want to shower and go to bed, all right?" He trudged out of the kitchen and through the family room on his way to his bathroom, where they soon heard running water.

A sarcastic huff blew out of Kenneth's nose. "That went well."

"What's wrong with you? Why did you force the issue with him?"

"Because you dancing around, being all polite, wasn't helping. I told you, we have to make him sit down and talk to us, whether he likes it or not, whether it's painful or not. That's the only way to get it out of him."

Suzy rubbed the inside corners of her eyes. Her head throbbed like an anvil beaten with a hammer. "Let's just go to bed and try to talk with him in the morning."

They got dressed for bed without a word to one another, which only irritated Suzy even further. Why did he always shut down and refuse to speak whenever they argued? That didn't help solve anything.

They lay in bed and watched television in silence until drifting off to sleep around eleven o'clock. Shortly after midnight, Suzy awoke to the sounds of screaming. She sat up, listened, as she tried to wipe away the cobwebs of sleep from her senses. *Oh, no. Not again.*

She shook Kenneth, whose loud snores reverberated around the room even with his head buried under his pillow. He moved slowly at first, but he soon sat up.

Suzy dashed out of bed and ran into the hallway toward Park's bedroom with Kenneth trailing behind her. Park's agonizing screams seemed to fill the house. She flew into her son's room and ran to his bedside where he screamed incoherently, flopping on his bed like a fish and wrestling with the covers.

Kenneth turned on the light and raced to the bedside next to Suzy. "Park! Park!" They both called out to their thrashing boy as they tried to control his violent spasms. His eyes were shut tight, his forehead and face sweaty. The dank, foul odor of urine hung in the air.

It took a solid minute to get Park under control and for him to awaken from the night terrors. Panting and breathless, he was pale and exhausted from the fight in his sleep. He looked down at the wet bedsheets and his soaked boxers. He got up and stormed off to the bathroom, slamming the door shut behind him and turning on the shower.

Without a word, Suzy pulled off the soiled sheets from Parker's bed and carried them to the laundry room. She returned, flipped over the mattress, and put on a fresh set of linens. Worry ate at her insides, and her palms turned clammy. *Something has to be done. He's getting worse.*

She put the pillows back in place and stopped by Parker's bathroom door. The shower had stopped running and she gently knocked.

No answer. Another knock. Nothing.

"Park?"

The door opened and Parker stepped out, a dark blue towel wrapped around his waist. He didn't say anything, but as he passed she placed her hands on his wet shoulders. He paused.

"I changed the sheets for you."

"Thanks," he whispered.

She leaned in and gave him a quick hug. "I love you, Park. It's going to be okay."

He nodded and then broke from her embrace. He walked to his room and shut the door behind him.

Suzy returned to her room. Kenneth sat in the middle of the bed, channel surfing. She walked around to her side of the king-sized bed and faced him. "We have to do something. It's getting worse, and he just can't keep going like this." How many more nights were they going to be awakened by Parker's frightening screams? This was at least the sixth. And each night, the screams were more terrifying than the night before.

Kenneth stopped surfing. The television channel had stopped on a tape-delayed, late-night talk show. He nodded while staring at the television screen. Almost a minute went by in silence.

"Kenneth?"

"I know," he said. "He's got to get over it somehow." He looked at her. "I don't know exactly how to do that or what we need to do to help, but he's got to overcome it." He turned away. "I just don't want him to run from it like he's doing. I don't want this to become a habit for him. It'll cause him bigger problems in the long run."

It was easy to understand what Kenneth alluded to, and

who could blame him? "You're thinking about your mom?" It was more of a statement than a question.

"I spent my whole childhood watching her refuse to confront dad's drinking and the beatings. She retreated, ran from it, and it slowly wore her down until she was only a shell of the woman I knew and loved, incapable of standing on her own two feet."

His eyes remained on the television, but Suzy doubted he was even aware of what was on the screen.

"I feel so helpless." His brow furrowed, jaws clenched, lips pursed tightly together. "I thought if she saw me stand up to him all those times, redirect his anger toward me and away from her, Chris, and Stacie, she'd learn to do it herself."

Suzy sat down on the edge of the bed.

Kenneth shook his head as he continued to stare blankly at Jimmy Kimmel. "I couldn't save her—and I couldn't save my own daughter, either."

"Oh, honey, please," she said, her voice barely above a whisper. "Please don't do this to yourself. There was nothing you could've done. There was nothing anyone could've done. I mean, nobody could've seen this coming. It just happened." Tears pooled in her eyes.

"A father is supposed to look out for his family, protect them, keep 'em safe. If only I'd gotten to her in time, I..." His voice trailed off, his sentence unfinished.

"If you had gotten down to the field, maybe you would be dead, too." Suzy sighed. "We can play 'what if' all night. What if I hadn't fired Misty and didn't have to work that night? I could've been there. Maybe I could've gotten to her, too." Her gaze drifted toward their bedroom door. "I suspect that's part of what's bothering Park. He probably regrets having Abby down there with the team. If he hadn't arranged for her to be there, maybe she'd still be alive."

She took a deep breath and exhaled. "For the last ten years, Park and Abby have been two sides of the same coin. Without Park, Abby never could've learned to be so strong.

Without Abby, Park never could've learned to be so empathetic and caring. Now, without Abby to balance the coin, I'm afraid for him. I'm afraid what he might become without her." She turned and faced Kenneth.

His hands were balled into tight fists as he continued to stare at the television. "I don't know what to do."

She crawled behind him on her knees and wrapped her arms around him. He leaned back into her embrace.

"We've already lost Abby," she whispered into his ear, "we can't lose Park." She gently rocked him until his fists unclenched and his body relaxed. "We've got to find a way to reach him, to help him."

Kenneth nodded and Suzy kissed the top of his head. He reached up and squeezed her arm. They sat for a moment in the middle of the bed, gently rocking in silence.

Suzy wasn't sure how best to approach Parker, nor was she sure how to help him, although she'd exhaust every resource to do so. Kenneth turned off the television and she let go of him.

"Thanks," he said as he turned around and adjusted his pillows. She got under the covers and lay next to him.

Suzy tried to relax, but uncertainty and anxiety still clung to her. Only one thing could be done right now. She clasped her hands together, closed her eyes, and prayed.

CHAPTER 25

Parker awoke in his bed as another gray dawn filtered through the blinds on his windows. He felt as though he'd just run a marathon. He took a few deep breaths and rolled over onto his back. He pried his eyelids open and blinked several times until the room came into focus. The ceiling fan spun in a monotone whirl, dispensing a cool, gentle breeze against his skin as the memories of last night came back to him.

There'd been no plan to quit in the middle of the game. It had just sort of happened, but the possible ramifications of his actions upon the team sank in for the first time. The fallout couldn't be good, but it didn't matter. The plan for moving on and getting out of town was still a go.

There was also Skylar. That'd certainly been a major bullet he had dodged. If they'd kissed and Summer had found out—Parker cringed at the possible outcomes. Still, it hadn't happened, thanks in large part to the mysterious girl who showed up at just the right time.

He sat up and swung his legs over the side and planted his bare feet on the carpet. His letter jacket lay on the floor, the steak knife protruding from the front pocket. Who slashed the tire? Why would they do that? A deranged fan, maybe, upset that he'd quit during the game everyone was using for some cathartic purpose. If so, it was proof positive that not only was everyone in this podunk town a hick, but their minds were as twisted as a crazy straw. He shook his head and stood, rummaging through a stack of laundry until he found a clean T-shirt, and then walked out into the hallway, pulling it over his head.

For the first time since the shooting, he found himself wanting to eat. Hunger pangs racked his body as he walked toward the kitchen. He passed the living room, where Mom sat in her favorite reading chair next to the piano, sipping coffee with an open bible in her lap. His bare feet shuffled into the kitchen, and he headed straight for the pantry.

Powdered doughnuts and microwaveable breakfast burritos? Breakfast of champions. He poured himself some orange juice, plated the food, and sat down at the table next to the bay window just in time to watch Dad perform the exciting task of raking leaves in the backyard.

The first three doughnuts had just gone down, his fingers covered in sticky white powder, when Mom walked into the kitchen. She stood behind the counter and leaned on her elbows while holding her coffee mug.

"Morning, Park." She took a quiet sip of her coffee.

He swallowed and took a giant swig of orange juice. "Morning," he replied, stifling a burp. He devoured his breakfast as though famished. Mom normally would've commented about the need to slow down, yet she just stood there, watching and saying nothing. *Something's up.*

He scarfed down the first burrito and, without pausing for breath, had begun working on the second, when Dad walked into the kitchen from the back porch.

Despite the coolness of the morning, tiny drops of perspiration covered his forehead. He pulled off his thick work gloves and sat down at the table while Mom poured him some ice water.

Here it comes. Better make the first move. "All right, get this over with," Parker said with an air of resignation. He sat up and took one last gulp of orange juice. "I'm done. I'm done playing football, I'm done with Briar Ridge High School, and I'm done with this town. There's nothing here I want, and nothing I want to be a part of, okay? I want out of here, I *need* to get out of here."

"What do you mean you're 'done?'" Dad asked.

"I mean exactly that. I'm finished. I'm cutting ties and moving on."

"You can when you graduate next May and go to college."

Here we go. Parker's stomach twisted, and he looked at his father. "I'm not waiting until next May. I'm graduating next month."

Dad sat back in his chair, eyes drifting away while Mom took several long gulps of coffee. The wind blew the thin, barren, outstretched ends of a tree branch against the top of the bay window, making a soft tapping and scratching sound as it bounced and twisted with the waves of cold air.

Clearly they hadn't been expecting this. Better to take advantage of their stunned silence and plow ahead. "I've got enough credits to qualify for graduation, so there's no need to hang around all spring. I've already checked with our counselor and with Principal Mooney, who have confirmed that I can graduate in December—if I want to—which I do."

Dad shook his head. "No," he said in a quiet but firm tone, quickly regaining his composure. "You're not running from this, Parker. You're going to finish school in May."

"Dad, I can't stay here, all right? I've got to get out of this town."

"You can't solve problems by running from them, son. That's my point. Believe me, if you start running now, you'll regret it, because it'll only make things worse for you. And I'm not going to let you do that."

Mom still hadn't said a word up to this point. She turned around and refilled her coffee cup. She blew across the top of it while she walked around from behind the counter and stood next to Dad, placing a hand on his shoulder. "I share your father's concern, Park. I really think you should try to work through this with us. We're still a family, and you don't run out on your family."

"I'm not running out on y'all, but it's impossible for me to stay here. In case you haven't noticed, I'm reminded twenty-four-seven by this place about what happened. My name is all over TV and the news, everyone talks about me wherever I go, and it's haunting me in my sleep." *Why can't they understand?* Parker's chest tightened. "The nightmares are getting worse, not better. In fact, I'm to the point now that I'm scared to shut my eyes because the next time I open them, I'll be lying in my own piss. I've just got to get out of here."

"You can always see someone about this. There's help out there that we can get you," Mom replied.

Parker scowled. "No, I'm not going to talk to some stupid shrink. I'm not crazy."

They spent the next ten minutes arguing back and forth with each side deadlocked against the other. Parker was adamant that he needed to get out of Briar Ridge. Mom and Dad seemed equally adamant about staying and working with them through the grieving process. It wasn't until he told them that he'd already applied for admission to a university that they seemed to realize it didn't matter how they felt.

"Which one?" asked Mom, who now sat at the table next to Dad.

"Red River State University in Dover. It's about a five-hour drive from here—far enough to get away and start over."

"And my next question is, how did you apply for admission since neither I nor your father signed an application?"

Parker glanced at the ceiling and massaged his forehead for a moment. "You didn't need to sign anything, Mom. I'm already eighteen and applications are done on-line now. Look, I'm guaranteed admission since I'm now in the top ten percent of my class due to some absences. I also qualify for some academic scholarships and Pell grants, which will help cover the cost of tuition. Believe me, I've spent two weeks looking into this, and it's going to work out."

Mom and Dad exchanged glances but didn't say anything.

"I appreciate what y'all are saying, but I have *got* to get out of here. I've got to go somewhere where I can move on, where I can put myself back together. This is an opportunity for me to do that, plus start my college education, which is something y'all have been preaching to me about for years. So, why wouldn't you be in favor of this?"

"Son, I don't care how you describe it, you're still running. I don't like it, and I won't support it." Dad drained the remainder of his ice water, stood up from the table, and walked out of the kitchen. He returned to the backyard and resumed the chore of raking leaves, though no leaf remained to be raked.

A few moments passed before Mom broke the silence. "Park, it's not that your father and I don't want you to heal and go to college. We do. We're just not in favor of the manner in which you've chosen to do so." She took a deep breath and sighed. "We're concerned that this is a bit rash and might actually be doing you more harm than good."

"I understand, Mom. But I've got to go. I can't stay here any longer." He leveled his gaze directly at her, set his jaw as if preparing to make a final, emphatic announcement. "I'm leaving."

She looked at him for a while, her blue eyes probing him before responding, and took another drink from her coffee mug. "Park, I know you think this is the best thing for you right now, but I just wish you'd slow this down a bit and rethink your decision. It's important, sweetie, and you need to make sure you've made the right choice."

She slid her hands halfway across the table as if she wanted to reach for him, take hold of his hands. "I know none of this has been easy. I just—"

"Easy?" Parker's lips curled into a snarl. "You've got no idea what it's been like, Mom."

She made no reply, but raised an eyebrow, a look of motherly concern plastered across her face. "Tell me."

Parker shifted in his seat. The memory of coming home from school and finding Abby crying on her bed after the McGonagill boys assaulted her came roaring back. Even though it'd been three years, it still stung as if it'd just happened yesterday.

"When the McGonagills beat up Abby that day at school, I spent the whole night with Abby, holding her, making sure she was okay. Remember?"

Mom nodded, but didn't seem to be breathing.

"Well, you know what I did when I was holding her? I spent the entire time telling her I'd never let her get hurt again, that I was her big brother and that I'd always keep her safe. I just kept telling her that over and over again." He tilted forward into the table. "Well, guess what? I screwed up, and she died right in front of me." A lump formed in his throat, but he swallowed hard to move past it.

"Oh, Park," Mom said softly, stretching her hands farther across the table.

He looked away and leaned back in his chair as the shooting flashed through his mind again.

"Easy?" he asked quietly, trying to blink away the gathering tears. "First, I had to see Joe Bob Swain take a bullet in his throat, blood squirting out all over the place. You should've seen the look on his face. He had no idea what had happened to him. He just looked at me, his eyes pleading for me to help him, but I couldn't. I couldn't even say anything to him."

He turned his head toward the kitchen. Trinkets and mementos of both him and Abby still covered the stainless steel refrigerator. Newspaper clippings containing write-ups about his on-field performances in past games and various pieces of Abby's artwork from school were held to the appliance by magnets.

"Park, it's okay to be angry," she said, her voice gentle but pleading. "Just don't let that change what you are."

He ignored the comment. "And Abby? She couldn't even run away." He shook his head at the memory of Abby standing in her walker, screaming for him to help her. "The way she was born, she never had a chance."

He faced her, felt the anger and guilt building within. "For the rest of my life, I'll never be able to get that scared look of hers out of my mind. Her face and those screams—I had to watch her die. To see her bleed all over me and watch her take her last breath—and now, knowing that it was my fault—" Parker cleared his throat again to keep from breaking down. A solitary tear trickled down his cheek.

"Park, it wasn't your fault, sweetie. It wasn't—"

"Yes, it was, Mom," he interrupted. "It's all my fault. If I hadn't beaten up Billy and Brian for going after Abby, none of this would've happened. Even if it did, if I hadn't gotten Abby to be on the sidelines, she never would've been down there in the first place." Parker's voice cracked as another tear fell from watery eyes. "But she was—and I was too slow to save her."

He wiped his eyes and paused to collect himself then pushed back his chair and stood from the table, hands on his hips. "So, no, Mom, things haven't been easy."

He stormed out of the kitchen and left her alone at the table.

CHAPTER 26

After spending the majority of the day reviewing on-campus housing options at Red River State and looking through their on-line course catalogue, he sorely needed a break from the house. Besides, Mom and Dad were shunning him. Why stick around for that?

Dad spent most of the day piddling in the backyard on unnecessary chores. The tool shed didn't need to be reshingled, Parker had already chopped enough firewood to build a log cabin, and mid-November seemed an odd time to fertilize a lawn. Even periodic glances at his father through his bedroom window went unacknowledged. *Whatever.*

Mom spent the majority of the day doing housework that had been neglected over the past two weeks. Piles of laundry took the brunt of her frustration. Something about whites must've made her angry. After rounding up all of Parker's dirty whites, she washed and dried them, and dumped them in his room only to return thirty minutes later and throw the same pile of whites into the washing machine. This insanity was repeated several times, but at least he'd have the cleanest undershirts and socks in Joe Wheeler County.

The only major interruption came after lunch when the doorbell rang. Parker shuffled to the door to find Coach Sinc standing on the front porch, leaning on his cane.

Uh oh. News of last night's loss had traveled quickly, with most of the finger-pointing leveled in Parker's direction. In fact, angry text messages and voicemails flooded his phone, but he didn't care. Still, he hadn't expected a visit by Coach Sinc.

He cracked open the door. "Coach?"

"Hi, Park. Can I come in for a minute? It won't take long."

If Coach was here to ask him to come back to the team, Parker could save him the trouble. Still, there was no point in being rude. Coach Sinc was a good guy. "Um…okay."

They each took a seat in the living room, Coach Sinc watching Parker intently.

"Park, I just want to get a few things off my chest, and then I'll be going."

Parker nodded, but found it difficult to keep eye contact with Coach Sinc.

"First, I want to express to you again my condolences about your sister. I can't even begin to imagine what you and your family must be going through, so I won't even try to say I know how you feel. But please know how very sorry I am."

A mumbled, "Thanks," was all Parker could muster.

"Second, I owe you an apology."

Parker's head twisted in Coach Sinc's direction. An apology? What for? Parker had been the one who had quit, in the middle of a game for crying out loud.

"I knew you weren't ready to go back out there, Park. I saw it all week long at practice. And I should've held you out of the game, but I didn't. I knew how much this town needed to see us take the field and how important it was to bring them a win. And I confess a part of it was my own selfish need to win, too. It's kind of hard to win without your best player. So…"

Parker crossed his legs and adjusted the clean, white sock on his left foot.

"Anyway. It was wrong for me to put you out there

knowing you weren't in the right frame of mind. I'm sorry."

Another muted nod.

Coach Sinc winced, and he rolled over to his left side. He thrust his hand into his pants pocket and retrieved a small bottle. He popped it open and quickly shoved three pills into his mouth. With one swallow, he forced them down, took a deep breath, and exhaled.

"Pain?"

Coach Sinc nodded. "Yeah." He twisted the cane in his hand, the tip making a soft grinding noise on the carpet floor. His eyes locked onto Parker. "Although I'll always carry the scars of what happened that night, the pain is only temporary. It won't last."

Parker shifted in his chair, the cushion suddenly feeling hard and uncomfortable.

"That's the funny thing about pain. It can either sharpen our mind and get our attention so we can focus on what we need to do, or it can make us want to withdraw, detach ourselves from everything, and slowly sink to the bottom. Either way, the pain isn't permanent. It'll eventually fade, and when it does we'll have to decide how to live with the choices we've made and how best to move forward without letting the memory of the pain overwhelm us."

Parker picked at something under a fingernail, glanced at Coach Sinc, and looked out the window at the sunless sky. How many days had it been since he'd last seen the sun? Fourteen? Fifteen?

"Well, I guess I better get going. That's all I needed to say." Coach Sinc struggled to his feet and Parker walked him to the door.

"I wish you the best, Parker. I truly mean that," he said, offering a hand. "If you ever need anything, if there's anything I can ever do for you, don't hesitate to let me know." He shook Parker's hand with a firm grip, and then limped back to his car.

Parker watched him hobble down the sidewalk. A mixture of emotions swirled inside him. Was there sadness at disappointing Coach Sinc? Sure, he could never imagine playing for a better coach or for someone he could respect more. But relief at turning the page on a chapter in his life seemed to melt every bit of tension and worry in his body. A weight had been lifted from his shoulders, and restlessness gnawed at him. Time to get out and enjoy the light now plainly visible at the end of the tunnel.

Who was there to share in the excitement of impending freedom? The options were slim. Mom and Dad? Out of the question. Teammates? Judging by the voicemails and text messages, none of them, including Tyler, were thrilled with him at the moment and would probably take a swing at him if they could. Summer? Although she remained the one person who knew him best, the recent breakup made things way too awkward. Skylar? No way, not unless he wanted Summer to hunt him down and cut out his appendix with a spoon.

No, flying solo fit. The town didn't want him, and he didn't want the town. He grabbed his letter jacket and told his parents he was going out for a while. Neither seemed all that interested, and both gave the impression they were still sore from their previous conversation that morning.

He threw on his letter jacket and stepped outside. A chilly mist hung in the air, the skies depressingly overcast as usual, but Parker didn't seem to mind as much now. A bounce in his step propelled him to his car, where the hubcap-less, temporary spare stood out like a sore thumb. He crossed to the driver-side door, opened it, and sat down.

A sharp pain struck in the middle of his back. He let out a cry and shot himself forward into the steering wheel. He twisted in his seat to look behind him, eyes scanning the backrest. A metal tip jutted out from the upholstery. His eyes focused as shaky fingers caressed the object. The knife point of a blade extended out from the car seat by almost an inch. Grimacing, he got out of his car and squatted next to the driver's seat to take a closer look. Someone had cut a small hole into the upholstery and shoved in the knife, the blade handle clearly visible from the back of the seat.

No way. He pulled the steak knife he had found in his tire from the pocket of his letter jacket. They matched.

Parker stood and looked around. A visual inspection revealed nothing that gave the impression that anyone lurked nearby, and he returned his attention to the steak knife. He pulled it out of his car seat. Turning it over in his hand several times didn't reveal any clues as to who exactly had done this.

Still smarting, he shoved the knife into his jacket pocket with the other one and tried to examine his wound. The knife had broken the skin. His fingertips revealed blood when he ran his hand over the point of entry. Fortunately, the puncture seemed minor since his thick letter jacket had insulated him. The intent had not been to kill but to harm. Someone was sending a message for sure. But who? And, why?

Going back inside the house to tell his parents what had happened would only freak out Mom. She'd call the police, and the last thing needed at this point was more attention. Dad was liable to go house-to-house searching for whoever had done it and then drag them into the street for a royal beat-down.

No, it was better to tell them later, after he had thought about this over a plate of tacos.

He got back into his car and drove to the west side of town toward Chateau d' Taco. A dull pain throbbed in his back, prompting guesses about who might have planted the knife and why they'd done it. How it had been done wasn't that big of a mystery since he routinely left his car unlocked in the driveway. Like most small-town residents, everyone in Briar Ridge left their front doors unlocked, but why anyone would want to literally stab someone in the back was beyond Parker's thinking. Maybe it was a zealous fan, extremely upset at him for quitting the team. Maybe the knife in the back symbolized his quitting, some lunatic equating Parker's walking out on the team as a form of stabbing the town in the back and this was a sick attempt to even the score.

The more he thought about it, the more it bothered him, and the more it bothered him, the more it reinforced his opinion of the town and the desire to leave it behind—for good.

By the time he pulled into the parking lot of the small restaurant, his stomach stopped growling. He got out of the car and walked into the restaurant, his back aching from the slight wound. He ordered a taco plate and sat down in one of the brown upholstered booths along the row of windows to keep an eye on his car.

He squirmed in his seat, trying to find a comfortable position for his back. The steak knives were the same for sure. That couldn't be a coincidence. They had to be from the same person. A stalker perhaps?

A waitress, smacking gum that could be heard on the far side of the moon, brought over his food and set it down in front of him. It was just now five o'clock, and the dinner crowd hadn't quite arrived yet. Only two other customers were present, both of whom sat by themselves scarfing down their food. They didn't seem to notice him.

He grabbed the first taco off his plate and was in the act of bringing it up to his mouth to take his first bite when a distinct color of hair appeared through the window.

His arm stopped in mid-motion as the strawberry-blonde girl stood outside the restaurant.

CHAPTER 27

The time for direct action had come, or so Marie told herself. She'd been watching Parker closely for the past two weeks, and she hadn't liked what she'd seen. In fact, each day seemed to exacerbate her anxiety. Every attempt to speak to him, to break through the clutter, only resulted in him tuning her out. More worrisome, he no longer *believed.*

This had happened with two or three others over the years, and so it was nothing new, but the reality of losing Parker hurt far more than the previous charges. This was the price for this line of work. Things didn't always turn out the way she wanted—it was that simple. After all, one of the greatest gifts had been the gift of choice, and he was just exercising it.

It was the consequences of those choices that made it all the more painful to watch. Normally, subtle hints were dropped along the way that would help charges reflect on their decisions, giving them ample opportunity to reconsider, but in this case time was of the essence. Imminent danger now loomed. And should events unfold unfavorably, events that could cost him his life, he would be lost forever. Gone. Into the cold, dark oblivion, never to be seen or heard from again.

The very thought made her sick.

No more sitting on the sidelines and working from a distance. No more being subtle. The time to act was now. Bold. Direct. Before it was too late.

But how would revealing herself to him turn out? There was no way to know. It was a huge risk. What if he freaked out? Or worse, what if he laughed her out of the room with his disbelief? He'd dismiss her and be in just as much danger as before. Whatever she did, it had to work. There would be no second chances.

Confronting him called for walking a fine line with what she could tell him. She couldn't warn him of the danger he was in, and she could not fully answer his questions, but just maybe the revelation of her existence could prompt him to rethink things before he acted.

But when she reached for the glass door of the restaurant, the sound of her name startled her.

"Marie, what do you think you're doing?" a hardened voice asked.

An old, dusty, denim-covered rancher sat on a bench a few feet away, his weathered hands rhythmically stroking a knife, shavings falling around mud-covered boots as he whittled a piece of wood.

"I'm going to save him, Markus. I'm not going to lose him if something happens to him."

"I understand you want to protect him, save him even." Markus shrugged. "But there's a proper way to go about it, and this isn't it." He shook his head, continued carving the piece of wood for moment. "You're just going to walk right up to the boy and say what, exactly?"

She opened her mouth, but hesitated to answer. The realization that she was unprepared made her uneasy. "I...I don't know yet." Really, she had no idea what to say to him. "But I'll think of something," she quickly added, trying to drum up a confident front.

Markus rolled his eyes. "You're not thinking this through. You can't reveal yourself to him."

"I did it once before, Markus. And it worked. I helped him."

"Yes, you did, and he was so young he probably has no memory of it. But he's not a scared four-year-old boy this time. You reveal yourself to him now, and he's definitely going to remember it, don't you think?"

Marie didn't answer. Her mind swirled, trying to process Markus's comments while attempting to devise a plan of action for confronting Parker. If he was to be saved, she had to find a way. He stopped whittling and motioned for her to join him on the bench. "Come here."

She hesitated at first, then slowly walked over and stood next to the wood and wrought-iron seat, but refused to sit.

"This is awfully rash, and I really wish you'd reconsider. You have no idea of the possible consequences that could unfold as a direct result of your actions." He shifted his weight on the bench and resumed slicing with his pocket-knife. "Has it even occurred to you this might do more harm than good?"

She took a deep breath. Her pulse raced, though she tried to remain calm. "Yes," she answered. "I'm aware of the consequences. I'm also aware of the danger he's in and what will happen to him if he dies."

"We can't control that," he replied. "And there's always risk with—"

"He doesn't believe anymore," she interrupted, on the verge of tears.

"I know," he replied in a huff, giving the wood a rigorous, almost menacing stroke of the pocketknife. "And that happens, you know that. But you can't go off the deep end when it does. You've got to keep talking to him, speaking to him, until he decides to listen again."

"That's my point. He's not listening. He no longer believes, Markus. And you know exactly what will happen to him if that man kills him. He'll be gone, and I'll lose him forever!" Her eyes grew moist and she clasped her hands together as she looked into the distance. "And I can't..." Her voice trailed off as she fought to keep from breaking down.

Markus leaned back and crossed his arms over his chest, watching her battle her emotions. "You're in love with him, aren't you?"

She turned, afraid to make eye contact. Her hands shook as she had to admit the truth. She swallowed. "Yes," she whispered.

Her confession hung in the air as they both veered into uncharted waters. How much trouble would this cause? Would she be removed from her charge and kicked out of the protectorate? Still, she knew only two things at the moment: she loved Parker, and she would do whatever it took to save him.

"Marie, you're standing at the precipice of an abyss right now." His words were soft, gentle. "I really need you to listen to me and step back from it."

When she made no reply, he continued. "Love is the most powerful emotion in the universe. It can inspire the greatest, most wonderful, most beautiful things." His voice lowered an octave. "But it can also serve as the catalyst for the wrong choices. Look at Lucifer. He had everything an angel could ever want, but his love for self led him down the wrong path."

"Oh, Lucifer was a pinhead. Besides—" She glanced over her shoulder. "—that's not even the same thing."

Markus stretched his arm along the top of the bench, striking a comfortable pose. "Okay, let me give you a personal example. I've never told you this. It's something I've never shared with anyone, but I kinda know what you're feeling. I had a charge once, Colette, a sweet eight-year-old girl. She was beautiful, gentle, and kind. Her father was Andre, a blacksmith who was quite fond of touching little girls, even his very own. One night, after watching him slither his hands all over her and listening to her muffled cries, something just snapped in me. I waited for him in his smithy that night, and when he'd gotten his fill with Colette, I appeared to him." Markus's voice, flat and monotone, trailed off, and he paused, no doubt reliving the memory of that night. "Only, I didn't take human form, I appeared to him in my angelic state. My radiance was so bright, I blinded him, robbed him of his vision. He cried and wet his pants like a baby, and I ordered him not to lay a finger on Colette ever again."

Another lengthy pause ensued, the whizzing sound of passing cars slicing through the cold wind along Wabash Avenue the only noise between them.

So Markus did have an idea. "Well, I bet it worked, didn't it?" she asked.

"Sort of. Although he never touched Colette again, the loss of his eyesight prevented Andre from working again. Without a means of support, Colette and her family became destitute. Her mother resorted to prostitution and ended up having her throat slit by a customer. Colette and her brothers and sisters were turned out of their boarding house and into the streets, where she ultimately died of cholera at the age of ten." He cleared his throat a few times, no doubt fending off the emotional pull of his narrative. "My love for Colette got the better of me. I harmed a human and set into motion a series of events that ultimately cost my charge's life." Markus sniffed and took a deep breath. "And that is why I can't let you continue as Parker's guardian."

She spun around. "What?"

Markus folded the pocketknife, slid it into his jeans pocket, and tossed the partially whittled stick of wood onto the sidewalk. "In hindsight, I shouldn't have let you talk me into keeping you after what happened in the cemetery— even the incident at the motel told me you were out of control—but I just can't allow you to remain as his guardian any longer. Your personal feelings are clouding your judgment, and you're about to take some enormous risks that can cause a lot of damage. I'm sorry, Marie, but—"

"What if I refuse?"

His jaw dropped and his eyes narrowed to an angry squint. "*Refuse?*" He spat out the word as if it were blasphemy. "What if I gave a direct order?"

"Markus, please don't do this to me. I just—"

"I beg your pardon. Don't do this to you?" He tilted back his cowboy hat, pulled a toothpick from his shirt pocket, and inserted it into his mouth. "How about you don't do this to me? After all I've done for you, I think I'm the one that's in a position to ask for favors."

She shifted uncomfortably and jabbed at a pebble on the sidewalk with the toe of her shoe. A lonely dried leaf tumbled in the cold wind and skittered across the pavement in front of her. She watched it spin and twirl, much like the chaotic swirl of emotions inside her.

"Marie, who let you into the Protectorate?"

"You did."

"Who saw something in you besides recklessness? Who made you into a guardian?"

"You did."

He slid the toothpick from one side of his mouth to the other. "Who was there for you in Hamburg during the Third Reich? Who helped you save your charge when everyone, and I mean everyone, was losing theirs?"

She pursed her lips. "You, Markus."

He leaned forward and spat on the sidewalk, his eyes boring holes into her with an intensity she'd never seen from him before. "Then I think you owe me one." The weight of his stare and all that it implied forced her to drop her head as her shoulders sagged.

She cast her eyes to the ground for a moment, studying the tiny fissures in the cement sidewalk as she recalled the events he had referenced. He had been the one who recruited her, made her into a guardian when no else would. He had always been there for her, and he'd supported her more times than could be counted. And yet…

"You didn't answer my question. What if I refuse to step aside?"

He dipped his hand into his shirt pocket and withdrew a thin, gold bar—the sight of which froze Marie to the sidewalk—and her stomach churned.

Markus stretched the length of the golden rod and then bent it back on itself until it formed a halo.

"You would use that on me?" she asked, barely able to get the words out of her dry mouth.

"I don't want to, but you're about to leave me with no choice."

She took a step back, fingers curling into her palms, the fists a clear sign of defiance.

"Don't do this. Look, if you care about Parker—if you care about him at all—then you'll listen to me and do exactly as I say."

She gazed at the street, watched the cars pass by for a moment as the wind teased her hair. Would he really fight over this? She shifted her attention back to him. "Again, what happens if I refuse?"

He scowled, pulled the toothpick from his mouth, and pointed it at her. "You'll be crossing the Rubicon if you do, understand? The point of no return. If you refuse to come with me, if you refuse to relinquish your charge, and if you reveal yourself to him, you do so at your own peril, as well as his. If Seth or any of the other fallen confronts you, you're on your own. Neither I nor any other guardian will intervene, understand?"

Marie pondered the consequences of going rogue while continuing to devise a plan. The rules said step aside. Yet every ounce of instinct screamed for her to go in the opposite direction. "If I leave him, you know he's going to die." It was a fact she knew as true as anything. Parker, even with another guardian, stood no chance against the enemy. There was not another guardian in all the Universe who would go to the lengths she would go to protect him.

Markus made no reply. Not the slightest trace of care or concern emanated from him. Sitting as still as a cement statue, he returned her declaration with a blank stare of indifference.

"You don't care, do you? This is just a game to you and Uriel, isn't it?"

"No, it's a war. It's violent and it's messy. And it's a war we will do anything to win. But just like all wars, there are sacrifices you have to make along the way."

Nearly every muscle in her body erupted at his last comment. She jabbed a finger in his direction. "Parker is *not* a sacrifice I will ever make. Ever."

"You may have to, whether you like it or not."

"What are you saying? That Parker has to be sacrificed for what you think is some kind of greater good? And if I get in the way, I'll be sacrificed as well?"

"That's exactly what I'm saying. We're at war against the most ruthless, most evil beings that would love nothing more than to wipe humanity from all Creation. And they wouldn't think twice about torturing and murdering a few former friends and colleagues along the way. What we have to do at times isn't pleasant or easy. And if you're not pre-pared to make some tough decisions in order to win this war, then you better take a long, hard look in the mirror. Because the stakes are higher than you can imagine."

"What you're asking me to do is wrong. We don't—"

"If you want to walk, then walk. Go ahead," he nodded. "Run back to Gabriel and deliver messages like Western Union. But if you pull some kind of stunt like you're talking about now, like refusing to relinquish your charge and re-vealing yourself to him, you'll be completely on the outside. You go off the reservation, I will not help you. If you find yourself in trouble, I will not come for you. No one will. Understand?"

Where was this coming from? After all these years, after all the things Markus had done to help, why was he taking such a callous stance? Was he finally showing his true na-ture or simply following orders?

"Is this Uriel pulling your strings or is this really you?"

Markus furrowed his brow. "Do you understand?" His stern voice punched the air with every syllable as he ignored the question.

So that's it. Either obey orders and leave Parker to his

fate, or risk saving him but be abandoned and exiled. "I understand," she murmured.

"Good. Now come on." He stood, unclasped the halo, and returned it to his pocket.

Disobeying or disappointing him was the last thing she ever wanted to do, but the thought of losing Parker left her no other choice. "No. I'm sorry Markus, but I'm saving Parker."

Marie abruptly turned around and closed the distance to the restaurant's doors in three quick steps. Markus barked out her name behind her as she pulled open the glass door and entered the restaurant.

She spotted Parker right away. What would she say to him? As she strode across the cheap linoleum, her mind worked feverishly to come up with something. She walked up to his booth and said, "Hello, Parker. Is the seat across from you taken?"

He held a taco in his hand, staring at her, his mouth open. "Um, no."

She sat down, settled into the smooth upholstery of the booth, and casually looked around the restaurant. Only two other customers were present, so they would have some modicum of privacy. Parker still stared at her. She turned and smiled at him.

"Do I know you? I mean, I've seen you before, but I don't think we've actually met. Have we?"

"Uh, well—" She fidgeted in her seat. "—we'll get to that later." This was a delicate situation. How to proceed?

"Okay. Then how about we get to your name?"

She smiled at his directness. "Marie. My name is Marie."

"Nice to meet you, Marie." He smiled, showing off his cute dimples, then looked down at his food. Both seemed unsure what to say next. An uncomfortable moment passed, and her mind went blank. She'd thought of this moment for years, of appearing to him and speaking to him in a normal conversation. She'd imagined what it would be like, how he would respond, what they would talk about.

Now that it was here, she could think of nothing to say.

He glanced out the window. She was so eager to talk to him, but it was proving to be much more difficult than anticipated. Maybe it would be best if she just got up and left. *No, this might be my only chance, and I'm going to save him.*

He looked back at her, his blue eyes lulling her into a sweet trance.

After a lengthy pause, he finally said, "Well, Marie, my food is getting cold. So, if you don't mind, I'm going to dig in." He grabbed the taco he'd been holding and took a bite.

She watched him chew as she inhaled the aromas of the Mexican food. The fajita meat, beans, rice, and spices appealed to her somewhat, but only for an instant. He took another bite of his taco and wiped his mouth with the napkin.

He grabbed his drink and looked out the window as he sucked his beverage through the straw in his cup.

Dr. Pepper, she reminded herself. *Eating Mexican food is the only time he ever drinks Dr. Pepper.* It was one of those quirks of his that she knew so well.

He set down his drink, turned to look at her. "Um, look. You can watch me eat my dinner if you really want to, but I gotta tell you, this is a little weird." He paused, allowing her another opportunity to speak.

When she said nothing, he continued. "Is there something you want? Something I can help you with? Look, I've seen you twice before." He propped his elbows on the table. "Once at the hospital a couple of weeks ago and then again last night at the game. Both times you were staring at me, so what's going on?"

Marie shrugged.

He sighed and reached for another taco as he shook his head. She didn't know why she said it—it certainly hadn't been planned—but it came out nonetheless.

"Wheezy," she said, seemingly out of the blue.

She spoke just as he took a bite, and the food almost fell

out of his mouth. He reached up with his napkin and tried to keep from making a mess. "What did you say?"

"I said, 'Wheezy.'"

He slumped back from the table until his back touched the booth, causing him to grimace slightly. He chewed his food slowly as his eyes locked onto Marie. He swallowed but didn't say anything. Marie sat quietly, waiting for him to respond.

"How do you know that name? Did we know each other in elementary school?"

Marie shook her head. "No, we weren't classmates." *Technically, that's true.*

"Then how did you know that's what they used to call me?"

Marie pondered her options. She could just come right out with it, or continue to be evasive until she could come up with something else. She looked at him. Good, she had his complete and undivided attention.

The more she thought about it, the more plowing straight ahead seemed the best choice. Her lips peeled back slightly into a thin smile.

"I know that name, because…because I'm your angel," she said. She held her breath and waited for him to respond.

Although he appeared stoic, she knew his mind was racing. Finally, a broad smile appeared on his face, and he stifled a laugh.

"Yeah, okay, weirdo." He took another sip from his cup. "Seriously, how did you know they used to call me that?"

"I told you, I'm your angel," Marie replied as matter-of-factly as she could.

Parker's jaw hardened. "You're a reporter, aren't you? Is that what this is about? You doing a little background research on me for your story?" Parker threw his napkin onto the table. "You people make me sick."

Marie took a deep breath. "Riley Parker Austin, I'm your angel. I've been your angel since the day you were conceived, and I have been with you ever since. I know everything about you, which is why I know the nickname the kids used to make fun of your asthma."

"You mean like a guardian angel? Whatever, freak." He rolled his eyes, picked up his fork, and stirred his Spanish rice into his refried beans. It was something she'd seen him do hundreds of times before, but she became mesmerized by his mixing of the two foods. Watching the fork scrape back and forth along the plate, she continued to think of the right words to say but nothing came to mind. Suddenly she became conscious of him staring at her. She looked up and caught his eyes looking her over. Heat rushed to her cheeks.

She cleared her throat and his eyes glanced back up to her face. "Yes, I'm your guardian angel."

He dropped his fork. "All right, knock it off with that angel crap. Who are you and what do you want?"

"Parker, I am your angel." Her earnest tone pleaded for him to believe her.

"Look weirdo, I'm done with this conversation." He shoved his plate and slid out of the booth.

"No, Park, don't go. Please stay."

He stopped and turned back toward the booth. He leaned in close to her and whispered, "I don't know who you are or what you're up to, but you're weird and a little bit creepy. So do me a favor and stay away from me."

He walked out of the restaurant and headed for his car. She slid out of the booth and followed him outside. As he reached into his pocket for his car keys, she blurted out, "Blurry Sesame Street!"

He froze. She took a few steps closer to him. "Blurry Sesame Street," she repeated. He slowly turned around, his eyes wide and his mouth open.

"How—" His voice was hoarse, disbelief written all over his face. "—how—do you know that?"

This was it. This was her chance. Her eyes watered. "Because I'm your angel, Parker. You were four years old and in the hospital with pneumonia. You were in ICU and your bed was encased in a plastic canopy."

He paused and she sensed his mind recalling that memory. *Yes, that's it, Park. Remember.*

"The plastic messed up my view. It made everything blurry."

"And you couldn't watch Sesame Street on the wall-mounted television."

"No, I couldn't," He said as he shook his head. "The plastic made the TV look blurry. Big Bird was just a big, yellow blob. I couldn't watch the show."

"And it made you sad. You were scared. Since you were in ICU, your parents couldn't stay with you, and you were left alone at night."

Parker nodded.

"Night was when you were the most frightened. You couldn't wait for the morning," she continued. "All alone in that hospital bed, with tubes and machines hooked up to you, your lungs fighting for every breath. Not really knowing what was happening to you, but wishing with all your might that your parents would just take you home."

Parker looked away, stared down at the asphalt of the restaurant's parking lot.

She let him linger for a while, and then asked, "So what got you through those nights?"

He stood motionless, obviously lost in thought. An attempt to speak produced nothing but a mumble. He swallowed. "A girl. A little girl stayed the night with me."

She stepped closer so that they were just a few feet apart. "Yes, a four-year-old girl stayed the night with you, every night you were in the hospital. She talked to you, she was your friend, she kept you company so you didn't feel so alone and scared."

Parker remained glued to the asphalt.

"And what was her name? You remember, don't you?"

"Marie," he replied softly. "She told me her name was Marie. My parents didn't believe me. They said I was hallucinating because of the pneumonia."

"Parker, look at me."

He hesitated, but eventually lifted his head and their eyes met.

"You didn't hallucinate. It wasn't a dream. That was me. I'm your angel."

Parker broke free and staggered a few feet to his car. He leaned up against the driver-side door and stared into the distance. Marie watched him but didn't move. This couldn't be rushed—better to give him a moment to let it all sink in.

They stood in silence as the dreary, cloudy skies darkened and the wind picked up. Ironic that although there were only a few feet between them, they were worlds apart.

She took a cautious step toward him. "I know everything about you." She smiled. "I know your favorite color is blue, and the scar on your knee is from a bicycle accident when you were seven. You love seafood but you're allergic to shellfish. You're deathly afraid of heights, and you can't make it through the movie *We Are Marshall* without crying."

She held her breath and paused again, giving him more time to comprehend, hoping he'd speak to her.

Nothing.

The seconds ticked by in silent agony until she couldn't stand it any longer. "Park, talk to me. Please."

He turned toward her, still leaning against his car. His mouth opened and he tried to speak but no words came out. He closed his eyes for a moment. "It's impossible."

"I know it's a lot at once, but I just—I just had to talk to you." She took another step, close enough now to touch him. What would he do if she reached for him?

His eyes popped open and he held out his arm to ward her off. "No, you stay away from me." Car keys jingled in his hand. "I don't know what's going on here, but I want you to leave me alone."

"No, Park. Please don't go. We need to talk."

He opened the car door, climbed inside, and cranked the ignition.

Marie dashed up to the car and rapped on the driver's

window with her knuckles. "Park, you can't leave. We have to talk. Please!"

His car sped out of the parking lot, tires screeching, and turned west on Wabash Avenue.

CHAPTER 28

Parker raced out of Chateau d' Taco's parking lot and headed west. Where didn't matter, just as long as it wasn't anywhere near Marie.

He left the city limits behind and headed toward Wheeler Lake. Six miles out of town, he pulled over at a rest stop that overlooked the water. It sat on a small, wooded hill with covered picnic tables, offering a nice view of the lake as the road below continued across the reservoir on a mile-long concrete bridge.

Parker got out of his car, snapped up his letter jacket, and went to one of the picnic tables. Though empty for the moment, the place could get busy on the weekends with high school students looking for a place to make out. Hopefully his classmates could keep their urges under control for a few more hours. What he needed now was solitude, time to think.

He climbed on top of the picnic table and sat down on the cold concrete tabletop, his feet resting on the bench seat, and looked out toward the reservoir. With his hands deep in the front pockets of his letter jacket for warmth, his fingers pressed against the steak knife he'd found in his tire. The dreary overcast skies at dusk would turn black soon, the temperature continuing to drop. With darkness fast approaching, the occasional cars crossing the bridge below already had their headlights on. Like twin pearls shining in a looming shadow, they moved across the concrete span in silence.

There's just no way. How could this be possible? *Angel.* He chewed on that word while recalling that episode from childhood when he'd almost died in the hospital. It'd been so difficult to breathe, lying in the plastic-enclosed bed, tubes and wires crisscrossing him in the darkened room. That's when she'd first appeared.

She'd sat in the chair beside his bed, and although he hadn't seen her face well because of the plastic canopy, he could tell she was a little girl his age. She introduced herself as Marie, and said she would be his friend. He'd been excited to have another child to talk to and keep him company. He couldn't remember what they had talked about, but she'd calmed him and eased his anxiety so much that he'd been able to drift off to sleep that night. But when he'd awoken in the morning, she was gone.

He told his parents about her, but they, like the treating physician, dismissed it as pneumonia-induced hallucination.

Yet, every night she'd appeared and sat with him until he fell asleep. He never forgot her, but had always assumed she'd been a figment of his imagination, a dream.

Now, sitting alone on the windswept hill by the lake, he knew it had been real. His mind reeled from the revelation. How was this possible?

As he continued to search for a rational explanation, the sound of his name startled him.

She stood a few feet behind the picnic table, the wind gently blowing through her long hair.

He frowned. "Don't sneak up on people like that." He glanced around the rest stop and saw no cars other than his own. "What are you doing here? I thought I told you to leave me alone."

"I'm sorry. I didn't mean to scare you."

He snorted. "Whatever. How long have you been back there?"

"Standing here? Just a few seconds, but I've been watching you ever since you left the parking lot." She took a step closer to the picnic table.

"What do you mean you've been watching me since I left the parking lot? How did you get here?"

"Well, it's kind of hard to explain, but I can see you all the time. It's like I'm an invisible person. You can't see me, feel me, or touch me, but I'm there. Just watching."

"But I can see you now."

She nodded. "Yes, because I've chosen to appear to you."

He shook his head. "I don't understand."

She stepped closer until she stood directly behind the picnic table. He was still sitting on top of it, but had turned completely around, facing her. "It means I can take human form, which allows you to see me."

His eyes studied her from head to toe. "So this is what you really look like?"

"I can look however I want when I appear, but this is what I prefer. The only restriction is gender. Since I'm a female angel, I can only take female form. When we appear, we're supposed to be able to interact as easily as possible and in a way that won't arouse suspicion. I think it's a silly rule, personally."

"Okay," he said, choosing his words with care. "So when I saw you in the hospital when I was four, you could appear as a four-year-old girl because you're a female angel?"

She smiled and nodded her head. "Yes."

"And when you don't 'appear,' as you say, you're watching me?"

She nodded again, her smile broadening. "Yes. That's right."

He said nothing as he contemplated this.

She put her hands in her jeans pockets. "I came out to check on you, see how you're doing. I know I laid a lot on you, so I wanted to see if you're okay."

He turned back around and faced the water. "Oh, I'm

just great. I'm being stalked twenty-four-seven by an invisible angel. Other than that, everything's cool."

She climbed on top of the picnic table, sat next to him, and gazed at the dark water below. "I'm not stalking you. I'm your angel. I'm with you all the time, just speaking to you and praying for you."

He turned and looked at her. "What do you mean you speak to me?"

"I speak to you all the time. I'm part of your conscience, that little voice inside your head that tells you right from wrong. You hear me every day, but it's up to you to listen to me—or to the others."

"Others? Like other angels?"

She shook her head. "No. Unfortunately, we aren't the only ones that speak to you, and we aren't the only ones that can appear. In fact, you ran into one a couple of weeks ago at Gibson's. If an associate of mine and I hadn't intervened, there's no telling what might have happened."

"Wait, slow your roll a second." Parker thought for a moment as he recalled that morning at the pharmacy. "Who exactly are these others you're talking about?"

"In a word, demons."

"Demons?" He shook his head. "This is crazy."

"I wish it weren't true either, but it is. They're the fallen. The ones who rebelled in the first Angelic War. And they've been taking it out on mankind ever since."

He rubbed his hand across his face and took a deep breath. "So demons are actually fallen angels. And they're fighting people?"

"Yes. And they hate you. They despise you more than anything because their rebellion was all about you."

"What do you mean?"

Marie crossed her arms and rested her elbows on her knees. "Lucifer and a lot of other angels resented the fact that man became the more cherished creature and that God would sacrifice everything for him. I mean, put yourself in their position. For a long time, you've been a powerful, celestial being. Loved and cherished. But then one day a new being is created, one infinitely inferior to you in every way. Yet, it's now the cherished favorite and given dominion over Creation. And what's more—you're told to serve it. That didn't go over too well with some. So they rebelled. And lost. But it all started because of you. And that's why they'll do anything to destroy you."

"Great. So, they're trying to off us every chance they get?"

"Not exactly. They're forbidden from directly harming humans. They speak to you, try to get you to do what you know is wrong, only they disguise it as temptation and help you rationalize it so you think it's harmless and okay. They're very good at it." Her eyes drifted to the water and lingered for a moment. "Other times they get inside your head and torment you into doing some pretty horrible things, things you would never imagine yourself ever do-ing."

"Like what?"

She sighed. "Like a when a mother drowns her own kids in a bathtub, or a depressed husband kills his wife and then turns the gun on himself. That's just the tip of the iceberg, I'm afraid."

"Dueling angels on our shoulders?"

"Something like that." She looked back out at the water and her eyes followed a car across the bridge.

"There was a demon that morning at the pharmacy. You saw him as the sickly looking man in the coffee area. They always look like they've got the flu because Lucifer can't recreate life. He's an imposter, a charlatan, so he can only make cheap knock-offs of the real thing."

He studied her for a moment. "What was he doing there?"

She shrugged. "I can't say for sure. They can be pretty unpredictable. If we hadn't shown ourselves, there's no tell-ing what it might have done."

This still wasn't making any sense. "How did you show

yourself? Trust me, if you had been in the pharmacy, I definitely would've noticed." Parker realized the compliment as soon as the words rolled off his tongue.

Marie pursed her lips and broke eye contact with him. Her mouth slanted in a sheepish grin. "Um, thank you." Crimson flooded her cheeks.

He hadn't meant to embarrass her. It just came out. But as he looked at her, the compliment had been an honest one. While not a knockout, she was pretty. Her strawberry blonde hair, green eyes, dimples, and cute little nose gave her an attractive appearance—a version of Scarlett Johansson, only without the airhead quality.

She cleared her throat and turned back to him. "Well, to answer your question, an associate and I posed as a father and daughter. We made sure it saw us, so it would leave you alone."

"How often does that kind of thing happen?"

"We run into them from time to time. There's one in particular, Seth is his name. He tends to cause us lots of trouble."

"I just...I'm still just trying to wrap my mind around this," he said. "This is real? This is really happening? You're really an angel, like from up there?" He motioned toward the sky.

She grinned. "There are more things in Heaven and Earth than are dreamt of in your philosophy."

He cocked his head to the side. The line seemed familiar. "Hamlet?"

She clapped her hands. "Oh, bravo. You did pay attention in Mr. Ellis's class."

"Um, thanks," he replied. "Okay, so if you're an angel, can't you fly? I mean, show me something. Levitate. Fly around."

She shook her head. "Afraid not." She got up off of the picnic table, turned around and faced him. "When I'm in human form, I'm bound by the laws of the Earth. So, like everyone else, I can't defy gravity or walk through walls. I have to follow the laws of nature that God created here. However, I can appear and leave as quickly or as often as I like. Think about it. I appeared right behind you out of nowhere. I didn't drive here, and I didn't walk here. Plus, how did I know where to find you? C'mon, Park. You know this is real, and you know what I'm telling you is true."

Parker leaned back on his hands. It was getting much darker now, the water below fading black to match the evening sky. He looked back at her. "So, how does this work? I mean what am I supposed to do now?"

She shrugged. "You live your life."

"Really? Well, it kind of creeps me out knowing you're watching me all the time. I mean, are you going to just magically appear every time I start doing something you don't approve of?"

"No, that's not how it works. I'm not here to judge you. I'm simply here to look after you, to remind you of what you know is right."

He thought for a moment. "So, if you're my angel, I can assume everyone has one, right?"

She nodded.

Parker sensed she knew exactly where this was headed. "So, that means my sister had an angel. And if you're here to look after me, then there was an angel that was supposed to look after her. Right?"

She nodded and looked down at the ground, avoiding his eyes.

He hopped to the ground in front of her. He stood, placed both hands on his hips. "So, what happened? Why is my sister dead?"

"There are some things I cannot explain to you, things you just can't fully understand at the moment, but, given time, you will."

"Nope. Not good enough. So what was it? Did her angel screw up, did God screw up?" He stepped closer, only a few inches separating them. "Or does God just not care?"

She looked up with soft eyes. "I told you, there are some

things you just can't understand right now, and it's pointless to keep talking about them."

"So why are you here? Why show yourself to me if you can't answer my questions?"

"When I watched you talk to your mother this morning and heard you say the things that you said, my heart broke for you. I could feel what the last few weeks have done to you. And I just don't want to see it change you, make you turn your back on everything you know and believe." She took a step back from him. "I—I just couldn't let that happen to you." She turned around, facing the dark lake.

"Why not?"

"Because I—" She stopped abruptly, as if catching her words. After pausing a moment and then taking a deep breath, she said, "Because I care for you."

But the tone was all wrong, as if those really weren't the words she originally wanted to say and had to settle for something else. Marie fidgeted with her hands. What was she nervous about?

He took a deep breath of the cold evening air and exhaled slowly, letting his body relax. His back still ached from where the steak knife had poked him, and fatigue weighed him down. He sniffled, ran his hand across his cold nose. The temperature was plummeting. This had been enough drama for one night.

"I'm going home," he said. He turned to Marie, who still had her back to him.

"Hey, did you hear me? I said I'm—"

"I heard you," she whispered. She stood as still as a statue.

He paused, waiting for her to explain. When she didn't say anything, he walked up beside her. "What are you doing?"

Her eyes were fixed on the edge of the woods just thirty feet away, scanning the shadows. She was looking for something, but what exactly? He glanced toward the trees. It was nearly dark now, quiet and still. Nothing stirred.

He looked back at her. "There's nothing there. It's just you and me."

Without taking her eyes off the trees, she shook her head. "We're not alone."

CHAPTER 29

If not for the tension in Marie's voice, Parker might've just ignored her and gone home. After all, they were at a popular make-out spot, so there was a good chance other people might arrive. But her tone implied something else. Something that wasn't good.

He scanned the trees again. "I don't see anything." Turning to her, he said, "There's nothing there."

Her eyes widened. "Get behind me." She spoke with urgency.

Two dark figures emerged from the trees, walking toward them.

"Where did they come from?" Parker asked.

She grabbed his arm. "Please get behind me and do exactly what I say. No matter what enters your mind, you have to be strong, okay? Just concentrate on my voice."

"What are you talking about? What's the matter?"

She jumped in front of him. "Just get behind me."

The two figures continued in their direction as if they were on a leisurely stroll and had all the time in the world.

"Remember, listen only to me," she whispered over her shoulder as the two strangers approached their picnic table.

He nodded. "I still don't know what you're talking about. Who are these people?"

"They're not people," she replied just as they stopped short of the concrete slab where Marie and Parker stood.

Parker squinted through the darkness and tried to focus his eyes. Now that they were less than ten feet away, the two strangers were more discernible. Definitely a man and a woman, but he could not make out much else except for their eyes. Both had the same eerie eye color that stood out in the darkness. It was a hue he'd seen before.

The woman looked from Parker to Marie.

"Yes, he recognizes you," Marie said. "Your eyes always give your kind away."

The woman made no comment in reply and continued to focus on Marie.

"Yes, he's been told what you are," Marie said.

"Who are you talking to?" Parker asked.

The man laughed and looked at Marie.

"He's smarter than you think," Marie shot back.

The man walked over to the picnic table and sat on top of it, his feet resting on the bench seat, his auburn eyes locked onto Parker as Marie shifted to stand between the two of them.

"Answer me," Marie demanded. "Why are you here?"

Parker glanced from the woman to the man to see if either made any reply, but not a single word escaped their lips.

"No, you're not. But if you're looking for a fight, you've found one," Marie said, glaring at the man.

"There's panic in your voice," the woman cooed aloud as her devilish eyes flashed in the darkness. She circled around Marie and Parker.

Marie backed up and turned to keep the woman in her sights, but glanced around the area as if looking for something.

"Markus isn't coming to help you," the man said, his voice dripping with mock pity. "Nobody is." He sat up, leering at Marie and Parker.

Thoughts of the shooting blindsided Parker. Horrific mental images of Abby pleading for him to save her swept through his mind like a tsunami. Gunfire and screams reverberated in his ears. The heaviest, most intense wave of guilt overwhelmed him, and he let out an audible cry.

Marie gripped his hand. "Parker!" She squeezed his hand more tightly. "Parker, listen to me! It wasn't your fault!"

The guilt abated for a few seconds, but soon returned stronger than before and crushed what little resistance remained. Tears pooled in his eyes. "I killed my sister." He sobbed as the tears streamed down his face. Marie's pleas faded to mute, and the thought of being responsible for Abby's death overpowered him.

He staggered from the emotional weight that crashed upon him, and a new thought entered his mind—an overwhelming desire to end the pain and join Abby.

"No!" Marie screamed and grabbed him by the shoulders. "Parker! Parker!" Her calls seemed to come as though from a great distance, making it difficult to concentrate on her voice. He tried to listen, but the thought of drowning himself in the lake or getting in his car and driving off the bridge seemed far more appealing. "Parker! Listen to me! It wasn't your fault!"

When he tried to turn away from her, she grabbed him to prevent him from leaving. "I will not let you take him from me!" A bright blue aura emanated from Marie's hand, and a streak of light shot from it as she pointed to the man sitting on the picnic table.

The blue bolt of angel fire struck him squarely in the chest, knocking him backward. He screamed in pain as he tumbled and fell off the table.

The urgent, suicidal thoughts disappeared, and Parker looked at Marie. He blinked, wiped the tears from his eyes. "What happened? What was that flash?"

Marie didn't answer. She spun on her heels and faced the woman, who was now behind them, her right hand giving off a distinct red aura. "Parker, you've got to get out of here," Marie said over her shoulder, shielding him from the circling woman. "When I tell you to go, run to your car and leave."

"I'm not leaving you here."

Marie shoved him away from her. "Go."

Parker staggered a few steps as a streak of red light shot toward Marie. She raised her right hand at the last second and a ray of blue light raced from her hand. The collision of lights exploded in a brilliant flash of fiery, yellow sparks that floated to the ground.

He could run for it now. He had a clear path to his car, but leaving Marie behind, even though she had told him to flee, just didn't seem right. Everyone at the stadium a few weeks ago had run from the danger, except for him. Without even thinking about it, he'd charged headfirst into harm's way to put a stop to the carnage. Running away hadn't been an option then, and it wasn't one now.

He turned to Marie just in time to see the man emerge from the darkness. The sinewy figure stood next to the picnic table facing Marie, pointing in her direction. Parker raced toward him just as the man threw a bolt of red light at Marie, hitting her in the back. Her scream pierced the air as Parker dove, his body barreling into the man and knocking him to the ground.

Parker scrambled on top of the man and hit him as hard as he could, his knuckles delivering crushing blows to the man's gaunt face. Images of Bobby McGonagill swept into his mind as Parker recalled the night of the shooting again. He remembered looking down at Bobby's broken and bloodied face, knowing the whole time he'd been too slow getting to Abby.

Now he'd been too slow to stop this man from hurting Marie, and another wave of guilt washed over him. He stopped beating on the man and rolled off of him as the most intense, profound sadness he'd ever felt settled over him.

He lifted his head and saw the woman standing near the picnic table, looking at him intently, an evil gleam in her devilish eyes. The feelings of guilt intensified. His body relaxed and went limp, his shoulders sagged, and he hung his head. His lips quivered and his eyes watered.

"Too slow," the man taunted despite blood pouring out of his nose. His yellow eyes flashed as he grinned at Parker. "You'll always be too slow."

Parker shifted back to the woman, who sported the same sinister grin as her colleague. A quick burst of blue light appeared from behind her, and the woman let out a blood-curdling scream. She collapsed onto the ground, smoke rising from her back.

Parker's sadness immediately vanished. Marie had been hit. Where was she?

A figure, doubled over, staggered toward him. Marie caught herself on the picnic table, her breathing labored and heavy. "Go," she said between breaths. "Hurry, get out of here."

"You're hurt. I can't leave you here," he said as he got to his feet.

She shook her head and grimaced. "I'll be fine. Get out of here before more of them show up."

"I'll get out of here when I know you're okay." Parker stepped toward her to check on her wounds. The stench of burned flesh wafted into his nose, and he gagged.

"No." She held out her hand to ward him off. "Please, Park, get out of here."

The man stirred on the ground behind him and struggled to stand. The woman moved as well.

"Park, I'm not going to tell you again, please get out of here."

Marie seemed more hurt than she let on. Her face contorted in pain as she tried to stand up straight.

He reached for her. "Please let me help you."

She drew back from him and then froze, her eyes widened. She turned toward the picnic table closest to the woods. "Oh, my God," she whispered. "No."

A shadowy figure sat on the table. A small flame appeared in the darkness as the silhouetted intruder lit a cigarette.

"That's it. I'm getting you out of here," Marie said. She grabbed Parker by the arm and led him away from the picnic table. The man and woman continued getting to their feet as Parker and Marie neared them. Parker delivered another punch to the man's face, sending him to the ground, and followed it with a fierce kick to his midsection for added measure. Marie blasted another jolt of blue light into the woman, who collapsed to the ground, jets of white smoke swirling across her limp body.

A voice called out from behind them. "You have nowhere to run, *outsider*." Its tone was cold and mocking.

Parker turned to look but Marie nudged him forward.

"Get in the car," Marie barked. This was not a request.

"But what about you?" he asked when he reached the car door and opened it.

"I'll be fine, just go."

"Who is that?"

"That's Seth. I'll explain later. Just go."

Why couldn't she just come with him? She didn't have to stay and fight. They could make their escape together. He was about to ask her to get into the car when Seth loomed behind her.

"He's behind you!"

Marie whirled around.

Seth took a long drag on his cigarette, the orange ember intensifying in the darkness. The small fire pulled away from his pale face, and he exhaled.

"Stop this foolishness, Marie. You can take your charge and run to the four corners of the earth, and I'll still be there, waiting."

Marie took a step back and flung her arms downward at her side. She clenched her fists, and the soft glow of blue light encircled them.

Seth didn't flinch. "Your devotion to protect your charge is admirable, but it's not enough." He turned his head from side to side, as if surveying the area.

Red lights, like tiny beacons in a sea of blackness,

emerged from every direction throughout the rest stop, completely encircling Parker and Marie.

"I did warn you about having feelings for your charge, how it would cloud your judgment. Now look where it has gotten you—alone and abandoned."

Parker's head jerked in Marie's direction. "What?"

A reluctant gaze met Parker's eyes, and Marie's mouth fell open. "Park—"

Seth seemed amused. "You mean you haven't told him yet? How you're now head over heels—"

"That's enough, Seth! Stop it!"

What Seth implied wasn't too hard to figure out, but the concept seemed far-fetched. Surely this wasn't happening. Was it?

"Um, Marie..." Parker couldn't finish the sentence. No. Impossible. Words couldn't even articulate it.

"Touching how you want to be the one to tell him yourself." Seth took a drag from his cigarette and exhaled a smoke cloud.

Marie squared her shoulders and cleared her throat. "Leave him alone, Seth." She pressed her palms together. "He's only one soul. Please, just let him go. *Please.*"

Seth raised an eyebrow. "Begging? That's not becoming of a guardian, Marie."

"Well, I'm not a typical guardian."

A thin smile creased Seth's smooth face. "No, you're not. You're different, that's for sure. All the other guardians know it. You're in touch with your true self, you know who and what you are, and there's power and freedom in that self-realization. It's what makes you better than the rest, and they resent you for it."

Seth glanced around the rest stop. "Look around. You've just been attacked and no guardian, no Venantium, has come to assist you. *Not one.* Even Markus—your friend and mentor—has cut you loose. Face it, Marie, you've been abandoned by your very own." He took another long drag from his cigarette.

Short, rapid gasps of breath came from Marie. She clutched her chest and cast a nervous glance at Parker.

White smoke hung in the air from Seth's exhale. "And the saddest part aside from forsaking you is the way you've been treated. You're a guardian, yet you've been made to feel ashamed, inadequate, and unworthy of that position. They've shunned you for centuries. They've called you names, mocked you, done everything they can to make you feel unwanted. And why? Because you didn't fall in line and goose-step with the rest of them. You were true to yourself and dared to act differently."

She shifted and hung her head.

"It doesn't have to be that way. You don't have to be alone and isolated anymore." His voice carried the words in rich, warm tones. His topaz eyes sparkled. "You, like everyone else, deserve to be free, to be yourself without fear of judgment or prejudice." He motioned with his hand. "Come with me. You'll feel included, accepted, like you belong. Everything you've ever wanted all these years."

He smiled, flashing his white teeth, and said softly, "Come with me and I'll spare Parker."

A cold gust of wind blew streamers of hair across her face, and she pulled them to the side. Her fingers fidgeted with the ends of her hair, coiling them in a nervous fashion as the ominous red lights from Seth's crew of demons crept closer.

"Why would you offer me this choice? You have me surrounded. You could finish me off and be free to do whatever you want to Parker."

He grinned. "Because I've never before met a guardian of your kind. You're exceptional. I see that in you. The other guardians see it, too, and they're jealous, so they mock you. But I say you deserve to be embraced for what and who you are. You deserve to be free."

She turned, closed her eyes, and muttered something.

He puffed on his cigarette. "If you're worried about losing your charge, don't be. He's already made his choice, and you know that. So, if you come with me you'll still have him. Forever."

She cocked her head toward Seth. "Maybe. But while he still breathes, I can always turn him back. I still might be able to save him."

Seth flicked ash from the end of his cigarette. "And should anything happen to him before you turn him, you will lose him for eternity. You're willing to lose everything on 'maybe'? C'mon, Marie. I'm offering you a sure thing— a chance to end your suffering and to be with your charge forever."

She closed her eyes again and her body seemed to slacken.

An outstretched hand beckoned. "You don't have to be alone anymore. Come with me."

Parker held his breath waiting for Marie's response. All this talk about isolation and wanting to belong struck a familiar chord, but surely she wouldn't go with Seth.

Marie opened her misty eyes. A faint smile appeared, the tiniest dimple forming. "I'm so sorry, Park. Please forgive me for what I'm about to do. It's not my intention to hurt you."

Oh no.

She straightened up, shoulders back, chin held high. "Like I told you at the church, Seth," her voice bellowed in a commanding tone. "Never this side of Hell would I leave and follow you."

She spun around and a streak of blue light raced from her hand. It collided in mid-air with something red and another explosion of bright yellow sparks flooded the ground. She turned and slammed both fists into Parker's chest, shoving him backward. He staggered, tripped, and fell into the driver seat of his car. Marie slammed the door shut and yelled at him to go.

He threw the car into reverse, turned around, and sped off as more flashes of colored lights erupted in the rearview mirror.

CHAPTER 30

Parker sped back to town, his mind racing faster than his car. The events of the past forty-five minutes left him reeling in a state of disbelief as he tried to process everything Marie told him and what he'd just witnessed. "This can't be happening."

Despite self-reassurances that he wasn't losing his mind, the crazy label would definitely be slapped on him if he ever said a word about this to anyone. It'd guarantee a one-way ticket on the happy bus to the funny farm. Crazier than Mrs. Calvin, they'd say.

As the city limits sign appeared in his headlights, a strange sense of foreboding took hold. His pulse quickened, his breathing sped up, and perspiration formed on his forehead. He couldn't pinpoint the exact cause of the anxiety right away, but something was amiss. Was Marie speaking to him? If so, she could be a little clearer with the hints. He shook his head. "This is so weird."

He pulled out his cell phone and called home. No answer. Within moments, he arrived at his house and turned into the driveway, coming to an abrupt stop underneath the basketball goal. Odd that the house was dark. His parents rarely went out on the weekends. He got out of the car, jogged through the open garage, and stepped into the back hallway that led to the kitchen. No television. Nothing stirred. All quiet.

"Mom? Dad?"

No response. Nothing. They had to be here. Their cars were in the driveway.

He hurried through the kitchen and into the family room.

As he entered, he caught a quick movement near his left side. *Swoosh!* A hard, tubular object delivered a blow to his stomach, knocking the air out of his lungs and doubling him over. He staggered a few steps. What was that—a baseball bat?

What just happened? He turned to look for his assailant but a boot flew up from the floor and smacked him square in the face, the blow whipping back his head and sending him to the floor.

He wasn't on his back but for a moment, when someone grabbed a handful of his hair and pulled him across the floor, the heels of his shoes cutting a swath through the carpet. His scalp burned like it was on fire. Dazed and winded, he tried but couldn't offer much resistance. As he was dragged through the family room and into the living room, a warm liquid ran out of his nose and into his mouth. He spat out his blood as he continued his attempt to break free of the intruder's grip. Whoever this was, he was physically strong.

A lamp glowed from one of the end tables—the only light in the room. The hand let go of his hair and a vicious kick caught him in the ribs. Parker recoiled from the blow and the sound of cracking bones. Instinctively, he pulled his knees up close and rolled away. Another kick, to the back of his head, almost rendered him unconscious.

The room spun, his eyelids grew heavy. As he struggled to orient himself, the sound of muffled cries caught his attention. He shifted his watery eyes and blinked a few times until his vision cleared.

His parents sat on the couch, hands bound behind their backs, and their mouths duct-taped. Both of them sported facial abrasions. His father's clothes and hair, unlike his mother's, were in disarray—a sure sign that he and the intruder had scuffled. Seeing that his father had fought back didn't surprise him. Dad would definitely go down swinging if he could.

Tears streaked his mother's mascara as she looked at him. He lay on the living room carpet, blood pouring out of his nose, looking into his mother's desperate, terror-filled eyes. He had to do something. Instinct said fight back, fight hard, fight with anything.

"Get up, Parker." The rough, calloused voice was unrecognizable. "C'mon. Sit up."

Parker tried to move, but pain racked his body. An elephant sat on his rib cage, the room continued to tilt, and his scalp still tingled. He managed to prop himself up and get onto all fours. More blood seeped through his lips, the metallic-tasting fluid wetting his mouth as he looked over his shoulder in the direction of the intruder's voice.

A man in his early forties stood facing him. He wore faded jeans, a worn camouflage hooded jacket, and scuffed and dirty work boots. A revolver stuck out from the top of his pants, and he gripped a baseball bat in his left hand. The leathery face was unfamiliar. No, he didn't know him, but the hooded jacket—hadn't he seen that before?

"Turn around and sit down," the man barked.

Parker slowly turned over and sat down, grimacing, but never breaking eye contact with the man standing at the end of the coffee table in front of the couch where his parents sat. His head still rattled and ached from the kick, and his broken ribs radiated pain throughout his body with just the slightest movement.

The man stood for a few moments, looking at Parker. Evidently, whatever he was up to he was in no hurry to complete. In fact, he seemed to be savoring the moment. He glanced in the direction of Parker's parents when his father began struggling to break free of the plastic zip ties that bound his wrists. The man smiled and laughed to himself. "Your old man's got some fight in him."

A faint odor of gasoline wafted through the air, and Parker scanned the room. Two small, rusty gas cans sat underneath his mother's piano bench. Parker had seen enough crime shows on television to know what that meant. Neither he nor his parents would leave the house alive.

"Yeah, going to even the score tonight, Mr. Quarterback," the intruder continued. "I meant to do it last night when I slashed your tire, but that girl showed up and then that stupid basset hound that peed on my leg came out of nowhere and started barking and made all kinds of noise."

Warm blood continued oozing from Parker's broken nose as he frantically raced to connect the dots despite the pain and grogginess.

"So I left you a little reminder this morning in your car. I hope you got the *point*." The man laughed at his own humor.

There had to be something in the room—anything—that could serve as a weapon. But whatever Parker was going to do, it had to be soon, before the man pulled out the gun, or else he wouldn't stand a chance. He spat more blood onto the carpet and tried to come up with an idea but nothing came to mind. *Think! Think!* There had to be something he could do.

Wait a second. What did the man just say about slashing the tire? The steak knives! *That's it!* Parker still carried them in the pocket of his letter jacket.

"Yes, sir. It's payback time. Eye for an eye, tooth for a tooth," the man said as he began to twirl the baseball bat. "You beat up my two little boys a few years back, then you turned my oldest boy into a vegetable. My wife and kids have been forced to move out of our house and go into hiding. The trucking company fired me. I got news people crawling all over the place talking about my kids. My life's a living hell, and it's all because of *you*. So, I'm going to finish what my boy Bobby started a few weeks ago."

So that's who this was—Daryl McGonagill. While he'd been talking and twirling the bat, Parker slid his right hand inside his jacket pocket and gripped the handle of one of the steak knives. He would have to move fast, but how quickly could he move with these broken ribs? His equilibrium was at an all-time low too, thanks to the kicks to the head.

"I'm going to fix some of my problems tonight," Daryl continued. "First, I'm going to do what should've been done a long time ago, and that's get even with you for beating up my two little boys." He stepped toward Parker's parents. "So, I'm going to beat your mom and dad to a pulp."

Daryl turned and swung the bat down into his father's left shin, just below his knee. Parker's father let out a muffled scream as his mother began crying hysterically, jerking her arms in a futile effort to break free of the zip ties that held her.

A volcano of anger and rage built within Parker, consuming him, threatening to erupt much like that day three years ago when he'd savagely beaten Daryl's two youngest boys for assaulting Abby. But a move was out of the question. Daryl was facing him and still too far away to reach quickly. What he needed was a distraction.

"Yep," Daryl continued. "I'm gonna beat your parents. Then I'm gonna blow both your kneecaps off just for the fun of it. And when you're hurtin' so bad that you beg me to finish you off—" Daryl shook his head. "—I ain't gonna do it. Instead, I'm gonna torch the place and watch you burn alive." An eerie smile creased his worn face.

The doorbell stopped Daryl in his tracks. He froze, uncertainty plastered across his face. He clearly had not anticipated an interloper. The doorbell rang again. Whoever had decided to drop by for a visit was pretty insistent. Daryl held up a finger to his mouth. "Sshh."

He snuck up to the living room window and peeked out from behind the curtain.

This was it. It was now or never. Parker looked at his parents and mouthed the words, "I love you." *I'm not going to be too slow this time.*

He shifted quietly into a coiled position, then sprang as fast as he could, ignoring the severe pain and lingering disorientation. He took three quick steps and then lunged with the steak knife as Daryl turned and tried to ward off the blow. Too late. The knife blade entered Daryl's left side just below his rib cage and sank all the way to the hilt, prompting Daryl to gasp, his eyes wide with shock. Parker slashed the knife forward toward the stomach, the blade exiting above the navel as he reached for Daryl's gun, his fingertips just grazing the handle.

The quick, sudden movement caught up to Parker as his knees buckled. He staggered against the living room window sill as Daryl retreated, his left hand covering the gaping knife wound.

Get the gun! Finish him off! But the pain in his ribs and the dizziness overwhelmed him. It was all he could to remain on his feet.

Blood poured out of Daryl's side and ran down his pants. He crashed backward onto the piano, the keys making a cacophony of choppy, eerie sounds as he tried to regain his balance.

Parker grunted through the pain, gripped the steak knife, and took a step in Daryl's direction. All that mattered now was killing Daryl and protecting his parents. He stepped toward him and then saw the gun as Daryl extracted it from his pants. *No!*

The hammer cocked and the first bullet struck Parker in the left shoulder, knocking him backward against the living room window. A scream erupted from the front door.

Parker staggered and slouched against the window sill, but somehow remained on his feet. Daryl raised the gun again and fired the remaining five rounds into Parker's chest, then turned and staggered off the piano toward the back of the house.

Parker fell face-down onto the floor. Sight and sound blurred together, everything growing dim and numb. Hands rolled him over, and his eyelids fluttered. A figure loomed over him.

"Parker! Parker!"

The plea in the girl's voice stirred him to focus. A brief

moment of clarity in his blurred vision revealed long strands of strawberry-blonde hair cascading in front of emerald green eyes.

Marie.

"Yes. Parker, I'm here, I'm here. Hold on!"

Had she been the distraction at the front door? A chill ran through his body. His eyelids grew heavy. A strange sensation of falling took hold of him, as though he were sinking through the carpet. Limbs became like sandbags, breathing became labored.

"No! Parker, stay with me! Do you hear me? Stay with me!"

The blurriness returned, overtaking everything. His chest heaved in a search for breath. Marie's words slipped into muted silence. The light grew dim, fading with each passing second, until nothing remained but darkness and the still, quiet void.

CHAPTER 31

Darkness. Thick, impenetrable—it consumed everything around Parker and left nothing visible. He existed in a black void, without shape or dimension. Was he blind? Maybe he could see his fingers if he waved them in front of his face.

Nope. Nothing, not even the sensation of bodily movement. No sound, no noise. Not even the faint whisper of breathing. There was no sense of direction or orientation, either. Standing, sitting, lying down—even floating—Parker couldn't tell.

Conscious thought was all that remained in an environment of nothingness.

Until the voice shattered the silence.

"…cannot touch him…mine." It came in fragments, like a garbled radio. Sweet, soft, intoxicating—where had it come from?

A second voice soon followed. "No…the truth…" Rough, with a hint of desperation, it wasn't as inviting as the first voice. Who was it? What were they talking about?

A slight draft of cold air, like breath, brushed against him. Still, he could see nothing, but something cold was approaching.

The sweet voice spoke again. "…claim him…it is written…"

With each syllable, the articulation grew more welcoming. Parker tried to fill in the gaps, but couldn't make sense of the broken conversation.

"You know the rules." The sweet voice dripped with honey.

"No...anything...him. I'll...his place...fall." The second voice was pleading.

The sweet voice countered in an almost singsong cadence. "Too late...no bargain...claim him."

A chorus of melodious voices cheered and echoed in support.

A sudden chill swept through him. Bitterly cold, it froze him to the core. Colder than anything he'd ever experienced. A coldness that actually hurt. Not like the tingling, prickly numbness one gets when staying outside in the cold for too long, but a blistering, burning kind of pain.

"Please! I'll...anything!" the second voice cried out in distress.

A third voice, low and curious, chimed in. "Would you...eternity...give up?"

"Yes," came the quick reply from the second voice. "Yes," it repeated, full of confidence. All trace of desperation gone.

The sweet retort came swiftly. "Doesn't matter...claim...remains regardless."

A long pause ensued. Seconds, minutes, hours—it seemed to last forever. Only the black nothingness and frigid cold existed. A cold that scorched and seared.

The third voice finally spoke. "Decision...is final."

The noise of running water echoed in Parker's ears. A stream of some kind, its fast current provided a relaxing rhythm. The cold, painful, dark void dissipated and his vision returned. Calm, at ease, almost refreshed, Parker stood in the middle of a tree-lined dirt road amidst the water's tranquil sound. The road curved and disappeared around a hill behind him. Oddly, he couldn't remember walking past the hill. In fact, no trace of footprints appeared in the dirt behind him either.

The road continued a short distance toward the stream until it came to a stone bridge that spanned the fast-moving water. Lush, green hills and snowcapped mountain tops appeared along the far horizon.

There had to be something to tell him where he was. Large, thick trees bordered the dirt road and lined the banks of the stream, providing the most inviting shade he'd ever seen. Each tree's brilliance and definition stood out. The colors seemed alive. He'd seen shades of green before, but nothing so dynamic as this. It made the images displayed by the best plasma and high definition television screens look like cheap, blurry imitations.

The clearest, starkest, and most enthralling color of blue permeated the sky. He stood for a moment, staring aloft, and tried grasping the awe-inspiring clarity. No clouds, no pollution or smog, no contrails from passing jet airplanes, just the clearest and most intense blue sky he'd ever seen.

He looked back at the bridge. A man stood at the far end of it, facing the water. He had a fishing rod, an old rusty tackle box on the ground next to him. A whirling sound emanated from the bridge as he gracefully cast the fishing line arching high into the air and then plunging into the rushing stream.

Maybe the fisherman knows what's going on. Curious, Parker started for the bridge, the sound of the stream growing louder and more pronounced. As he walked closer, the man at the end of the bridge came into sharper focus. He appeared to be around sixty, medium height and build, thick head of dark hair with streaks of gray. Dressed in olive-colored pants and a long-sleeved navy blue flannel shirt under a vest adorned with a million zippers and pockets, he bore a striking resemblance to an actor whose name Parker couldn't recall at the moment. Clooney? Crowe? No, that wasn't it.

At the foot of the bridge, Parker scanned the banks of the stream. The water curved from either end, making it impossible to see where the stream came from or where it led. He watched the fisherman for a moment, holding his rod, studying the water, and gently reeling in his line. Oblivious to everything but catching fish. Should he call to him or walk right up to the old guy?

The water beckoned. The rhythmic sound of the current hypnotized him, but even more captivating was the crystal clear, translucent quality of the water. It was the cleanest, purest, most beautiful water he'd ever seen. Like everything else, the color and clarity of it were so striking it took his breath away. He could stand and gaze at the water forever, bask in the warm sunshine, and be perfectly content. Oddly, with the exception of the man on the bridge, the place had a feeling of familiarity. Like a recurring dream.

Parker snapped out of his trance at the sound of the fisherman recasting his line, and he walked out onto the bridge. It seemed old, like something that had been built ages ago. Made out of large gray stones, the bridge had no flooring but the dirt road. The chalky dirt and tiny pebbles ground under his feet. The fisherman's attention was still fixated on the rod and reel, despite Parker's presence only a few feet away. Just as he was about to say hello, the man turned and smiled.

"Hello, Parker." The third voice.

Although the words came from a gruff old fisherman, they carried a gentle undertone with soft traces of care and concern. Lines creased the old man's weathered face like a cracked windshield as he smiled. With an air bordering on something like a grandfather—close to affectionate, yet distant enough to be objective—he sized Parker up, but said nothing more.

If the old man wanted to have a staring contest or play the quiet game, he could do that by himself.

Parker edged to the side of the bridge, looking out at the moving water as a cool, gentle breeze blew against his skin. He closed his eyes and let the sun's warmth wash over him for a moment. It was so nice to feel the sun again, to stand in a place far removed from the cold, painful void. A place so inviting and relaxing. If there was a better place to be, he didn't know it.

Still, as desirable as it was to just stand and bask in the sunshine and the soft caresses of the wind, it was time to figure out what was going on here. Time to get some answers. Hopefully, Captain Ahab here had some.

Parker propped his elbow on top of the smooth surface of the railing and leaned into the stone as the fisherman reeled in his line in quick, jerky movements. The first question was on the tip of his tongue when the old man nodded up the road.

Parker scanned ahead to the point where the dirt road disappeared behind the trees as it curved around the next hill. Something moved behind the trees, heading toward them.

Curious, Parker stepped away from the side of the bridge and into the middle of the dirt road for a better look. The object was clearly a person, but he could not make out much else. He took a step forward as if to move off the bridge and up the road to close the distance, but the long fishing rod suddenly thrust in front of him, blocking his path.

The old fisherman smiled, but gave a slight shake of his head. Clearly, leaving the bridge and stepping foot on the other side was out of the question.

In a moment, the mysterious person emerged from behind the trees as it came around the curve, and Parker lost his breath again. As she skipped toward him, her ponytail flipped back and forth behind her.

Tears formed quickly in his eyes. "Abby," he whispered.

The sight of her bounding down the road brought back her last words to him as he held her in his arms. He'd just reached her amid the chaos and frenzy of the shooting. She'd lain on her back, her body riddled by gunfire, covered in blood. He'd dropped to his knees and propped her in his arms. Frantic, he'd called her name as he'd checked for signs of life, hoping that by some miracle she could hang on until an ambulance arrived.

Sleepy, glassy eyes fluttered open. She'd managed a weak smile, and without any trace of the nasal sound that always accompanied her speech said, "I'm skipping, Park. See how fast I can go?" Her eyes slowly blinked then closed a final time with her last breath.

The road, trees, and hills—everything spun like a carnival ride. He bent over and placed his hands on his knees, staring at the ground. Teardrops darkened the dirt below. Relief washed over him, and the heaviness that had been pressing down and nearly suffocating him these past few weeks lifted.

Abby stopped skipping and strode toward him, beaming from ear to ear. Her strong legs gave not the slightest hint there'd ever been anything wrong with them. Seeing her stand fully erect without having to stoop or hunch in her walker—he hadn't realized how tall she actually was.

The fisherman withdrew his rod as Abby stepped onto the bridge. She lunged forward and threw her arms around Parker, squeezing him tightly.

They stood in the middle of the dirt road hugging one another as the wind rustled the nearby tree tops. The rippling stream continued to sing its relaxing and rhythmic song. He held her, not wanting to let go.

She finally raised her head and locked her eyes with his. "Good to see you, big brother." Her voice was strong, clear.

"Yeah," he said hoarsely. "Good to see you, too." A playful rub of the top of her head elicited a laugh. Music to his ears. The awesome wonder of seeing Abby again left him speechless.

She laughed, rolled her eyes, and shook her head. She stepped back and took hold of his hands. "Oh, it's so much fun here, Park. It really is! I ride horses every day and play with ponies. And I run and play games with other children, too. And sing all day and night!"

He hung on her every word. Her face lit up with a joy he'd never seen from her before as she continued describing how happy and content she was. She went on and on about how this was truly home for her and how each day seemed better than the one before it.

"But, Park, don't be sad or angry anymore about what happened. It wasn't your fault. You didn't cause any of it," she said. "Please let it go. I'm happy here. I mean, I'm exactly where I belong. I'm home." She smiled again, her blue eyes sparkling like sapphires. "Okay?"

He nodded, his mouth dry. A lump formed, and he swallowed hard to get rid of it. "Okay," he managed to say.

"I love you, Park."

He cleared his throat. "I love you too, Abby." The words somehow seemed cheap, inadequate to express what his heart wanted to say.

She nodded toward the road behind him. "Now, go get back on the football field."

Surely she'd misspoken. Parker cocked his head to the side, looked at her quizzically. "What?"

She grinned. "You heard me, big brother. Get back out there and play football. That's where *you* belong."

Impossible. "No, I can't. It's—"

"No, it's not too late. It's never too late. Get back out there, I always loved watching you play."

He wasn't sure how to respond. Quitting during the middle of a game? A sin from which there was no forgiveness. Besides, did he really want to play football again? Was there any choice now?

"Time to go back, Park." The fisherman's voice interrupted his thoughts.

"But I just got here," he said, turning around to plead his case for more time with Abby, but the road was empty, the bridge vacant. Even the fishing rod and tackle box were gone. The only thing present was a basset hound, sitting where the fisherman had been.

"It's okay, Park," Abby said. "We'll see each other again someday."

No. He'd barely had any time with her. How could he possibly go back so soon?

She nodded. "It's okay."

He turned and took a step back up the bridge. The basset hound rose up on all fours and waddled past him toward Abby. The hound's tail wagged and his long, droopy ears skirted the top of the dirt road. It was the same dog from the alley behind his house that had chased away Daryl McGon-agill when Parker broke up with Summer. What had Daryl said? Something about a basset hound barking at him the night he slashed his tire.

Standing in the middle of the stone bridge, Parker took one more look at Abby. She stood in the road, the basset hound sitting next to her, both of them looking at him. Abby smiled again, reached down, and gently patted the dog on its head. It panted and wagged its tail in response.

A bright light appeared in Parker's peripheral vision, quickly enveloping him. He squinted, blinked a few times, and tried to focus, but the brightness only increased. He tried to remain focused on Abby and the dog, but the bright light that swirled around him blinded him.

Abby! Abby! No, please don't go! He raised his hand to shield his eyes, but the light overpowered him. He shut his eyes to block it out, hoping to see her again when the light faded.

CHAPTER 32

The scent of disinfectant and rubbing alcohol filled Parker's nostrils, tickling the little hairs inside. The odor always made his nose itch whenever he visited his mother at work. As the smell continued to permeate his senses, the impulse to reach up and scratch his nose tugged at him. Somehow, however, his body failed to cooperate.

He tried opening his eyes, but they felt as heavy as a ton of bricks, and the attempt drained him. As he rested for a moment, a garbled noise interrupted the quiet. It sounded like someone being paged over an intercom. The name wasn't recognizable and the words seemed to be jumbled together.

Although tired and weak, he tried forcing his eyes again. With great difficulty, he pried them open. Blurry vision obscured everything, keeping his sight out of focus, but it did allow enough orientation to provide some bearings.

He lay in a bed, his head elevated, arms at his sides. *Where am I?*

With each blink of his eyes, the fuzzy, distorted vision came into better focus, though his eyelids proved difficult to keep open and required a few pauses to rest. A television, mounted on the far wall across from him in the semi-dark room, displayed muted images of a football game. Several vases of multi-colored flowers sat on a shelf underneath the television.

A window, its blinds open, offered gray light. Soft, periodic beeps emanated from a machine next to the bed. Wires seemed to connect him to it.

Closing his eyes again, he processed his surroundings. *Hospital.*

He took a deep breath and exhaled, trying to clear his mind and focus on exactly what had happened. Fighting with Daryl McGonagill he recalled with ease, but everything afterward seemed hazy. The sound of running water had a ring of familiarity to it, as did trees and a fisherman, but there was something else. What was it?

He opened his eyes again and tried to move, but only a few fingers responded with spasmodic jerks. Maybe he'd have better luck with his legs? An attempt to bring up his knees only resulted in a twitching of his toes. Why was his body so weak?

"Parker?"

Something moved at the corner of his eye. A figure emerged, sitting up on a couch beneath the window sill.

"Parker?" His mother repeated his name as she leaned forward and gently took hold of his hand.

He shifted his eyes and looked at her. A few lacerations littered her face, but they seemed to be almost fully healed. No obvious bruising or swelling appeared either.

Speaking, like bodily movement, proved difficult. His muscles failed and exhaustion overwhelmed him. A squeeze of his mother's hand might work, but only a few fingers obeyed. Evidently it was enough.

"Parker!" She stood, gripping his hand, and leaned over him. "Oh, thank you, God, thank you." Her eyes filled with tears.

It would be nice to say something, let her know he was okay, but how to communicate?

"Park, you're in the hospital, sweetie. You're going to be okay," she said, wiping her eyes. "Your father is in the cafeteria. I'm going to go get him. I'll be right back, honey, okay? I'll be right back."

She planted a kiss on his forehead and dashed out of the room. Parker tried to follow her with his eyes, but she moved too fast, and the act tired him. His eyes closed again, demanding rest. Drifting off to sleep sounded appealing, but he fought off the temptation when someone else stirred in the room.

His eyelids proved more difficult to open this time, requiring effort from a fast-draining reservoir of energy.

"Hello, Park." Marie's soft voice spilled from the corner of the room. "I thought..." Her voice cracked and trailed off. She shuffled to the side of his bed and clasped his hand. "I thought I was going to lose you forever."

He tried to say something, to ask if she was okay, but only mumbled something incoherent.

"It's okay." She looked deep into his eyes, "You don't have to speak. Just think to yourself, and I'll know what you're saying."

Wait. There'd been a fight with other demons, and she'd been hit. *Are you okay?*

"Yes, I'm fine. I heal quickly," she said with a faint smile.

He'd gone home and been attacked by Daryl McGonagill. They'd fought. *What happened?*

"It was a trap. Seth knew if you were threatened, I would get you out of there, which I did. But that was exactly what he wanted. He wanted you to go home, where he knew Daryl was waiting for you. I tried to speak to you about it, to let you know of the danger, but he blocked me, and I couldn't get through to you clearly enough." She gripped his hand more tightly. "I'm so sorry. I should've seen it coming."

Then what happened?

"After Daryl shot you, you were clinically dead for sixteen minutes until the EMTs revived you on the way to the hospital. You were airlifted to Harris Hospital in Fort Worth, went through some pretty intensive surgery, and have been in a coma for the past eleven days."

Are my parents okay?

Marie nodded. "Yes. Your father has a fractured tibia, but other than that they're fine, although watching their son die in front of them was pretty traumatic, as you can imagine."

McGonagill? Where is he?

"Dead. He was found in the cab of his truck, parked in the alley behind your house where he bled out."

Parker breathed a sigh of relief, his body relaxing. He'd melt into the sheets and fall into a deep sleep, if only hospital beds were more comfortable. Oh, well. He'd just have to get used to it for the time being.

Peace spread over him like a blanket, as when he'd stood on the bridge near the stream of sparkling water in his dream.

Water? Bridge? Had that really been a dream? Other events came back to him with greater clarity now. *Abby?* His eyes shifted to hers. *I dreamed I saw Abby. Was that really just a dream or was it real?*

Marie smiled. "Does it really matter?"

The conversation between the voices in the dark void. *You offered to take my place?*

She pursed her lips and nodded. "Yes." Her voice choked with emotion. "I would do anything to save you, Park." She stared hard into his eyes. "Anything."

Her fingers caressed his hand in tender, smooth strokes. There was something behind her touch. Something that went far beyond just care and concern.

"I offered to fall in your place. One soul sacrificed for another. That act voided Seth's claim on you. It was an offer I would've gladly followed through with."

So why didn't you?

"I didn't have to. I'll explain later, but suffice it to say my offer was very pleasing to someone and that's all that mattered. As a result, you're alive and I'm still your guardian."

He summoned every ounce of strength that remained for the moment. His hand gripped hers as he looked at her intently, drinking her in with his eyes. Her long, curly, straw-berry-blonde hair cascaded like a beautifully colored water-fall around her face. Two glassy emeralds, seas of green where any man could lose himself, stared back. Waiting.

She had been there for him, always. Through thick and thin. Right or wrong, win or lose, stand or fall, she'd remained at his side. And when he'd jeopardized his soul, she'd stepped up to commit the ultimate sacrifice, because she—

His dry lips parted. "Marie." His voice came out thick, hoarse. Barely audible.

She sucked in a quick breath and then paused. "Yes?" she whispered. Her eyes widened and her mouth hung open.

"Thank you."

She smiled, bit her lip, and bowed her head, her cheeks turning redder than her hair.

A soft orange glow filtered through the window, and the room brightened. Dawn. The breaking of the new day brought the first rays of sunshine he'd seen in weeks.

Marie raised her head and looked at the window as the sun peeked over the horizon. "'Arise, fair sun, and kill the envious moon, who is already sick and pale with grief.'" She remained fixated on the sun as a broad smile showed her dimples. "I love the sunrise, Park," she said. "It tells us that the darkness of the night is gone and whatever happened yesterday is forever behind us and in the past. It says today is a new day, full of hope, promise, and unmerited grace. It reminds us that no matter how dark things may get, dawn will always come when we need it most."

A huge sense of comfort washed over him as the warm, heavenly sunlight filled the room. He grinned, marveling at the majestic sunrise.

୧ଏେ୨

Seth sat at one of the small round tables in the cafeteria,

next to his associate, and read through the obituaries of the local paper with quiet bemusement. The young woman at his side held a cup of steaming coffee in her hands in a vain attempt to warm herself, which was stupid. Hot liquids cooled too quickly, and any benefits derived from them faded even faster. Smoking provided much better relief, but unfortunately humans now banned it in hospitals.

For days they'd watched and waited. Being patient was tough, but what choice did they have, especially with the family hunkered down in such a public place? Thoughts swirled through their minds of what they could do to them if only they were allowed.

"He's awake." Seth spoke without looking up from the paper.

The young woman stopped staring at Kenneth. "What? He's out of the coma?"

Seth nodded. "His mother is on her way here to get her husband. Watch."

She turned and looked toward the cafeteria's main entrance. In a few moments, Suzy darted into the cafeteria, scanned the crowded room, and dashed over to Kenneth's table where he sat picking at some scrambled eggs.

"Parker's alone. Let's get him," the young woman said, her voice trembling with excitement.

"No," Seth answered firmly. Why was it so difficult for others to follow orders? "He's not to be touched. Besides, he's being protected right now."

"I hate waiting," she complained through gritted teeth as Suzy beamed with the news that Parker was out of the coma.

Kenneth's face lit up. Suzy handed him his crutches and helped him to his feet.

Their joy was disgusting. This shouldn't be happening anyway. His soul had been rightfully claimed, but they had been swindled at the last second by a cheap trick. Dishonesty, hypocrisy—that was how they played the game, all under the guise of "love."

Seth's colleague gripped her coffee cup so tightly her hands shook, black coffee swirling in her Styrofoam cup until the small chalice imploded in her grasp. A river of black liquid spilled into her lap.

He quietly slid a napkin to her and tried to hide his displeasure over the ruining of a pair of Escada jeans. "Settle down." He watched Suzy and Kenneth make their way toward the exit. "I have a plan. And I'll deal with them myself."

He picked up the paper and resumed reading the obituaries. A small laugh escaped his lips.

About the Author

Scott Abel works in state government and is the author of several short stories and the young adult paranormal romance novel, *Sunrise*.

A native Texan, Abel was raised a PK (preacher's kid) and grew up listening to his father, a masterful storyteller, every Sunday. Whether it was sermons from the pulpit or episodes of *The Twilight Zone*, powerful stories that tug at the emotions and stretch the mind captivated him.

As he began his own journey through life as a football coach and college administrator, he remained a sucker for a good story—plus chocolate and peanut butter. Now, as a husband and father, he's discovered he's got a few stories of his own to tell.

As an author, Abel is firmly entrenched in the shadowlands where the line between light and dark isn't always so distinguishable. He invites you to step through the thin, misty veil separating the known from the unknown and venture with him into the realm of *Sunrise* where the supernatural is not only possible—but natural.

In addition to his writing endeavors and work in state government, Abel is also a public speaker. He often speaks to organizations, non-profits, and churches on leadership, communication, teamwork, and motivational messages.

Abel has a bachelor's degree and a law degree from Texas Wesleyan University, but is a rabid, life-long fan of the TCU Horned Frogs. He lives in the suburbs of Austin with his wife and two precocious daughters, who enthusiastically assist him in his search for the perfect combination of chocolate and peanut butter.